HAWAIIAN LOVE

HAWAIIAN LOVE

Jeanne McCann

iUniverse, Inc.
New York Lincoln Shanghai

Hawaiian Love

iUniverse, Inc.

For information address:
iUniverse, Inc.
2021 Pine Lake Road, Suite 100
Lincoln, NE 68512
www.iuniverse.com

ISBN: 0-595-32046-5

Printed in the United States of America

This book is dedicated to the romantic and ground breaking gays and lesbians who stood in line for hours to be married these last few months. All of you are creating history and will one day look back and recognize your contributions to all of our lives.

I would also like to recognize the brave and talented police and firefighters all over the world that daily put their lives on the line without question. Every day you set out to protect and serve and we all want to thank you for your dedication.

Thank you.

Acknowledgements

As always, many others besides the author contribute to a story. I would like to thank my partner, Pam, my friends who wait for the next story to be published, and my family who loves to tease me about being a romance writer. I would also like to thank my editor, Holly Vierk who is trying to teach me the value of a comma, with no great success.

CHAPTER 1

"Shanni, I'm really glad you decided to come with us to Hawaii." Janice's white teeth gleamed against the pink skin of her face. She lay basting in the hot sun, her body coated with SPF 15 sunscreen. Janice's blond hair and blue eyes matched her freckles and still pale complexion. Her cheeks were already showing signs of sunburn as she lounged negligently on her towel.

"I'm glad I came too," Shannon smiled in response. She, on the other hand was already a deep brown, her olive skin complexion matched her dark brown hair and eyes. She tanned very easily, much to Janice's dismay. "I'm enjoying just being able to relax."

And Shannon was relaxing. Hawaii was her favorite place to unwind. She loved the water, the beaches, and especially the heat. It always made her feel sensuous and decadent. The air around her was perfumed with a blooming hibiscus tree behind them, the turquoise water sparkling. The sand was white and soft as she pushed her toes comfortably through it. Even the smell of tropical tanning oil made her smile as she watched others languishing comfortably on their towels. No one moved quickly in Hawaii, slow and happy was the mood.

"You needed this. You have been working way too hard." Janice commented as she spread more sunscreen on her arms.

Shannon had needed a vacation. She had been working non-stop the last few months taking on every filming request that passed her way. This was good for her pocketbook, but not for her spirit. But traveling to Hawaii and single life was still a little painful. She and her ex-girlfriend Anita had vacationed every winter in Maui the last four years they had been together. After they parted ways, Anita had spent her latest vacation in Hawaii with her new girlfriend, one she'd had long before she and Shannon had separated. At least Shannon was on a different island, away from some of the memories that plagued her. Anita and Shannon had grown comfortable with each other, more roommates than lovers. But it had hurt her deeply when Anita had told Shannon she wanted out of the relationship. Shannon missed the companionship. She could admit that their relationship wasn't full of passion, but whose was?

"Hey girls, how's the beach?" Melody Anton, Janice's girlfriend of eight years, along with Hanna Bryce and Olivia Charles, joined them. Melody was a very healthy woman of five-ten clad in a one piece bathing suit and a pair of shorts. She worked out constantly to keep herself in shape, due in part to her job as a firefighter. Her chosen career required physical strength and agility. Mel was dedicated to her profession and since peoples' lives depended upon her, she worked out religiously to maintain her body. Even with her diligent focus she had sustained an injury a month earlier. But that didn't stop her from enjoying her vacation. Her hair was cut short, and her auburn hair was liberally shot through with silver. Her eyes were a deep brown and her face was full of appealing laugh lines. Her face was a window to her feelings and she was a woman who enjoyed her life. Hanna and Olivia were both on the short side; Hanna was blond and a very plump five-three. Olivia was also a little on the full figured side, her hair a light brown, and her hazel eyes full of humor and affection. Hanna was a very talented chef and she and Olivia enjoyed the fruits of her work, making their waistlines fluctuate with their meals. The word diet was not in their vocabulary. All three women were showing signs of a healthy tan and the relaxed laid back attitude that was so much a part of the islands.

"Good, hot, but relaxing." Jan sat up to greet her girlfriend. "It's about time you guy's got up."

"Hey, we aren't early birds like the two of you." Melody teased Janice as she spread her towel on the sand next to her own before flopping on it and sneaking a quick kiss from her, while Hanna and Olivia made themselves comfortable on their own towels. They had staked out their spot days before, close to the beach and shaded with trees. The sun could get down right grueling after a couple of hours.

For the last four days, Shannon and Janice headed for the beach a good two hours before the other three women, who elected to sleep in. Since the five of them had been friends for over ten years, they knew each other's habits, good and bad, and accepted them. Janice and Shannon took the ribbing about their early rising with good humor and returned the teasing with barbs of their own. What were friends for if not to zero in on each other's quirky habits?

"The beach is pretty crowded today," Olivia commented as she and Hanna pulled out their snorkel gear.

"There's lot's of people. The waves are very rough, watch yourself going into the water."

"You guys want to snorkel with us?"

"No, I'll pass," Melody responded, and Janice just shook her head no.

"I'm staying here." Shannon was just fine lying on the beach reading her latest mystery novel.

"Okay, come on sweetie. Let's go out by the coral reef."

"Be careful, it's really heavy surf out by the reef," Janice cautioned. She'd been watching the water all morning. There was a strong wind, and combined with the high tide, the waves were very dangerous.

"We will." Olivia and Hanna headed for the water chattering to each other playfully, flippers hanging off of their arms.

"Mel, how's your back?" Melody was recuperating from a serious back injury due to an accident at work. She and Janice were both firefighters for the city of Seattle. Melody was a lieutenant in north Seattle, who had recently gone out on a call at a burning warehouse. One of her team had gone down inside the building and she and another firefighter had carried him out of the flames. It had not been an easy task and she had suffered a serious back strain. She was on injured reserve status until she recuperated, relegated to office work and some vacation time. These types of injuries happened in her line of work and Melody dealt with it just like everything else, with good humor and hard work. She was intent on getting back into shape and active duty.

"Good, I did all of my exercises this morning and it feels great."

"Honey, a little swimming might be good for you."

"So would a little morning delight," Mel grinned at her girlfriend, a gleam in her eyes.

"Morning delight," Jan chuckled, rolling her eyes. "I can't believe you said that out loud."

Shannon tuned the two of them out, smiling at their banter. She was used to it. It was a part of their relationship. They would tease each other with affection, never running out of things to talk about. Shannon enjoyed their easy way with each other. She wanted a relationship that was as open and loving. She sat up and gazed out at the beautiful shoreline, enjoying the incredible view and the scenery. There was nothing like Hawaii, with its brilliant water, colorful flowers, and weather. But there was something else that tugged at

Shannon whenever she visited. Something spiritual and sacred surrounded Shannon, and it made her feel protected and a part of the islands.

They were staying at an elegant Four Seasons Resort in Kona, right on the water. It was a beautiful complex that had everything a traveler might need. It contained restaurants, a private lagoon, and any other amenities a person could imagine. The five of them had gravitated to the beach in front of their rooms. It was large and relatively quiet. Shannon watched as children and their parents frolicked in the surf, jumping the waves, snorkeling in the clear blue water, and shrieking with pleasure. She started to lie back down when she caught a faint cry that sounded very much like a call for help. She stood up quickly, shading her eyes as she scanned the beach.

"Help!"

Shannon heard the muffled cry again and moved closer to the shoreline, as she scanned the water looking for someone who might be in trouble. "Janice, Mel, did you hear that?"

"What?"

"A cry for help."

"I don't hear anything."

"Shush." Shannon strained to hear, shading her eyes from the sun as she continued to search the crowded shoreline.

"Help, help!"

"There he is!" Shannon burst into a run. "He's being pounded by the waves on the reef!"

While Janice and Mel watched in disbelief, Shannon raced into the water and started swimming with strong strokes in the direction of the coral reef about one hundred and fifty yards off the shore to the right of where they lay. No one else seemed to have noticed that a young boy was experiencing trouble in the water.

"Mel, go get some help! I'm going out with Shannon." Janice struggled through the high waves and began swimming after her friend. She wasn't as comfortable swimming as Shannon but she followed after her.

Mel raced to the hotel lobby while Shannon swam toward the young boy. He tumbled against the reef as high waves pummeled his small body. Shannon prayed she would reach him in time. When she was only twenty feet away, he disappeared from her view. She swam those final twenty feet even faster and dove into the water. She saw the unconscious child twisting and turning against the jagged coral reef. She grabbed his arm and pulled him to the surface. Her lungs burned. Waves rolled the two of them over and over and Shannon pulled the boy's tiny body tightly against her as they slammed against the sharp reef. Pain shot through her as the coral tore the skin of her back and legs. She sucked in a mouthful of salt water and gasped for air. Still, she managed to keep the boy's face above water. She choked, gagged, tightened her grip on him, kicking heavily, and swam with one arm toward shore. Her body screamed with pain and exhaustion, but she couldn't stop now.

"There they are!" a man yelled as Shannon broke through the waves, holding the boy's face above the water.

She felt hands grabbing her arms, pulling her out of the surf and on to the shore, the boy taken out of her arms as she fell to her knees, gasping. "Is he breathing?"

"The paramedics are working on him. Let's get you out of the water, honey." Janice and Mel tried to help her. Janice had been one of several swimmers who had helped Shannon get the boy to shore. Shannon was unaware she was kneeling in the shallow surf on her hands and knees, as she forced herself to breath, her body screaming with pain.

"Is he breathing?" She couldn't stand up; her knees were too weak.

Simone Moreau was a senior paramedic for the town of Kona Hawaii, and had been a medic for over twenty years. Normally, she could be found in her office doing mounds of paperwork since she was in charge of a staff of twenty-six. Today, she was in the field with two of her younger medics, observing and training. They had responded to a possible drowning at the resort, which unfortunately, was something that happened periodically in the heavy beach surf around the island. Tourists and the island bound were equally at risk, as the waters around the main island of Hawaii could be treacherous. The island was formed by lava flow from Mauna Kea and Mauna Loa volcanoes, many years earlier, leaving the shoreline rough and in many places very deep. Undertows and rough surf claimed many a tourist and islander if they weren't respectful of the water. She watched two of her junior medics as they worked on the young boy.

"He's not breathing. I'm going to begin compressions," Barry Levin explained as his partner, June cleared the young boy's airway and took his pulse. "How long has he been without oxygen?"

"This woman pulled him out of the water." A man in the growing crowd of onlookers spoke up.

Simone turned to Shannon and saw the exhaustion and pain on her face. "Here, let's get you seated and warm."

"Oh, Shanni, what happened to your back and legs?" Olivia cried out in horror.

"Is he breathing?" Shannon repeated, as she painfully tried to move. She just wanted to make sure the boy was going to be okay.

"Not yet, but give the medics some time." Simone reassured her. "How long was he under water?"

"Not long, he was just going under when I reached him, maybe ten minutes or so, I'm not exactly sure." As Shannon spoke, the boy coughed and choked loudly, before throwing up the salt water that had filled his lungs. They rolled him on his side as he struggled to breathe.

"Jason, that's my son Jason!" A frantic woman dropped to her knees next to the young boy. "Is he okay?"

"His pulse is strong, and he's breathing normally." Barry covered the shivering boy with a blanket as June prepared a gurney so they could transport him to the ambulance. "We need to take him to the hospital to be looked over by a doctor. He needs to be checked out, but it looks like he is very lucky."

"Jason, I'm so mad at you. You were not supposed to go in the water without me, honey." She smothered the little boy with kisses.

"Ma'am, let us get your son into the ambulance and then you can talk to him."

"We need to take care of your injuries now that the boy's okay." Simone spoke to the drained woman who stood silently watching the paramedics work. She was being supported by two women, one on either side of her. Her body slack from exhaustion and shock.

"I'm fine. I just need to go get cleaned up." Shannon turned stiffly, intent on heading up to her hotel room to lie down. She hurt like hell and she hissed in pain as she tried to move.

Simone saw the extent of her injuries and winced. She knew first hand what coral could do to skin. "You aren't going anywhere but to the hospital. Your back, arms, and legs need to be cleaned and taken care of."

Shannon's eyes were already glazed with pain and she just wanted to return to her room. "That's okay, there's no need."

"Are you the woman who saved my son? Thank you so much. What's your name?" Shannon almost cried out as the oblivious woman overwhelmed her, hugging her energetically. Her back screamed as the woman's hands touched it.

"Shannon, my name is Shannon," she gasped, closing her eyes to keep from crying.

"Shannon, I can't thank you enough."

"It's no problem." Shannon started to feel lighted headed and her knees began to buckle, her stomach churning.

"Oh my, you're bleeding," the woman cried out. "Someone help her!"

"I am, ma'am." Simone couldn't help but notice how pale Shannon had gotten and reached out to support her. "June, we need another gurney."

"Right, boss."

"Can you hold her while we wait for the gurney? We need to get her to the hospital." The tall blond medic spoke quietly but with such authority that Mel didn't question doing what she asked. She recognized knowledge in the woman's demeanor.

"Certainly. Shanni honey, Janice went to get your pack so you have your wallet with you. We'll meet you at the hospital."

"I'm not going to the hospital." Shannon's face was beaded with sweat, her eyes all but shut as she tried to ignore the pain that moved through her body.

"Honey, you need to go, please?"

"I'm fine. I just need to go to my room and get cleaned up. I'll be fine."

"Shannon, what's your last name?"

"Dunbar."

"My name is Simone Moreau, and you need to get to the hospital. Coral cuts can get infected very quickly if you don't take care of them."

Shannon smiled up at the tall beautiful woman standing next to her. "What a beautiful name, it suits you perfectly."

Simone was pleasantly startled by the comment and the smile on the beautiful, injured woman's face. June met them with another portable gurney.

Shannon sighed heavily and stared at the woman who had spoken so gently to her. She was beautiful; her soft eyes a pale blue, her hair short and ash blond, with streaks of lighter blond sprinkled throughout. An abundance of full curls adorned her head, her nose thin and elegant to match her high cheekbones, but it was her mouth that caught Shannon's attention. Her lips were full and arrested in a slight smile, her perfect white teeth offset by her deeply tanned face. She was tall and lean in her navy uniform of shorts and matching shirt, but obviously very strong as her bare arms and legs attested to. Shannon started to object to going to the hospital again, but the slight smile, the gentle hand on her arm, and the direct gaze, kept her silent. She just nodded her head in agreement, all the while staring at the woman who somehow made her feel safe. Shannon let her guard down and put herself in the woman's capable hands.

"Good. Now, can you lie on your stomach? You will be more comfortable and we can take a look at your injuries." Shannon sighed again as she bent over and did as she was told. She hurt all over and was finding it difficult to talk, her stomach rolled uncomfortably.

"Shanni, we'll follow you to the hospital. Olivia went to get the jeep." Hanna reassured her while Mel and Janice watched. "Oh, my God," Hanna exclaimed as she saw how much damage Shannon's body had endured.

Simone and June rapidly loaded Shannon into the ambulance as the large crowd of people watched quietly. While June climbed into the back of the ambulance Shannon glanced at the little boy laying quietly beside her, his mother kneeling next to him while the other paramedic continued his examination.

"How's he doing, Barry?"

"Good, Simone. We're trying to keep him warm and quiet until he gets checked out by the doctor."

"June, can you cover Shannon up and start an IV drip?"

"Will do."

"I'll meet you at the hospital." Simone closed the ambulance doors and turned to walk to her vehicle, colliding with three very worried women. "I'm sorry."

"Can you tell us how bad Shanni is?" Janice's voice trembled with emotion as she spoke.

"She's taken off a large amount of skin from her back, arms, and legs and some of the areas are quite deep. Coral cuts are worrisome because they can become easily infected. The hospital will scrub the lacerations and sterilize the areas. She will be put on heavy antibiotics to handle any infections." Simone spoke quietly, realizing the women were terrified for their friend.

"Can you give us directions to the hospital?" Mel inquired as the four of them clustered together.

"Why don't you follow me?"

"Thank you. Olivia is parked right over there."

"It'll take about thirty minutes to get to the hospital from here."

"We'll be right behind you."

Simone climbed into her Range Rover and waited as the four women climbed into their jeep. She smiled when the two women in the front seat shared a short but intimate kiss. She'd had an inkling that they might be gay, but it wasn't easy to tell anymore. She was a good example of that. Very few people actually knew she was gay, primarily because she was a very private person. She glanced in her rearview mirror to see if the jeep was still following her as she headed out of the resort grounds. Thankfully, the day was light as emergencies go. She would continue to observe Barry and June for the rest of their shift after visiting the hospital. Her job required that she complete quarterly reviews of all of her paramedics. It took her a little over a week to complete but it was essential to their training, followed up by a mound of reports. The required paperwork was the worst part of her job and it was a large piece of it. She missed working in the field as a paramedic but she enjoyed being in charge and helping to groom new medics. She covered shifts when they were short-handed, but it wasn't as often as she would have liked. She was also a member of the search and rescue team when it was called out. She was an accomplished diver and paramedic and over the years, her skills had been put to the test in many rescues around the islands.

Simone pulled into the driveway of the hospital and parked next to the ambulance in the slots designated for emergency vehicles. The four women in the jeep continued into the visitor's parking lot and pulled into an open stall. She waited for them outside the emergency entrance and observed their easy camaraderie. It was now fairly obvious that they were two gay couples and it made her curious about their friend, Shannon.

"Right inside these doors is the emergency desk. Go check in there and they will come locate you when they have some news about your friend. It will probably be a while before they have her settled in a room and can assess the extent of her injuries. She's in no danger though."

"Thank you, we don't even know your name," Olivia admitted, smiling at Simone. "You've been so nice."

"It's Simone Moreau, and you're welcome." Simone smiled in return.

Olivia couldn't help but admire the stunning woman. She looked like an athlete, her uniform should have muted her appeal, but it only enhanced it. Her eyes were large and gentle, a pale blue that gazed steadily at the four women. She had a calmness to her that made you want to trust her. "Good luck to all of you."

"Thanks again."

Simone wagged her fingers at Trina seated at the emergency room desk as she whisked by her and entered the emergency room. She was very familiar with the hospital and for many years ran in and out of emergency as she gained experience as a paramedic. She knew many of them very well and one of the doctors even better.

Her ex-girlfriend was one of the emergency physicians on staff. It was how they had met years earlier. Liz had been relentless in her pursuit of Simone and they had dated on and off for almost three years, never actually living together. Their relationship had not been a smooth one and they fought as much as they made up, most of their fights revolving around Liz's inability to accept that Simone wanted to remain a paramedic. Liz could never understand that Simone had a satisfying career and didn't want to be a doctor. Liz accused her of being unmotivated, whereas Liz was determined to continually push herself. She was highly driven, and had her sights set on running a hospital one day. Having a girlfriend who was a lowly paramedic tarnished her rising star. Liz wanted the sex part of the relationship but not the commitment and that would never be enough for Simone. Even being seen in public together was against Liz's rules. She wanted nothing to stand in the way of her career. Simone had been hurt deeply that Liz never placed any value on what Simone did for a living and it had gradually eroded their imperfect relationship. It had broken Simone's heart when she had finally admitted to herself that it wasn't working. It had taken Simone a year to completely separate herself from Liz. It had only been the last four months or so that she could run into Liz and not feel an ache and the loss in her heart. She grieved for a relationship that would never be and a love that had faded slowly.

"Hey, Simone, how're you doing?"

"Good Tess, how about you?"

"Wonderful, thanks. Your medics are just finishing up in room six. Boy, that young woman took a beating. She's a mess." Tess was a talented head nurse at the very busy hospital. Simone had known her for over ten years. She was a fixture at the hospital and Simone knew that Tess and her dedicated nursing staff were the reasons why the hospital ran so smoothly.

"She saved a young boy's life."

"That's what we were told."

"How's the boy?"

"The doctor's with him now, but all his vitals are good. His mother is a little shocked. I think she just realized how close she came to losing him."

"Let me know what the doctor says, please?"

"I will, and your kids did real well," Tess grinned. She delighted in teasing the new paramedics. She also had enormous respect for Simone. She knew any paramedic trained by Simone and her crew would be skilled and knowledgeable.

"They're very good."

"I know you trained them," Tess responded with affection for her good friend.

"I'll be in room six with the young woman." Simone blushed with Tess's comment. "Could you let the four women in the waiting room know what's going on with their friend? They're very worried."

"I can do that."

"Thanks, Tess."

"None needed, it's good to see you. You look wonderful."

Tess was the emergency room nursing manager and Simone had spent many an evening with Tess and her family. They had become close friends. "Who's on duty, today?"

Tess placed her hand on Simone's arm in support, her gaze soft on Simone's face. "Doctor Irvine is." They both knew Simone would rather not see Liz. Liz, at times would try to convince Simone to sleep with her. It was more of an irritation than anything, but it hurt Simone deeply. Tess was one of the few people who knew about Liz and Simone. Tess was not fond of Liz but had kept quiet while Simone was with her. Tess had not been able to ignore the selfish behavior by Liz toward Simone. Tess was protective of Simone's feelings, and woe anyone who tried to hurt her again. Simone was family to Tess.

Simone slipped through the curtain in room six and watched as Barry made Shannon comfortable while June reported her vitals to a nurse.

"We started a saline IV drip on site for fluid replenishment. Her pulse is steady and her breathing normal."

"Thanks, June, good job. Well, young lady, you did a number on yourself. I hope the young man you saved appreciates what you did." The nurse patted Shannon's hand as she looked at her back. "I want the doctor to see you first before I begin cleaning you up. I'll go get him."

"Thank you." Shannon lay flat on her stomach, her head on a pillow. She was in a lot of pain and still felt quite nauseous.

"You're welcome, honey. I'll be right back."

"Simone, June and I need to fill the rig and head back to base."

"Go ahead, Barry. I'll meet you back at the station in a bit. If you get another call beep my pager."

Simone waited until Barry and June left the room before she pulled up a chair and sat by Shannon's head. "Shannon, how are you doing?" Simone's voice was as gentle as her blue eyes.

"I've felt better," Shannon replied, turning her head so she could look at Simone. "How's the boy? I think his name is Jason?"

"He's fine. He's very lucky you were there."

"Someone else would have helped him."

"Shannon," Simone touched her cheek lightly. "You saved his life."

Shannon stared at the beautiful woman seated next to her and smiled. "I'm just glad he's okay. He's going to be grounded for a year according to his mother. Apparently he snuck out of their hotel room without her."

Simone grinned at Shannon. "He deserves to be grounded, but I don't think he will be."

Simone continued to smile at Shannon, still touching her cheek. She admired the dark brown eyes, the long thin nose, and the pronounced cheekbones. Her olive complexion was enhanced by her deep tan. She was very appealing with her straight dark brown hair tied in a ponytail at the base of her neck. She looked European to Simone and beautiful despite all of her injuries. "Your friends are out in the lobby, worried to death."

"I'm okay."

"You're pretty banged up, and they obviously care a lot about you."

"We've known each other for years-Melody and Janice have been together for eight of those years, and Hanna and Olivia for twelve."

"I thought you were lesbians-me too," Simone said and almost laughed as she saw surprise register on Shannon's face. "Where is your girlfriend?"

"I don't have one."

The curtain slid open before Simone could respond.

"Hi Shannon, I'm Doctor Irvine."

"Hello, doctor. Here, I'll get out of your way." Simone started to get out of her chair.

"Can you stay?" Shannon asked softly, looking up at Simone with such vulnerability that it tugged on Simone's heart. She couldn't leave her by herself.

"Certainly," she smiled and remained standing by Shannon's head.

"Let's take a look at you. My, oh my, you took quite a bit of skin off. We need to clean these coral scrapes and cuts very carefully and start you on a strong antibiotic. You may run a slight fever for a couple of days, but you should feel more like yourself later in the week. If you run too high a temperature or don't start feeling better in a couple of days, I want you right back here." The doctor continued examining Shannon, and his probing was painful. She was close to crying, her eyes brimming with tears.

Simone saw Shannon struggling with her emotions and she reached out and placed her hand over Shannon's, where it lay on the pillow next to her head. Shannon turned her hand over and clasped Simone's hand in her own. Simone held tightly to her fingers and locked her gaze on Shannon's face. Shannon's eyes remained trained on Simone's face. It helped to calm her as waves of pain moved through her body. Simone had such a soothing manner and her eyes remained gentle and watchful.

"Shannon, I will check on you after the nurse scrubs your back, arms, and legs. You are going to need someone to change your bandages a couple of times a day and I want you to stay out of the sun and surf at least through Wednesday, but after that the salt water will help with the healing. Keep all tanning oils and lotions away from your wounds. You need to keep them very clean. Aloe Vera gel is the only thing that you should use. Do you have someone who can help you?"

"Yes." Shannon answered with difficulty, swallowing to keep from getting sick.

"Then, I will leave you in very good hands. I'm very glad you saved that little boy." The doctor briskly left the room.

"Okay, Shannon I'm going to get started. This is going to be very painful when I scrub your backs and legs with an antiseptic. I'm sorry, but I need to do this. I will be as gentle as I can, I promise. You just tell me when you need a break." The nurse spoke briskly as she prepared to begin.

"Simone, you don't need to stay." Shannon squeezed her fingers, staring at the compelling woman standing quietly next to her.

"Would you like me to stay?" Simone had no plans to leave. She felt a connection with Shannon and she wouldn't let her deal with this alone. She couldn't explain why she needed to remain with her; she just knew she had to.

Shannon gasped when the nurse started to work, her fingers tightened around Simone's hand. "I want you to stay."

Simone smiled and leaned in closer to Shannon's face as she spoke softly. "Tell me why you are single."

"Now?"

"Yes." Simone knew if Shannon could be distracted she might get through her painful ordeal with a little less discomfort.

"Let's just say I don't believe in open relationships or sharing. My ex-girlfriend thought I should be accepting of her rather frequent forays into the single world." There was more to it then that. Shannon had found out that her relationship had been built upon lies and falsehoods. She had trusted her girlfriend and that trust had been destroyed more than once. Shannon hissed as the nurse scrubbed a particularly sensitive area of her back. She took a big deep breath and continued to speak. "We stayed together a year longer than we should have."

Shannon took deep breaths to deal with her pain while Simone placed her other hand on Shannon's arm gently stroking. Shannon's eyes filled again with tears and her fingers tightened around Simone's. "So what do you do for a living?"

"I'm a cameraperson for the Fox News Network in Bellevue."

"You film sports events?"

"Yes, and interviews and practices, whatever is happening."

"How long have you been a cameraperson?"

"Eight years, I studied filmmaking and camera work in college. How long have you been a paramedic?" Shannon was struggling very hard to handle the pain; tears slid down her cheeks, and she was extremely pale.

"Twenty-three years."

"That's amazing. So are you with someone?"

"No, I'm single."

"Why?"

"Why? Because my girlfriend and I parted ways a while ago."

"Why?" Shannon had to lay her head down on her pillow but she still clutched Simone's hand, her eyes never leaving Simone's face.

Simone smiled and bent very close to Simone's face, speaking in a whisper. "Don't you think we should save some of this for our second date?"

The smile on Shannon's face was sweet, especially considering how much pain she was dealing with. "This has been a hell of a first date."

"I think so." Simone's smiled bloomed.

"Do you think that our second one could be less painful?"

"I should hope so." Simone chuckled, grinning at Shannon.

"When?"

"Why don't we see how you feel over the next couple of days and then plan something?"

"Really?"

"Really Shannon, I want to go out with you." Simone couldn't explain it but she really wanted to get to know Shannon. She liked the woman she was beginning to know. Given the circumstances, Shannon was a very charming woman.

"I can't wait." Shannon's eyes slid shut for a minute before she opened them and gazed once again at Simone. "You're very beautiful."

"Thank you and you're very brave."

"Shannon, I'm going to give you a little break before we start on your arms and legs. I also want to get you a shot for the pain. I think the doctor will okay it." The nurse spoke as she stopped her painful scrubbing.

"Thanks."

"You're welcome, honey. Simone, are you going to stay here?"

"Yes."

"Good, I'll be right back."

Simone sat down on the chair, her hand still clasped with Shannon's, her other hand resting on her arm. "So tell me, is it exciting to be a cameraperson?"

"I think so. I love my job. I get to see all kinds of sports, professional, college, high school, men and women. So your badge says Lieutenant Simone Moreau, are you the boss?"

"I'm in charge of all the paramedics on this island; my boss is on the main island."

"Wow, that's very impressive. You must have worked very hard to be in such a position."

Simone smiled. "Shannon, I am forty-five years old, I'm one of the oldest."

"You certainly don't look your age. I never would have guessed you were forty-five."

"You can't be much older than twenty-five."

"I am thirty-one."

"I am fourteen years older than you."

"Are you trying to back out of our date?" The little bit of irritation in Shannon's voice made Simone grin.

"Not at all, but I am a lot older than you."

"I don't think so."

"Shannon, do you want any of your friends in here with you?"

"No, but if you need to leave, go ahead."

Simone bent over until her face was level with Shannon's where her head lay on the pillow. "Shannon, I'm not going anywhere until you get released, okay?"

"Okay, but will you get in trouble for missing work?"

"Honey, I'm the boss, I don't get in trouble." Simone grinned mischievously. Shannon felt the twinge of attraction tickle her body despite all of her pain. What a strange thing to have happen. "How long are you staying in Hawaii?"

"Three weeks, and we just arrived on Friday evening."

The curtain rustled and the nurse re-entered the room. "Okay Shannon, the doctor said you can get a pain shot along with a mild sedative. It is going to make you very drowsy. Do you have someone here to take you home?"

"My friends are out in the lobby."

"Okay then, you will feel the affects almost immediately."

Simone watched as the nurse administered the pain medication into Shannon's IV. She knew that Shannon would slowly drift off to sleep. They had waited to see how bad her injuries were before giving her any medication. She was relieved that Shannon would be spared any more pain while they scrubbed the rest of her body. Simone knew first hand how painful coral cuts could be. She'd experienced a few herself, but nothing as extensive as Shannon's.

"Whoa, that's pretty fast acting." Shannon's eyes immediately began to droop.

"Let go, Shannon," Simone instructed, stroking her cheek.

"But, I won't see you again." Shannon's words were slurred as she struggled to keep her eyes open. She was afraid to close her eyes. Simone would be gone and she might not ever see her again.

"I promise you will see me. I'll stop by your hotel this evening to check on you, and we have a second date to plan."

"You are so beautiful…" Shannon's words trailed off and she dropped into sleep.

"She's a pretty tough girl," the nurse admitted as she began to scrub the back of Shannon's upper thighs. Simone winced as she watched. "Yes, she is, and a hero."

"Why don't you go talk to her friends while I finish up in here? She should be ready to go home in about an hour."

"I hate to leave." Simone still held on to Shannon's hand.

"She's out Simone, and it's a blessing. Go talk to her worried friends before they drive Tess crazy."

"Okay, come get me if she awakens."

"I will."

Simone stroked Shannon's cheek one last time and pulled her fingers out of her grasp. "I'll be back, Shannon," she whispered to her. For some reason, Shannon had worked her way into Simone's heart in a little less than an hour. Simone didn't question it; she followed her feelings. Emotion deep inside of Simone told her it was something she needed to do.

Her long stride took her quickly out of the emergency area and into the waiting room where she saw all four women seated in chairs looking tired and extremely worried. All four looked at her expectantly. "Shannon is fine. She has been given a pain shot and sedative that knocked her out. That's a good thing, because it is very painful to endure the nurse cleaning her scrapes and cuts."

"Will she be able to go back to the hotel today?"

"She will be released in about an hour but she will be very groggy and maybe a little ill. She'll need to be watched carefully for a fever and infection."

"We'll watch her." Olivia promised as she clasped her girlfriend's hand tightly and tried not to cry. "She's going to be okay, isn't she?"

"Yes, in a couple of days she will feel much better, and she will be able to go back out in the sun and swim."

"Good, she needed this vacation. I can't believe this is happening. The little boy's mother has already told the hospital she is paying Shannon's bill here and at the hotel. And there are newspaper reporters that keep coming in and asking questions. Tess keeps throwing them out." Janice spoke as she and Mel shared a hug. They were scared to death for their good friend.

"Tess can be a terror," Simone admitted with a chuckle as she sat down across from the women.

"She's terrific!" Mel responded, ready to defend Tess. Her show of unabashed loyalty to Tess helped Simone go with the idea she had been considering. Simone's instincts were usually right about people, except for Liz. She knew these women were loyal and caring.

"I would like to make a suggestion and if you don't like it, I'll understand. Shannon needs to stay in bed for the next couple of days and her bandages will need to be changed quite often. Since you're all staying in a hotel room, I would like to suggest that the five of you stay in my home for the duration of your vacation. It will be much easier to take care of Shannon and more convenient for all of you. I have three bedrooms and a daybed in my den. I live on the water so you could lay on the beach, swim, or snorkel. I think Shannon will be much more comfortable in a house instead of a hotel."

The four of them were shocked at the generosity that Simone was offering. It took them a moment to respond and it was Hanna who replied. "Why would you make such a nice offer, you don't even know us?"

Simone smiled at the four women and took a deep breath before she responded. "I'm a lesbian, so I think that might make you more comfortable. And to be honest with you, I am not sure why I am suggesting this. For some reason Shannon has touched my heart, and I really want to make it easier on her to recover. I know that doesn't sound very plausible, but that's the reason."

Simone waited for the four of them to react to her words. She had no idea if they would take her up on her offer. Mel was the first to respond. "Do you have a girlfriend?"

"No, I'm single. I have been for awhile."

"And you would welcome five unknown lesbians into your home?"

"You aren't unknown to me. The four of you are sitting in a hospital waiting for your dear friend who saved a young boy she didn't know. I'd say I know you very well."

"Can we talk about it and let you know?" Hanna asked.

"Of course, I'm going to go back in and check once more on Shannon. Then I need to call in to work and check on everything. I'll be back in about ten minutes, will that be enough time?"

"Yes, and Simone, we want to thank you for everything," Olivia spoke softly. She liked the woman sitting across from them.

"No thanks are needed. I'll be back in ten minutes." Simone stood up and headed back into the emergency room. She couldn't believe she had just opened her home up to strangers. But she had meant what she said. She would do anything to make Shannon comfortable.

She slipped into room six and stepped up to Shannon, who was sound asleep as the nurse finished scrubbing her arms. "How's she doing?"

"She's totally out and I'm very glad. Her arms and legs are as bad as her back. She's going to hurt like hell tonight and tomorrow."

"Is the doctor going to give her some pain pills?"

"He already has but they may make her sick to her stomach." Simone stood close to Shannon's head and placed her hand on her hair while she slept. "I am just about ready to put some bandages on and we can get her out of here. The best thing for her to do is sleep through most of the next couple of days."

"I'm going to make sure she does. Can I use the telephone in the office?"

"Sure, honey."

Simone spoke to a few of the other nurses as she went into the office and used the telephone. She knew all of them by name. "Eric, its Simone, how are things going?"

Simone was on the telephone for a couple of minutes and then returned to Shannon's room. The nurse was almost finished with the bandaging as she wrapped gauze around her arms. "It is going to be difficult to get her home comfortably, because the backs of her legs and back are extremely tender."

"What if we make a bed for her in the back of my Rover?"

"That'll work."

"Good. I'll be right back."

Simone rapidly returned to the waiting room in time to see Tess shoving a reporter out of the emergency room doors. "I told you to stay outside," Tess admonished as she turned to a hospital security guard. "If one of them tries to come back in I want you to shoot them, Randy."

"Yes, Tess." The security guard grinned at Tess. He knew she didn't mean it but he also knew she expected him to keep them out, and he would. Tess was a force of nature and you only crossed her once. You wouldn't be allowed a second chance.

Simone smiled as she sat down across from the four women again. "Shannon is still sleeping and the nurse is just about done bandaging her. She is going to have to remain on her stomach so no matter whether you decide to stay in my home or the hotel, I think we should make a bed in my Rover and transport her that way. It's the best way to keep her comfortable. One of you can ride with her and make sure she is not disturbed."

"Simone, we need to ask you one question."

"Okay."

"What is it about Shannon that touched you?" Janice inquired as the four women waited for Simone to respond.

"She didn't hesitate to save a young boy's life and she never once asked for help after being horribly injured, her only concern was about the boy. She has four loving and loyal friends. She wants a girlfriend that loves her enough to be committed to her and her alone, and she's gorgeous. Oh, and I forgot to mention, she is proud of her career as a cameraperson and she thinks my being a paramedic for over twenty years is amazing. I think that about covers it"

Mel began to chuckle as the other three women grinned. "You know more about Shannon in two hours than her ex-girlfriend learned in a couple of years."

"Isn't that a shame for her ex-girlfriend?" Simone grinned as she responded, her eyes twinkling with mischief.

"We've made a decision."

"Good."

"We have decided to take you up on your offer with a couple of concessions."

"And those would be?"

"We pay for all the food and beverages, and any other expenses. We also pay for any utilities for the time we stay there. You did invite us to stay for our full vacation?"

"Yes, I did. I will agree to your buying food and beverages but utilities are already taken care of."

"Okay then, you'll have five roommates for a few weeks. We decided that Olivia and Hanna will go back and check all of us out of the hotel. They can pack everything up. Janice and I will go with you to take Shannon to your house. Olivia and Hanna will need directions to get to your place."

"I'll write them down and give you my telephone number and my cell phone number."

"Good, Hanna has her cell phone with her. We'll give you the number."

"Does Shannon have any relatives that should be notified?"

"She has an older brother, but they aren't very close. Her parents are both dead. I'll get the number from Shannon and call him later."

"Okay, I'll go write down the directions so you can get going. My home is about forty minutes from your hotel."

Twenty-five minutes later Simone, Mel, and Janice, along with help from an orderly, had settled a sleeping Shannon on blankets in the back of Simone's Ranger. Janice sat next to her holding her limp hand while Mel sat in the front with Simone. Mel hadn't missed the gentle hand that had pushed Shannon's hair out of her sleeping face, nor did she miss the concern on Simone's face when Shannon murmured in pain as they moved her. She was curious as to how a stranger could, in two hours become so attached to Shannon. She thought it was almost magical.

"How long have you lived in Hawaii?" she asked Simone.

"All my life, I was born here."

"It must have been wonderful to grow up in such a beautiful place."

"I liked it. I went to college in California for four years at Stanford, but I came right back here afterwards. I missed Hawaii."

"Are you Hawaiian?"

"Only because I was born here, not by race. My dad was stationed here during Pearl Harbor and he fell in love with Hawaii. When he met my mother in France, he married her, and brought her back here to live. He was originally from France also."

"That explains your name. It's a beautiful name."

"Thank you. I was named after my dad's mother."

"Are your parents still here?"

"No, they both have passed away."

"I'm sorry."

"No problem."

"So why are you single?"

"Because I choose to be," Simone grinned at Mel.

Mel laughed and responded, "Touché, I probably sound like a grand inquis-itor."

"You sound like a concerned friend."

"Thank you, I love Shannon. She's a sweet person."

"Tell me about her."

"I met her the same time I met Janice. They played on the same softball team. When Janice and I got together, Shannon was a natural part of the deal." She went on to explain meeting Hanna at a softball tournament, and that Shannon and Hanna had actually dated briefly. But they made better friends and Hanna soon met Olivia. She explained, too, about Anita Roosevelt, and that all four friends had known Anita had cheated on Shannon more than once. They had all been afraid to bring it up with Shannon because she wasn't ready to hear it. They had watched their friend's heart get broken repeatedly.

"Anita wanted an open relationship," she said, "and Shannon finally moved out. Shannon just wants someone to love her enough to be committed to her, but she's been single since that breakup. What about you?"

"What about me?"

"Simone, we're having a conversation. You're supposed to contribute."

Simone laughed. "I work long hours and I don't date. In my spare time I scuba dive or swim."

"Good, that's a start," Janice piped in from the back.

"How's she doing?"

"Sleeping like a baby."

"Good, let's hope it lasts. She's in for a long night."

"So why did you and your girlfriend break up?"

"How do you know I had a girlfriend?"

"Simone," Janice groaned.

"Okay, she's a doctor at the hospital we just left, and she didn't like the fact that I don't want to be anything more than a paramedic. We fought all the time about it and we finally broke up. She also didn't want anyone to know we were together. No one at the hospital knew she was gay and she wanted it to remain that way. Most people at the hospital know I'm gay and it was a problem. I got tired of hiding our relationship. I have been single for over a year. What do the two of you do for a living?"

"We're both firefighters. I'm on medical leave right now."

"You both are firefighters? Are you okay?"

"I strained my back during a fire, and yes we are both firefighters."

"That must be hard on your schedules."

"A little, but I am in charge of the North Seattle station so I work pretty regular hours. Janice still works shift work but we get by, don't we, Janice?"

"You bet we do."

Shannon cried softly in her sleep and Janice stroked her head and began speaking softly to her as the other two women remained silent until she settled back down. "I can't believe this happened."

Simone glanced at Mel after she spoke. "There are going to be a lot of irritating reporters trying to get information about Shannon. They don't know that she's going to my house but it won't be long before they find out."

"Are you worried about the attention?"

"No, I am worried about Shannon's health. You might want to meet with a reporter and answer all of the questions once so they'll leave her alone."

"That's a good suggestion. Do you know any particular reporter?"

"I do. One of my friends works at a local television station. She's who I would go to. She's an excellent reporter."

"That's a good idea."

They turned into a long driveway that had an open gate and drove up to park in front of an elegant entryway to a fairly good sized house. The yard was large and immaculate, full of gardens, and a sloping green lawn. Huge flowering trees and birds of paradise, along with towering palm trees made the yard look very natural and part of the paradise that was Hawaii.

"Let me go get the room ready for Shannon before we move her." Simone suggested as she stopped the Rover and prepared to get out.

"Sounds good, can I help?"

"Why don't you stay with Janice, it will just take a minute."

"Okay."

Simone walked to the front door and opened the double doors, then entered the home. She disappeared from view as Mel and Janice watched. "What do you think, Mel?"

"I think Simone is wealthy, honey. Look at this house." They both stared at it with a little awe.

"That's not what I meant."

"I know what you meant. I think she likes Shannon a lot. For some reason she wants to help take care of her. I think she is very genuine and very nice."

"So do I, do you think Shannon is going to like being here?"

"We'll have to wait and see."

"Mel, Janice, I thought we could carry Shannon in on this stretcher." Simone came out of the house carrying a roll under her arm.

"You have a stretcher in your home?"

"I do a lot of instructing to paramedics and first aid classes and I keep a lot of supplies in my home."

"So how should we do this?"

"Can you roll Shannon up on her side while I slide this under her? Then we will roll her back on to the stretcher and carry her in."

"Sounds like a plan."

The three of them worked silently and successfully as they transferred Shannon onto the stretcher and started to move her into the house. "The bedroom is down the hall on the left, all the way to the end." The three of them moved quickly but Janice and Mel couldn't help but see the large living room and front entry with the intriguing masks hanging on the walls. The hallway was wide and as they entered the bedroom it was all Janice could do from keeping her jaw from dropping open. The room was enormous and centered against the far wall was a canopied bed. There was white tropical netting that was draped sensuously around the four bed posters to the floor. It was the sexiest bedroom Janice had ever seen.

"Wow, this is a beautiful room!" Mel exclaimed as she helped them lift Shannon's sleeping body onto the bed.

"Simone, Shannon's back is bleeding. Maybe we need to put something down so she won't bleed on the bed." Janice knew that it was Simone's bedroom.

"Don't worry about that, let's just get her into bed and I will check her bandages after she's settled."

Shannon didn't even moan as they gently rolled her onto the bed. Simone pulled up her bandage on her back and checked her bleeding but everything looked okay. "Janice and Mel, why don't you take Shannon's bathing suit off and if you want to put something loose on her? I have a nightshirt laid out. I'm going to check the kitchen for food. I doubt if there is any, so I'll stop by the store on my way home from work. Shannon might feel better later if you put some ice on her back and legs. She's going to run a temperature for awhile. And she might feel a little nauseous. You'll need to take her temperature every couple of hours and make sure it doesn't go too high. I've put a thermometer on the bathroom counter. Come on, and I will show you the other bedrooms so you can choose where to stay when Olivia and Hanna get here."

Simone showed them through the one story rambling home and then the patio and the path to the beach. It was an incredible house laid out to take advantage of the view of the beach and the tropical breezes. "Please make yourself at home. My telephone number and cell phone number are on the counter in the kitchen. Call me if Shannon has any problems. I just need to check in at work and clear my calendar tomorrow so I can take the day off. I should be back in a couple of hours."

"Simone, Shannon will be fine. We can't thank you enough."

"You don't need to thank me. See you later."

Mel and Janice watched Simone leave and then turned to each other. "Can you believe this place, it is amazing. I can't believe she invited us to stay here. Don't you think she's incredibly generous?"

"I do. Honey, Simone suggested that we speak to one reporter and answer questions so they will go away. What do you think?"

"I think it's a good idea. Why don't we write some things down?" After removing Shannon's bathing suit to make her more comfortable, the two of them sat in the living room working on a statement while Shannon slumbered in the back bedroom. Periodically, they checked on her, but she slept undisturbed even when Olivia and Hanna arrived with more news.

CHAPTER 2

"There was no bill at the hotel, the boy's mother requested that it be sent to her, and the hotel even ran interference for us with the press. Everyone was so nice and helpful. They sent someone to help us pack everything and then snuck us out the back where Olivia waited in the jeep. You should see the flowers Shannon already received. They are out in the jeep."

"How is Shannon?" Olivia asked as she unloaded some of Shannon's things in the hallway.

"She's still sleeping. I need to take her temperature in a few minutes." Janice responded.

"This place is amazing!" Hanna's eyes were large with surprise.

"It's incredible. Let me show you your bedroom and you can unpack." Mel grabbed some of the luggage on the floor.

"We need to get to a store and pick up some groceries and things." Olivia reminded them.

"Simone said she was going to stop by a store on her way home from work. She should be home pretty soon." Mel responded leading the way down the hall.

"She's very generous opening up her home to us."

"That's why I think we need to pay for all the food and stuff, and make sure we clean up after ourselves." Janice piped in grabbing some of their things.

"Maybe we should do the cooking?" Olivia volunteered.

"We should ask her first."

"I'm going to go and take Shannon's temperature. Why don't you guys go unpack and then we'll decide who gets to go find a store." Janice placed her suitcase in the bedroom she and Mel had chosen.

"We passed a shopping mall on our way here. It's only ten minutes away."

"Good, we can make a list of what we need after we get settled." Hanna and Olivia began to unpack their things in their bedroom as Mel did the same with her things in the other room.

"Mel, guys, Shannon has got a temperature of one hundred and one, and she feels very warm to the touch. She's still sleeping but what should we do?" Janice asked her voice full of concern for their injured friend.

"Simone said to get ice packs and put them on her back and legs."

"Okay, can you go find a towel and I will get some ice."

Thirty minutes later the three women unpacked and were all seated in the living room, taking turns going into Shannon's room and holding an ice bag to her back and legs. She had become restless in sleep, obviously experiencing a lot of pain. The four women were at a loss as to what to do. "Maybe we should wake her up and give her pain medication?"

"She can't take one for another twenty minutes according to the prescription."

"She's in a lot of pain."

"I know, honey."

The front door swung open and Simone walked in with two large grocery bags in her hands. "Hi, how's Shannon?"

"Restless and running a temperature. Here, let me help you," Mel responded as she took a bag from Simone.

"There are more bags out in the car."

"I'll go get them." Hanna jumped up and headed out the front door.

"Simone, what do we owe you for the groceries?" Janice asked as she followed her into the kitchen.

"Nothing."

"That wasn't our agreement."

"I didn't have anything in the house so this is normal restocking. You can buy everything from now on."

"How do you feel about one of us cooking? Hanna is a gourmet chef."

"You're kidding?"

"Nope, she used to cook for a living. Now she plans the menus and runs the kitchen at a major hotel in Seattle."

"What does Olivia do?"

"She works with handicapped children. She's a teacher and a therapist."

"You're an interesting foursome. I am going to check on Shannon and then put everything away. We can plan something for dinner after that. And I am not a great cook, so if Hanna wants to cook, I would welcome it." Simone smiled as she headed out of the kitchen. "I was able to take tomorrow and Wednesday off from work, so I can help take care of Shannon."

Simone could hear Shannon's restless movement as she walked down the hall. The pain medication was probably wearing off. She entered her bedroom and went straight to the bed. Shannon had thrown off her covers and she was naked except for her bandages. She was tan all over with no apparent tan lines and it made Simone smile. She was very fit and her back end was sleek and muscular. It was a very appealing sight but Simone pushed everything away as she approached the bed. She placed her hand against Shannon's forehead and winced. She was running a temperature, her face beaded with perspiration. Janice entered the room and joined Simone. She was surprised to see the look on Simone's face and her hand affectionately stroking Shannon's cheek.

Janice recognized the expression and was amazed. Simone looked like she was falling in love with Shannon. "She's got a temperature of one hundred and one and she's dripping with sweat. We have been putting ice on her back and legs to cool her down. I think it's almost time to wake her up and give her a pain pill."

"Why don't you rouse her and I'll get another ice bag. She may be a little groggy and seeing a familiar face will help."

Simone left the room and Janice sat down beside Shannon and shook her gently. "Shanni, wake up, honey."

Shannon grumbled and moaned as Janice continued to try and awaken her. Shannon slowly opened her eyes and looked sleepily at Janice. "Where am I?"

"You're in Simone's home. She offered to let us stay here. How are you feeling, honey?"

"I feel kind of sick to my stomach and I have to go to the bathroom."

"Let me help you."

"Janice, I'm naked."

"We thought you didn't need to wear clothes against your bandages. We have all your stuff here. What do you want to wear, how about a pair of underwear and a tee shirt?"

"Okay. Where is everyone? Is Simone here?"

"Everyone is in the kitchen and Simone went to get an ice bag."

"Please, get my clothes."

"I'll be right back. Let's put the sheet over you until I return."

Simone met Janice as she left the room. "Is she awake?"

"Yes, and she wants to put some clothes on. She's feeling a little sick to her stomach."

"That's probably the pain medication. I have ginger ale in the kitchen that may settle her stomach."

"I'll be right back."

Simone entered the quiet room and noticed Shannon's eyes were open and following her as she crossed the room to her. "Hi, how are you feeling?" She spoke softly as she watched Shannon's reaction.

"I've felt a lot better. It was very generous of you to bring all of us to your home."

"It's nothing." Simone smiled. "You might have an upset stomach from the pain medication. Janice went to get you a glass of ginger ale just in case. It will settle your stomach."

"That sounds good." Shannon smiled. "I thought you were a dream."

"I'm not a dream." Simone chuckled as she reached out to touch Shannon's hand.

Shannon turned her hand over and laced her fingers with Simone's. "Thank you."

"Shannon, you don't need to thank me, I want you here."

"Why?"

"Because I feel a connection with you and we need to get to get to know each other better before we can have our second date."

Shannon grinned. "I remember that."

"Good, because I'm not going to let you forget." Simone smiled at Shannon. Janice waited outside the door intrigued and eavesdropped.

"Simone, I'm feeling a little sick to my stomach and need to get to the bathroom."

"Let me help you."

"I'm naked."

"I know." Simone grinned down at her.

"I'd rather you saw me naked when I was more appealing than being wrapped up like a mummy."

"I'll tell Janice to get your clothes."

"I'm right here, Simone."

"Okay, I'll leave you to get dressed and then I need to change your dressings. You need to take another pain pill and you might want to try and eat some soup and crackers."

Simone slipped out of the room as Janice approached the bed. "She has taken time off from work to take care of you and she stayed at the hospital even after you went to sleep. She's the one who brought you here and put you in her bed."

"This is her bed?"

"Yes and her house is amazing. She lives right on the beach. Her living room has two large sliding glass doors that open up the back of the house to a big patio and the beach."

"Did she see me naked?"

"Yep," Janice grinned down at her.

"Oh God," Shannon groaned with embarrassment. "Give me my clothes so I can get dressed."

"Let me help you, honey. You might be kind of dizzy." Shannon started to sit up and cried out as her shredded skin on the back of her thighs touched the bed. She stumbled to her feet unsteadily.

Janice slid her panties on her legs and Shannon bent over to pull them up. She almost fell to the floor she was so dizzy. "Janice, where's the bathroom? I'm going to be sick."

"Over here, honey. Hold on to me." Janice got her to the bathroom and Shannon bent at the waist as she vomited into the toilet. Janice held her hair and rubbed her neck as Shannon was violently ill. When she finished, Janice wiped her face with a warm washcloth and slid a tee shirt on her. She then walked Shannon back to the bed, where Shannon gingerly sat down.

"Can I come in?" Simone asked from the doorway.

"Yes. She's dressed."

"Shannon, I brought you the ginger ale and an ice bag for your back. It might help keep your temperature down."

Shannon's eyes again locked on to Simone as she approached the bed. "Ginger ale would be nice, thank you."

Simone handed the glass to Shannon and Janice decided to leave the room. She was going to report what she saw to the other three women. She was amazed by the reaction Simone and Shannon had to each other. You would have thought they were a couple they were so in tune with each other.

"Do you want some soup and crackers?"

"Maybe in a little bit. My stomach is still not very settled."

"How about you take this pain pill and then I check your bandages."

"I will have to take my shirt off."

"Shannon, I have already seen you naked. I think you're beautiful."

Shannon blushed as she gazed at Simone. "I can't believe you still want to go on a date with me."

"I want to do more than date you but we'll start with that," Simone announced with a sexy smile.

"You haven't even kissed me."

"Is that an invitation?" Shannon was flustered that Simone was flirting with her. "I think we will wait on the kiss until you are feeling a little bit better. Now, let's have you roll on to your stomach and slide your shirt up so I can check your back and legs for infection."

Shannon slowly rolled onto her stomach and Simone gently slid her shirt up over her shoulders. She lay with her head on the pillow as Simone's gentle fingers slowly pulled her bandages away from her skin.

"Shannon, I'll be right back I need to get fresh bandages and tape. The rest of your friends would like to come in and see how you are doing."

"Okay."

"Hi Shanni, how are you doing, sweetie?" Hanna approached the bed and bent over to kiss her. Olivia followed her and then Mel.

"I'm okay, guys. I'm sorry I ruined our vacation."

"You didn't ruin it. We have three weeks of sun and surf and we are staying in a beautiful home right on the beach. It's perfect, other than you were hurt so badly." Mel reassured her.

"I'll be fine, tomorrow. I just need a night of sleep. I'll be fine, really." Her friends didn't have the heart to contradict her. It would be longer than one night before Shannon felt better.

"Okay, I'm going to remove all of your back bandages and replace them with clean ones. Can one of you help cut the tape for me?" Simone requested as she sat down next to Shannon on the bed.

"Sure, I'll help." Olivia volunteered. "Shannon, Hanna is going to cook dinner tonight for everyone and make you some soup. Mel, why don't you and Janice talk to her about what you have prepared for the reporters?"

"What reporters?"

"The reporters that tried to talk to you at the hospital and chased us around the hotel, they were everywhere."

"Why?"

"Because they want to interview you," Hanna stopped in mid sentence when she saw Shannon's back. "Mel, you tell her."

Hanna hugged Janice as she realized how much damage Shannon's body had sustained. "Shannon, Simone suggested that we choose one reporter to answer all their questions so they will go away. It's a good suggestion."

"Why do they want an interview?"

"You saved that boy's life, and his mother has already done several interviews. She's telling them you're a hero."

Shannon tried to keep her moan quiet but to no avail as she laid her head down while Simone pulled her bandage off. "I'm sorry, Shannon. I've got to get this bandage off and I'm trying to be gentle."

Simone's eyes glistened with unshed tears as she pulled the remaining bandage off. The last thing she wanted to do was hurt Shannon. The fact that Shannon didn't do more than moan quietly was amazing to Simone. "I'm swimming with a wet suit from now on." Shannon grumbled quietly.

Mel chuckled. "I think that's a wise idea."

"How does it look?"

Simone glanced up at Shannon's four friends who stared at Shannon's back with disbelief. They looked at her uncertain as to how to reply. Simone reached out and clasped Shannon's hand gently as she spoke. "Shannon, you are deeply cut in places and missing lots of skin."

"Great." She laid her head back down, tears leaking from her eyes.

Simone continued replacing all of Shannon's bandages on her back, legs, and arms, while the rest of the group left the room and began preparing soup for Shannon and dinner for the rest of them. Hanna busied herself getting to know the kitchen, while Victoria and Janice made a quick trip back to the market with Hanna's list.

"Shannon, I'm done."

"Thanks, Simone. I appreciate everything you're doing." Shannon hurt so much she could barely talk.

"I want you to stop thanking me, please. I want you here."

Shannon turned so she could look at Simone's face as she sat on the side of the bed. "This is an awful way to get to know me."

"I'm not complaining, except that I wish you weren't in so much pain." Simone smiled at Shannon. "Do you think you can eat some soup and crackers and then take another pain pill? If you get something in your stomach you might feel better."

"I'd like a little soup. Can I get up and sit at a table?"

"Sure, but you may find it a little painful. Let me help you."

Shannon stood up unsteadily on her feet. "My hair is a mess." She grumbled as Simone supported her arm while she walked down the hall toward the kitchen. "Hey, guys."

"Hi, sweetie, how about you eat some of this chicken noodle soup and some crackers." Mel suggested as she watched Shannon with loving eyes. Shannon was one of her best friends and she wished she could make her feel better.

"I'd like some, thanks." Shannon sat gingerly on the chair. Simone left the room and returned almost instantly with a blanket in her arms.

"Shannon, why don't you put this blanket over your legs?"

"Thanks." Shannon gazed steadily at Simone.

"Here you go, honey." Hanna placed a bowl of hot soup and a plate of crackers in front of her. "Here is some more ginger ale for your upset stomach."

"I'm going to change my clothes. Do any of you need anything?" Simone asked while Shannon dipped into her soup.

"Not a thing. As soon as the girls get back from the store, I'm fixing dinner. Is there anything you don't eat?"

"No. So you really are a chef?"

"For years." Hanna grinned at her. "That's why Olivia and I are pleasingly plump."

"I'm looking forward to dinner." Simone smiled and left the room heading down the hallway. After she entered her bedroom, Mel sat down next to Shannon and spoke. "She's a nice woman."

"Yes, she is." Shannon agreed.

"She's quite taken with you."

Shannon blushed. "I'm kind of taken with her."

"Boy, Shannon, couldn't you think of an easier way to get noticed?"

"Mel, you are so funny."

"Shannon, we're all very proud of you."

"I just got there before any of you and believe me I wish one of you had beat me to the water."

"Hey girls, wait until you see what we got at the store. Mel, Janice needs some help with the bags." Olivia had two full bags in her arms. "Hey, Shanni, I'm glad to see you up."

"Thanks, Olivia."

"Did you find all your things in the bedroom? We unpacked all your books."

"I did see them."

Simone chose to enter the kitchen at that time and Shannon's eyes followed her as she crossed to the table. She was wearing a pair of shorts and a tee-shirt, looking much younger than forty-five. "Hanna, do you want to eat outside?"

"That would be terrific. I've got two bottles of wine here. We can start with that."

Within minutes, all six women were in the kitchen. Shannon remained seated at the table while the rest were put to work by Hanna, either cutting vegetables, preparing a salad, or drinking wine. It was a friendly group and Simone fit right in as they bantered back and forth. As she passed Shannon, carrying plates and napkins outside, she winked at her, drawing a smile to Shannon's face. Shannon joined them outside while they sipped their wine, and Hanna grilled pork chops on Simone's gas grill.

"Simone, how did you end up with such a beautiful place on the water?"

"It was my parents. I grew up here. When they passed away, I became the owner."

"It's a beautiful home."

"Thanks, I like it."

Shannon sat quietly enjoying the sun and her friend's conversation but she quickly found herself getting tired and her legs were bothering her quite a bit. Her eyelids started to droop as the other women visited. Simone was watching her very closely and didn't miss her paleness or the exhaustion on her face. Shannon's eyes slid closed as she struggled to stay awake.

"Shannon, let's get you back in bed. You must be very tired." She suggested.

"I am. I can't seem to keep my eyes open." Shannon stood up unsteadily and Simone slipped an arm around her waist to steady her. Shannon leaned against her as she slowly walked into the house toward the bedroom. "Goodnight everyone, see you in the morning."

"Goodnight, honey." They watched as the two women left the patio.

"She looks like she is in a lot of pain. It makes we want to cry." Janice admitted.

"She'll be okay in a couple of days, sweetie."

"Simone sure is a doll. She's taking wonderful care of Shannon."

"She is very nice and I think there is a romance brewing between her and Shannon. Did you see how they watch each other?"

"It's really sweet, don't you think?"

"Simone, this is your bedroom isn't it?" Shannon asked as they entered the room.

"Yes."

"Are you going to sleep with me?"

"Do you want me to?" Simone smiled and watched Shannon respond as she stood next to the side of the bed.

"Yes." Shannon returned the smile.

"Can you crawl in bed and get some sleep?"

Shannon reached up and touched Simone on her cheek. "You're being so nice to me."

Simone turned her face until her lips touched Shannon's palm, kissing it softly. "I like you, Shannon, and I want to get to know you."

Shannon sighed as her fingers touched Simone's lips. "I like you too, and I can't wait until I feel a little better so we can go on our date."

"Soon," Simone moved closer to Shannon.

"Simone, could I have a hug?"

"Of course," Simone gathered her gently in her arms until Shannon rested against her body. Shannon placed her face against Simone's and relaxed. Simone smelled so wonderful, her scent a mix of citrus, coconut, and lilacs.

Simone just about gasped as Shannon's body settled against her own. She was surprised at the raw pulsating, hunger she felt for Shannon. This was something new to Simone. She raised her hand and stroked the back of Shannon's head.

"Simone, do you feel what I feel?" Shannon whispered quietly as she tucked her face tighter against Simone's.

"What do you feel?"

"I'm unbelievably attracted to you and I've just met you. I don't feel uncomfortable or nervous I just want to be with you."

Simone smiled as she tightened her arms around Shannon. "I feel the same way."

"What are we going to do about it?"

"I suggest we get you feeling better and go from there."

"I think that's a good idea." Shannon hugged her one more time and then moved out of Simone's arms. "Go eat dinner, Hanna's a terrific cook."

"I'll check on you in a little bit. You feel a little warm, Shannon."

"I think I'm running a temperature again."

"Here, you sit down and let me get the thermometer." Simone went to the bathroom and returned to take Shannon's temperature. It was elevated again. "It's one hundred. I'll go get an ice bag. You get comfortable and I'll be right back."

Shannon rolled onto her stomach and relaxed the best she could. She wanted everything over with. Her back, legs, and arms throbbed and she was feeling nauseous again. What crummy timing she had. Here she was in the bed of a gorgeous lesbian and all she could do was sleep.

"Here, honey, I'm going to lay this ice bag on your back. I'll check back in a little bit and see how you are doing." Simone leaned over and ran her hand over Shannon's head. "Go to sleep, please."

Shannon looked up at Simone and smiled. "Thank you, again."

Simone bent over and lightly kissed Shannon on her cheek. "You're very welcome." Simone watched as Shannon's eyes slid shut. Even after a day like Shannon had, she still looked so appealing, her hair over her shoulder, her hands tucked against her face as she began to breathe deeply while she slid immediately into sleep.

"Is she sleeping?" Olivia whispered from the doorway.

"Yes." Simone turned away and headed back down the hall with Olivia. "She needs to sleep. She hasn't seen the worst of her injuries yet. She's going to feel pretty bad until the antibiotics kick the infection out."

"Simone, this may sound rude but what is the attraction between you and Shannon?"

"It's not rude, you're her friend. I'm not sure it's something I can explain completely. I feel connected to her, like I have known her for a long time. I want to get to know her, and I am extremely attracted to her."

"Have you told Shannon?"

"Yes."

"She's attracted to you."

"I know." Simone grinned. "Now, we have to get her feeling better so we can go on a date."

Olivia burst into laughter as they both walked out of the house to join the other women for dinner.

"Hey girls, what's so funny."

"Simone and Shannon are going to go on a date when Shannon feels better." Olivia shared as she sat down.

"Good for them." Mel chuckled. "Is she asleep?"

"Yes, hopefully for a long while."

"Let's eat, ladies." Hanna suggested. "Anyone want any more wine?"

The five women sat outside until the evening became late as the warm breeze and the conversation kept them occupied. They all took turns checking on Shannon, who though still running a temperature, slept heavily even when they changed her ice bags. Janice and Mel were the first to call it a night and then Simone decided to turn in. "I'm going to go crawl in bed. Hanna, thank you for the incredible meal."

"Wait until tomorrow night. I have big plans."

"I've set the coffee pot to turn on at seven. I'm not working tomorrow but I'm usually up by then. Feel free to roam around and use anything."

"How's the beach here?"

"Good, there is a slight drop off if you go left, but if you stay in front of the house it's pretty flat. Be careful of going out too far, there is an undertow at the change of tides."

"I think we are going to get up early and go snorkeling."

"Maybe after Shannon feels better I can take all of you to a beach I know that has turtles and manta rays swimming in the bay."

"That would be cool."

"Great. Goodnight then, I enjoyed the evening."

Simone slipped into the house while Hanna and Olivia sat on a lounge chair listening to the waves crashing on the beach. The evening had been very pleasant. Simone was open and friendly, and there were none of the usually lags in conversation. They had shared stories of each other and Simone had talked a little about herself. The care with which she watched over Shannon impressed and reassured all of them.

Simone entered the dark bedroom and went straight to the bathroom. She quietly cleaned up and then changed into her nightshirt before checking on Shannon once more. Shannon was still running a temperature and her shirt was damp with perspiration as she fought off the infection that tried to take hold in her body. There was nothing Simone could do except pray she'd sleep through most of the discomfort. Simone went to the other side of the bed and crawled under the covers. She didn't want to bump Shannon and disturb her but Shannon murmured in her sleep and moved closer to Simone, tucking herself tightly against Simone's back. Simone rolled over and tucked Shannon's head on her shoulder, slipping her arm around her neck. Shannon's arm snaked around Simone's waist as she settled back to sleep. Simone smiled and closed her eyes as she willed her body to relax.

Simone had been asleep for over an hour when Shannon began to cry in her sleep obviously in a lot of pain. Simone turned and stroked her cheek, whispering quietly to her to settle her down. "Shannon, do you want another pain pill?"

"Yes." Shannon's voice was hoarse.

"I'll be right back."

Simone returned with a glass of water and her pill. "Here you go, honey." Shannon took her pill and laid back down as Simone got back into bed. Shannon turned to her immediately, her head nestled on Simone's shoulder and her arm resting on Simone's stomach.

"I feel so cold." Shannon shivered her body clammy with perspiration.

"It's because you have a temperature." Simone gathered her closer to her. "Go to sleep."

Simone kissed Shannon softly on her forehead and then gently on her cheek. Shannon lips slid against Simone's cheek before finding her mouth and kissing her softly. "Goodnight."

Simone was astounded at how such a short kiss could have thrilled her so much. She trembled at the reaction her body had to the one sweet kiss. It was like a bolt of lightning shot through her. Shannon's fingers clutched at Simone's nightshirt as she slipped back into sleep again, while Simone lay awake for quite awhile, trying to settle her growing attraction for Shannon, before she finally fell asleep.

CHAPTER 3

It was after six before either of them woke up again and it was Shannon who woke up early to find herself draped completely across Simone's body. Simone's face was tucked against Shannon's neck, her arms holding Shannon gently. Shannon watched as Simone slept, marveling at her long eyelashes, her perfect eyebrows, and her blond curls surrounding her beautiful face. Shannon couldn't help but notice they were hip-to-hip, Simone's long legs cradling Shannon's body. Shannon felt the familiar rush as she felt Simone's full breasts intimately pushing against her own. Shannon laid her head back down and shut her eyes. She wanted the moment to last forever. Simone stirred against Shannon and tightened her arms around her as she opened her eyes.

Shannon and Simone stared at one another, as awareness of each other's body was all they felt. "How are you feeling?" she asked Shannon with a smile.

"Okay, better, I think."

"Do you need another pain pill?"

"I think I will wait until I have eaten something."

"You don't feel like you're running a temperature."

"How did you sleep?"

"Wonderfully, I like sleeping with you," Simone teased her.

Shannon grinned at her. "I like sleeping with you."

"Good. I'm going to go hop into the shower. Can I get you anything before I do?"

"No, I'm good. I don't suppose I can take a shower?"

"No, I don't think that would be wise."

Shannon started to slide off of Simone but Simone stopped her with a touch of her hand to her cheek. "Good morning," she repeated as she kissed Shannon softly.

Shannon returned the kiss, her fingers sliding into Simone's hair as she deepened the kiss. It was full, soft, and perfect. Simone pulled gently away from Shannon as they stared at one another. Shannon slowly moved off of Simone's body, their eyes still watching each other carefully. Neither one had been prepared for the feelings that the kiss had unleashed.

"After I take my shower I would like to change your bandages."

"Okay, but I need to clean up a little myself. I'm a mess." Shannon grimaced. "I'd like to wash my hair."

"I can help you with that if you want." Simone rummaged through her drawers as she spoke. "Shannon, I have emptied a drawer for you to put your things in."

Shannon was completely caught off guard by Simone. She had known her less than twenty-four hours and she was staying in her home, sleeping in her bed, and putting her clothes in her drawer. She sat on the side of the bed while Simone entered the bathroom and shut the door. Shannon really liked Simone, at least what she knew of her, and heaven knew her attraction to her was overwhelming. She stood up a little unsteadily, her back and legs stinging as she moved. She was going to locate some coffee. The house was silent as she padded barefoot down the hallway, the rich scent of fresh coffee luring her into the kitchen. The back sliding glass door was open and Mel and Janice were laying together on a chaise lounge, arms around each other as they drank their coffee. Shannon smiled as she watched them. They were a very healthy, loving couple who had weathered through some bad times, and were enjoying their life with each other.

Mel and Janice had met on the job years earlier while Janice was still involved with someone else. Mel had been instantly attracted to Janice and her odd sense of humor. But Mel never approached women in relationships, it was a golden rule. For months, Mel thought she had hidden her feelings well until one evening Janice had stayed late after a company dinner party. Mel and Janice left the restaurant at the same time, chatting about work. It was Janice who stopped Mel from getting in her car.

"Mel, can I talk to you a minute?"

Mel turned to Janice with concern. "Sure, is everything okay?"

"No, I have feelings for you and I need to know if you have any for me?" Janice stared at Mel, her heart in her throat. It had taken her weeks to say anything.

"Aren't you with someone?"

"Yes."

"Janice, I don't date women in relationships." Mel responded with a hint of anger.

"You didn't answer my question."

"Janice, it wouldn't matter how I felt. You're in a relationship."

Janice continued to watch Mel silently. She had her answer. She'd been fighting feelings for Mel for such a long time.

"I've got to go." Mel knew if she didn't leave soon that she would reveal her thoughts to Janice.

"Mel, wait." Janice clutched her arm. "Let me explain, please?"

Mel turned and waited for Janice to continue, her heart pounding in her chest.

"My girlfriend knows I am attracted to you. I've been honest with her. She wants out of our relationship as much as I do. We are friends, not lovers. We haven't slept together in months."

"What does this have to do with me?"

"I am wildly attracted to you and I think you might be interested in me. Am I right?"

Mel looked into the beautiful, vulnerable eyes of a woman she'd been fantasizing about for months and melted. "Yes."

Janice's smile bloomed on her face as she moved closer to Mel. "I'm glad."

"I can't be with you." Mel stated as she moved to get into her car.

"Yes, you can. I'm moving out of my house next weekend into an apartment of my own. I will be single."

"And recuperating from a breakup."

"Mel, I didn't break up from my girlfriend because of you. We broke up because we aren't in love each other."

"Why would you be interested in me?"

"Because I'm in love with you."

Mel's mouth dropped open. "You don't even know me."

"Yes, I do. You are honest, hard working, funny, and sexy. You are a dedicated firefighter and have a reputation for being a team player and an excellent leader. I've been paying attention for a long time."

"I won't date you unless you are single." Mel was losing the battle with her feelings.

"Good. How about dinner after next weekend?"

Mel almost grinned at Janice. She was tenacious as hell. "I'm on shift through the next couple of weeks."

"We'll find a night." Janice smiled. "I'll call."

Mel watched Janice get in her car before she let herself grin. What a surprise her evening had become.

It had taken Janice exactly one month to get Mel in bed with her, but it had taken a good year to gain Mel's trust that Janice wouldn't fall out of love with her and move on. Mel still had brief periods of insecurity when she worried that Janice might be losing interest in her. But Janice was patient and completely committed to Mel. She worked hard to keep their love healthy and full.

Shannon smiled as she gazed at the two of then while pouring herself a cup of coffee and made the return trip to the bedroom. She wasn't going to live in a tee shirt for the day. She was going to get dressed and get back to her vacation.

She was still rummaging through her suitcase when Simone came out of the bathroom in a robe, her blond hair still wet. Shannon's tongue almost fell out of her mouth; Simone was gorgeous. "Shannon, the bathroom is yours."

"Thanks. Simone, can we talk a minute?"

Simone turned to Shannon, her soft, blue eyes large and trusting. "Certainly, is something wrong?"

"Nothing is wrong; I just don't want to take advantage of you and your kindness."

"Shannon, you're not taking advantage of me. I invited your friends to stay here because I wanted to spend more time with you. As you can see, I have a very large, empty house. Your friends have been nothing but gracious and friendly."

"But we need to pay you something." Shannon wasn't sure what to say to Simone. She didn't want to hurt her feelings.

Simone smiled and sat on the bed next to Shannon. "Do you feel uncomfortable here?"

"No."

"Do you want to get to know me?"

"Very much."

"Your friends negotiated with me to pay for all the food and drinks while you're here. Also, Hanna volunteered to cook a few gourmet meals. After last night I'd be crazy to turn down a deal like that."

"You opened your home to us."

"I'm glad to do it."

Shannon stared at Simone's beautiful face and smiled. "You're something else."

"How are you feeling?"

"Much better, I only hurt when I move, sit, or breathe," Shannon quipped. "I just need to get cleaned up and I'll feel better."

"Do you need some help with your hair?"

"If you don't mind, after I wash up and change clothes I'd like to wash it."

"The bathroom is yours."

"Thanks." Shannon grabbed her overnight bag and headed for the bathroom.

Simone watched Shannon until the door closed and then sighed. What was she doing? She had known Shannon for one day, one pretty emotional day, and she had moved her and her friends into her home. Simone never did spur of the moment things; she was a planner. Everything she did was well thought out and all of her options reviewed. This was so out of character for her. Kissing Shannon hadn't helped anything. She was even more attracted to her. She tugged a pair of shorts and a tank top out of her drawer and dressed before heading for the kitchen. It was too late to change her mind; she would just have to live with her spontaneous behavior. And she had been honest with Shannon. She actually enjoyed everyone's company.

"Good morning." Olivia exited her bedroom and joined Simone in the kitchen.

"Good morning, did you sleep well?"

"Perfect, the sound of the water is so soothing."

"You both must have been exhausted after yesterday."

"We were. How is Shannon doing?"

"Much better than last night, I think getting some sleep has helped considerably. She isn't running a fever this morning so she may have weathered the worst of her injuries. She is still very uncomfortable and sore."

"Simone, do you mind if I ask you a personal question?"

"Certainly."

"What possessed you to invite all of us to stay with you?" Olivia grinned as she spoke.

Simone chuckled. "I asked myself the same question this morning and then I answered it. I was really impressed with how all of you supported Shannon.

You seem to be very caring women. I'm also intrigued with Shannon and to be honest with you, more attracted to her as I spend more time with her."

"She's attracted to you."

"Are you sure it isn't just gratitude?" Simone's voice betrayed her insecurities. Her previous relationship had eroded her self confidence. Simone had no doubts about herself except when it came to a personal relationship, having spent the last several years hiding her feelings and her relationship from everyone made her faith in herself tenuous.

Olivia chuckled as she placed her hand on Simone's arm. "Honey, I know gratitude and I know attraction. It's not gratitude I see on Shannon's face when she looks at you."

Simone was interrupted from responding by the entrance of Hanna. "Good morning."

"Good morning, Hanna. Do you want a cup of coffee?"

"I do, thanks, morning sweetie." She slipped her arms around Olivia and kissed her.

Simone felt a little envious as she watched the two women. They were so much in love and she wanted to find that. She needed to find it. Her life was too empty if she couldn't share it with a woman.

"How is Shannon?"

"Better. She is getting cleaned up and then I'll change her dressings. She isn't running a temperature so it looks like she has ducked an infection. She is still going to be very uncomfortable."

"We should call your reporter friend and answer some questions so we can put an end to any questions from other reporters." Olivia suggested.

"Good idea. Do you want to talk to Shannon about it?"

"Sure." Hanna and Olivia followed Simone into the back bedroom. Shannon was sitting on the side of the bed, dressed in a pair of shorts and a tank top.

"Hi guys."

"Hey Shannon, you look pretty good considering what you looked like yesterday." Hanna commented with a grin.

"I feel pretty good, I just need to wash my hair and I'll almost be back to normal."

"Do you need some help?"

"No, Simone has volunteered."

Hanna and Olivia looked at each other with a grin. There was no doubt about Shannon's attraction to Simone. She couldn't keep her eyes off her. "Do you want to wash your hair before we change your bandages?" Simone asked, placing fresh bandages on the bed.

"Yes, please." Shannon eyes traveled over Simone's body until she looked into her eyes. Shannon had just a hint of a smile on her face meant only for Simone. Simone returned the smile as Hanna and Olivia quietly slipped out of the bedroom.

"How about we do this in the bathroom sink? I think it is deep enough to wash your hair."

"Okay." Shannon followed Simone into the bathroom.

Simone turned the water on and checked it until it was warm enough. "Can you lean over? Let me know if this is too painful." She placed a towel over Shannon's shoulders and Shannon bent slowly, her back and legs stinging as she stretched her wounds. Simone gently gathered up Shannon's long thick hair and slowly rinsed it with the warm water. She was surprised at how much hair Shannon had and how many different shades of brown there were.

"I think its wet enough." Simone poured shampoo into her hand as Shannon waited patiently. "Are you okay, Shannon?"

"Yes." Shannon didn't feel the pain she only felt an overwhelming attraction to Simone. Never had she felt such a crushing need that completely dwarfed the pain of her injuries.

Simone slowly rubbed the shampoo into Shannon's hair, massaging her head as she worked the suds into the strands of glistening hair. Shannon could have moaned out loud as Simone sensuously rubbed her scalp. Shannon would never be able to wash her hair again without remembering Simone and her reaction to her. While Simone rinsed the soap from Shannon's now clean hair, Shannon breathed slowly trying to keep from groaning. She wasn't alone in her feelings as Simone's body reacted to the woman standing intimately next to her. She almost shook as she tried to hide her response to Shannon. She tried to focus on rinsing the soap away and not on Shannon's appealing neck.

"There, I think I've got all the soap out." Simone wrapped Shannon's head in a towel. "Come on and sit on the bed and we'll dry it."

Shannon headed for the bed and Simone kneeled on it behind her as she removed the towel and began to rub her hair dry. Not a word was uttered but Shannon watched Simone in the mirror over the dresser. Simone looked up to find Shannon's eyes staring at her and ceased her movements. She stared back waiting for a reaction from Shannon, her hands resting softly on Shannon's shoulders. Shannon reached up and grasped hold of Simon's hands as she turned to face her.

"Simone, I need to kiss you," Shannon whispered, her eyes large and trusting.

"Yes," Simone whispered back as she bent to meet Shannon's lips with her own. She was unable to keep her moan silent as Shannon's mouth hungrily covered hers. Their tongues touched and they tasted each other thoroughly. Shannon's fingers reached up to run through Simone's blond curls as Simone's hands cupped Shannon's cheeks. It was the kiss that overwhelmed Shannon as she fell under Simone's sexy spell. She wanted to run her hands over Simone's well-toned body, to slide her lips over her breasts, licking and tasting her way until she feasted on the very center of Simone. She wanted Simone's hands on her body in the very same way.

Shannon pulled slowly away from Simone, her hands still cradling her head. "You're incredibly beautiful," she whispered.

"I think you're gorgeous." Simone fingers traced Shannon's lips.

"Simone, I could really care about you, but I'm only here for a couple more weeks." Shannon whispered, leaning into Simone, her lips sliding along her cheek and neck.

"Shannon, I know I could have feelings for you. Why don't we see how the next few weeks turn out? And if we both still feel the same way, we'll work it out, I promise." Simone turned her head so that Shannon's lips met hers in a soft, gentle kiss.

"But what if I fall in love with you?" Shannon uttered the words she had been afraid to say.

Simone's heart stumbled and she smiled at Shannon. "Would that be so bad?"

They shared another full kiss and than sat holding each other quietly. Two weeks was long enough to fall in love Shannon thought. Simone didn't need two weeks. She'd fallen in love with Shannon the minute they'd kissed.

"I think we need to dry your hair and change your bandages," Simone whispered as she held Shannon gently against her.

"Then what?"

"You need to be interviewed by a reporter friend of mine so that the other reporters will leave you alone. Then what do you say about a day on the beach?"

"I like everything but the interview." Shannon reached up and clasped Simone's hand in her own.

"I promise you, Christa is a very nice woman for a reporter. It's better her than having them follow you where ever you go."

"Okay, as long as you're there with me."

"Honey, I'm not going anywhere," Simone promised, lifting Shannon's hand up and kissing her fingers. "Now, let's dry your beautiful hair and then get the interview over with."

CHAPTER 4

Forty minutes later, the six women were seated in the living room waiting for Simone's reporter friend to show up. Then they were all looking forward to a day on the beach, or at least a few hours on the beach in Shannon's case. She sat quietly on the couch, her hand grasped protectively in Simone's.

The doorbell rang and Simone stood up and went to open the door. A well-dressed woman in a red skirt and matching jacket hugged her quickly in greeting.

"Hi Christa, you look terrific as usual." Simone returned the hug. "Come on in."

"Thanks for calling me. There are a lot of reporters trying to get an interview with Shannon."

"Shannon wants to get this over with as little attention as possible. Let me introduce you. Shannon Dunbar, Christa Neiland, a reporter from the local television station. These are her friends, Mel, Janice, Hanna, and Olivia."

"Hello ladies, it's nice to meet all of you. Shannon how are you feeling? I understand you were injured saving the young boy."

"I'm fine. How is Jason?" Christa sat on a chair across from Shannon as Simone resumed her seat next to Shannon. Simone couldn't help but smile when Shannon slid her hand into Simone's as she talked to Christa. It didn't go unnoticed by Christa. She would have to ask Simone about that at a later time. Christa hadn't known Simone was seeing anyone and Simone would have told her.

"He's fine. In fact, he's back swimming in the water, with his mother watching him like a hawk. He seems to have come through his ordeal unscathed. His mother was adamant that her son wouldn't be alive if it wasn't for you."

"I don't think that's the case. I just was just the first one to get to him. Others on the beach would have helped him."

"Well, if you don't mind I'd like to bring the cameraman in to take some video while we talk."

Shannon looked a little startled and turned to Simone. "It'll be okay, Shannon." Simone reassured her with a smile.

Christa watched the exchange and was surprised at how solicitous Simone and Shannon appeared to be. "Shannon, I promise we'll turn the cameras off if you become uncomfortable."

Shannon's gaze returned to Christa and she smiled. "Okay, if Simone trusts you, I can trust you. I've just never been on this end of a camera before."

Christa was not immune to the smile that transformed Shannon's face. She's beautiful, Christa thought, her brown eyes large and trusting, and her dark brown hair full and hanging straight to the center of her back. No wonder Simone was entranced with her. And it was obvious that Simone was enthralled. Christa knew Simone well and she saw the attraction on Simone's face whenever she looked at Shannon.

"Christa, the rest of us will be in the kitchen." Simone squeezed Shannon's hand as she stood up.

Shannon's eyes followed Simone and her friends until they disappeared from view. "Shannon, before I bring my cameraman in, I'll explain a little bit of what will happen. I'll ask you your name, where you're from, and what brought you to Hawaii. Then I will ask you about that day at the beach and how you noticed Jason. The camera will be behind me, so you and I can just talk. I will take the tape back to the studio and edit it for airing. It will be shown this evening on the news."

Shannon sat quietly on the couch listening to Christa speak. She shook her head in response. "Should I change into something different?"

"No, I think you're just fine." Christa wanted to capture the fact that Shannon was still on vacation. "I'll go ask the cameraman to come in. You should be interested in this. I understand you are a cameraperson."

"Yes, primarily for sports events for Fox Sports Network in Bellevue."

"I know the station. You must be very good."

"I've been behind a camera for quite a few years."

"I'll be right back." Christa smiled as she went to the door and motioned to her cameraman out in the van. He met her at the door and entered the room.

"Shannon Dunbar, this is Frank Miller, Frank meet Shannon, a fellow cameraperson from Seattle."

"Nice to meet you Shannon, who do you work for?"

"Fox Sports Network."

"Cool, you get to go to all the pro games and stuff?"

"Yes, professional, college, and some high school tournaments."

"Very cool, what's your favorite?

"Women's professional basketball and the Mariner games are fun."

"I'd love to do that."

Christa smiled as she watched the exchange. Shannon had relaxed considerably and chatted comfortably with Frank. "Okay, Frank, we'd better get started."

"Will do, Christa."

"Do you have enough light with Shannon seated on the couch?"

"Yes, I'll stand behind you to your left."

"Good. Alright, Shannon, let's get started. First of all, tell me who you are and what you do in Seattle."

The interview went by quickly, Christa very professionally drew Shannon's story out, and within an hour had everything on film. Shannon had been quite reserved when it came to admitting she saved a young boy's life, but Christa had a tape of Justin's mother. She wasn't shy about giving Shannon credit. It would be a good piece. Christa was very good at what she did.

"Frank, why don't you go out and warm up the van? I'll be right out."

"Okay, Christa. It was nice to meet you, Shannon."

"You too, Frank. If you ever make it to Seattle, look me up. I'll get you into a game or something."

Frank grinned at her. "I will thanks. Hey, I'm glad you're okay."

"Thanks."

Christa waited until Frank left before calling to Simone in the kitchen. "We're done out here."

Simone came out immediately and headed for the couch and Shannon. The rest of the women followed. Shannon smiled at Simone as she sat next to her on the couch, reaching for Shannon's hand. "How did it go?"

"Good. It's a good interview. I'll get out of your hair now. I'll call when I know for sure when the tape will run. And I'll drop a copy off later this week."

"Thank you, Christa."

"No problem, it was my pleasure, and it was an honor to meet you, Shannon. Justin was very lucky you were at the beach yesterday."

"Thanks." Shannon blushed with embarrassment.

"I've got to go get some more work done." Christa stood up. "Simone, call me." She looked at Simone pointedly.

"I will, Christa."

The women waited until Christa left before Mel turned to Simone and spoke, "She doesn't look gay."

"She has a girlfriend who is a lawyer. I've known them both for a long time."

"She was very nice." Shannon smiled at Simone. "She's going to ask you what's going on between us."

"I know." Simone chuckled. "She's a very nosy reporter. I say it's time to hit the beach, ladies. That is, if you're up to it, Shannon?"

"I think I can sit on the beach for a while."

"Great, I'm going to get my suit on and grab our snorkel equipment." Janice rushed out of the room.

"I'll go change into my suit." Simone stood up and left the room.

Mel sat down next to Shannon. "How are you doing, sweetie?"

"Good, Mel. Thanks for asking."

"You and Simone are okay?"

"Yes, we're more than okay. I like her Mel, a lot. And she likes me."

"Tell us something we don't know. You're only here for three weeks."

"I know." Shannon looked at Mel. "But I want to spend as much time as possible with her. I need to."

"Okay honey. But be careful." Mel's face was full of concern for her best friend.

"Thanks, Mel, but I think I'm already in love with her."

"Oh, Shannon," Mel responded, but was interrupted before asking any more questions.

"Wow," Shannon whispered as she caught sight of Simone.

Simone reentered the room wearing a Samoan wrap around her waist, and a bathing suit top. Shannon's eyes devoured Simone as she walked toward her. "I've got a couple of large towels and we can bring the chaise lounge for you to lie on."

"A towel will be fine." Shannon rose slowly from the couch. Her back and legs had stiffened up while she sat. She gingerly walked to the back door where Simone joined her.

"Shannon, do you need a pain pill?"

"No, I just need to lie in the sun for a while."

Simone took Shannon's hand and walked outside. The other four women watched them in silence. "What are we going to do about Shannon and Simone?" Hanna asked.

"Nothing, I like the two of them together," Janice responded as she and Mel headed for the back door.

"So do I, but they're only going to have a little more than two weeks together."

"Mel and I fell in love in one weekend. What makes you think it can't happen to Shannon and Simone?"

"But they live on separate continents."

"I guess they'll just have to figure things out." Janice was an eternal optimist. She believed everything could be worked out given time.

The four followed the path down to the beach and found Shannon and Simone embracing at the edge of the beach. There was something incredibly beautiful about two women kissing on a sun filled Hawaiian beach. They moved apart as the four other women joined them still holding hands. Simone spread their towels side by side while the other women dropped their towels on the beach and shed their shorts and tops. They all headed for the water intent on cooling off in the mild surf. Shannon sat cautiously down on the blanket as Simone removed her wrap and sat down on the towel next to Shannon. Shannon all but choked as she looked at Simone in a bathing suit. She was incredibly sexy with her long tan legs and her full breasts. Shannon found it hard to believe Simone was interested in her. She knew she wasn't unappealing, but Simone was beyond anything she had ever imagined. She was gorgeous.

"Simone, why don't you go swimming with them? I'll be fine here."

Simone turned to face Shannon, leaning on her elbow watching her with a smile. "I like lying here next to you just fine."

"You're so beautiful I find it amazing that you want to date me."

"Honey, I don't want to date you. I want to make love to you and spend every waking minute with you."

Shannon gasped softly as she reacted to Simone's words. "Oh wow! I feel the same way. I am so attracted to you."

They shared a kiss and a pledge then laid back holding hands in the Hawaiian sun as Shannon's friends enjoyed the water, swimming and snorkeling for several hours. Shannon slipped asleep as the heat and sound of the surf relaxed her, Simone's hand making her feel safe and secure.

"Is she sleeping?" Hanna asked as she flopped on to her towel.

"Yes, she has been for about twenty minutes. It's good for her. She's probably still exhausted. Swimming against the tide with Jason's limp body would be
difficult on anyone." Simone held Shannon's slumbering body against her own,
Shannon's arm tucked around her waist, her head resting on her shoulder.

"Simone, we all appreciate your letting us stay here. I personally want to
thank you for being so wonderful to Shannon. She's a very special person to
us."

"Hanna, you may find this hard to believe, but I think Shannon's pretty special myself."

"I know you do, and I like the two of you together."

"Thanks, if this is meant to be, we'll figure it out."

Hanna smiled at Simone. "I like you, Simone."

Simone smiled at Hanna's comment. "I like you too."

"What do you say to pasta for dinner?"

"I suggest we take a break and go out for dinner, that's if Shannon is up to
it."

"Sounds good to me." Olivia joined Hanna on her towel.

"Simone, this beach is perfect. The snorkeling is amazing. I can't imagine
owning property here."

"I don't own the beach. In Hawaii, the beaches belong to all Hawaiians and
everyone can use them. You have to allow access from your property to the
beach. My parents were able to buy the property a long time ago because they
used to allow non-Hawaiians to purchase land. Now, the government regulates
all land purchases. Non-Hawaiians cannot own land, they can lease in perpe-
tuity."

"That's very cool."

"Yes, it is. It guarantees Hawaiians will retain a part of their heritage. We
have very few places that still teach the Hawaiian language, let alone the history, or the dance."

"That's so sad."

"Many of the children leave the island for greener pastures. We have a large
number of people on welfare on the islands. Work is hard to find, especially if
you don't finish high school, which a lot of kids don't do. We need to have
more opportunities for kids growing up besides tourism."

"It really means a lot to you."

"It does. I run a training program for high school kids who want to become
paramedics. I really enjoy working with them."

"That's a very generous thing to do."

"So are you guys up to going out on a boat on Saturday and doing some diving? We can snorkel and fish, and spend the day on the water."

"That sounds like fun. Do you have a boat?"

"No, but some good friends of mine do, and I know they would love to take us out."

"Cool."

"We better wake Shannon up and go inside. We've been out in the sun for quite a while." Simone nuzzled Shannon's cheek. "Shannon honey, time to wake up."

Shannon moved closer to Simone as she slowly opened her eyes. "How long have I been sleeping?"

"Not long." Simone kissed her softly. "You needed it."

All of them headed back up to the house to clean up and think about plans for dinner. The five other women took showers while Shannon grumbled about how she didn't see why she couldn't take one. Simone grinned at her as she headed for her own shower. "You know you can't get your back and legs wet yet, but I promise you I will change your bandages. I think we should put some aloe vera on your scrapes. It will help them heal." Shannon was showing a little irritation about her injuries and it made her even more appealing to Simone. She had every right to complain.

Shannon went off to find an iron while Simone showered and dressed. She may have bandages all over her back and legs but she was going to do her damnedest to look her very best. She was also going to remind Simone that this was their second date.

She carried her freshly ironed clothes into the bedroom and caught her breath as she saw Simone. She was wearing a pair of white pants and a pale yellow sleeveless blouse. She looked tan, sexy, and gorgeous. "You look terrific."

"Thanks." Simone smiled. "Are you ready for me to change your bandages?"

"In a minute." Shannon laid her clothes down on the bed before closing the space between her and Simone. "I need to kiss you."

Simone wasn't going to argue as she closed the gap between them, their lips meeting in a ravenous kiss. All thought left as they shared kiss after kiss. Shannon's lips traveled down Simone's neck as her tongue tasted the skin that beckoned to her. Her hands trembled as she ran her hands through Simone's blond curls while their tongues dipped and tasted each other's mouth. The sound of the telephone ringing made them pull away from each other, both having to catch their breath.

"Simone, it's for you. It's Christa," Janice called from the kitchen.

Simone kissed Shannon quickly and then answered the telephone. "Hi Christa."

Shannon left Simone on the telephone while she cleaned up in the bathroom. She finished her makeup and joined Simone once more. "Let's get your bandages changed. We need to watch the news tonight. Christa is airing your interview at five forty-five. She is going to drop off a copy of the tape tomorrow."

"That's nice of her. Do you know her very well?"

Simone blushed as she began to remove Shannon's bandages from her back. "She was my first girlfriend."

"She was your first?"

"Yes."

Shannon turned and looked at Simone for a moment. "She must be very special."

Simone smiled and leaned over to kiss Shannon before responding. "You might say it was the shortest relationship in history. Neither one of us knew what we were doing or what we wanted. It was a mistake to think our friendship had more to it. We have been friends ever since. What about your first lover?"

"It was in high school and it lasted several months until she decided dating boys was also in the picture. She broke my heart for about five months until I started college and went to my first lesbian party." Shannon chuckled. "I recuperated very quickly."

"How many relationships have you had?" Simone asked as she spread aloe vera gel across Shannon's back.

Shannon breathed deeply as the deep wounds reacted to Simone's attentions. "Two serious ones, one that lasted a little over four years and another that lasted six. What about you?"

"I've had a few more than two but I would say I've had one serious one that lasted for several years."

"Do you want a relationship?" Shannon felt Simone hesitate, her hands stilling their movements.

"I want a real relationship. I want to fall in love, and I want to be with a woman I respect, who respects me. I want to fall asleep every night with her and wake up every morning knowing that at the end of my day I have her to come home to. I want to make love to my lover on Christmas Eve and New Years and all the important holidays and anniversaries."

Shannon smiled as she listened. Simone was perfect. She was saying everything that Shannon wanted, and Shannon knew she wanted it with Simone. Now all she had to do was convince her. She already knew deep in her heart that Simone was the one for her.

"What do you want?" Simone began to work on Shannon's legs.

"I want to be able to share everything with a woman. I want to fall in love and stay in love. I want to be with someone who thinks making love with me is as important as telling me she loves me. I want to hold hands at the movies and watch the sun go down at night with our arms around each other. I want to lay in bed on Sunday morning and drink coffee and cuddle."

"There, your bandages are changed." Shannon rolled up until she was sitting next to Simone.

"Thank you."

"You're very welcome. I'll let you get dressed and then we can watch your interview." Simone stood up and started to leave the room.

"Simone, is there someone you still care about?"

Simone turned toward Shannon, a slight smile on her face. "There is only one woman I care about. I am rapidly falling in love with her and hope she is with me. This same woman I am going to take to a movie and hold her hand. Now, I'd like to take her out to dinner for our second date."

Shannon grinned at Simone as Simone winked at her and left the bedroom. Shannon rushed into her clothes; she didn't want to miss one minute of time with Simone.

"Hello, Ms. Celebrity, your interview will be on in about ten minutes. How does it feel to be a real hero?" Mel teased her as Shannon joined them in the living room.

"I'm not a hero." Shannon sat down on the couch as Simone came out of the kitchen with Hanna and Olivia. Their eyes locked on each other as Simone came over to sit with her.

"You look terrific." Simone spoke quietly as Shannon reached for her hand.

"Thanks." Considering what Shannon had gone through, she felt pretty good. She was wearing a pair of tan slacks and a black tank top. She had a shirt to throw on when they went outside to hide her bandages.

"Shush. Christa is on television. Wow, she's one pretty woman," Janice muttered as Mel grinned at her. She knew Janice only looked. Time and trust had made Mel feel secure most of the time. Besides, she was right. Christa was a knockout.

"We have a story of heroism and a happy ending to a very scary episode that took place yesterday on one of our local beaches. Christa Neiland is here with the very interesting story."

The whole thing didn't last more then three minutes but Christa had included clips of her interview with Shannon, along with Justin and his mother. She was very grateful that Shannon had come to the rescue of her son and wanted the world to know that Shannon was a hero. Christa went on to explain Shannon's injuries and how she was recuperating while enjoying the rest of her vacation in Hawaii. It was a very nice story that made Shannon self-conscious and the others very proud of her.

"That was good, Shannon. You should be proud of what you did."

"I am just glad Justin is okay. Now, can we go to dinner, please?"

Simone hugged her as they all headed for Simone's Range Rover. She knew the way to the restaurant and she had the largest car. The six women visited for the twenty minute trip while Shannon and Simone held hands and kept glancing at each other.

Simone pulled into a restaurant that overlooked the beach and they all piled out. She led them in to where a handsome man waited at the desk. "Hi Simone, we have your table ready."

"Thanks, Leon."

"No problem, enjoy your meal."

"Do you come here often?"

"My parents and I would come here for special occasions, birthdays, anniversaries, and stuff. The restaurant has been here for many years." The view was spectacular, overlooking the jagged lava fields that ran right to the sand beach, where the jewel blue water lapped against the beach. The beach was ringed with coconut trees that stood stately almost as if guarding the beach from intruders.

"Tonight is a special occasion," Mel responded, hugging Janice.

"Yes, it is," Simone agreed, staring at Shannon.

The dinner was fun, the food excellent, and all Simone wanted to do was to go home and touch Shannon. They sat side by side and periodically held hands through out the evening, or brushed shoulders and arms and all it did was make Simone more agitated. From the looks Simone was getting from Shannon, she was feeling just as frustrated.

"Can we go home?" Shannon whispered, staring at Simone.

"Yes."

"Simone, do you have to work tomorrow?"

"Yes, and Friday. I mentioned that a friend of mine has a boat and he would love to take all of you out on Saturday to swim, snorkel, or fish. Would you like to do that?"

"What about you, Shannon? Do you think you can go in the water by then?" Olivia inquired, concern for her friend injuries making her cautious.

"The doctor said the salt water would be good for me. I should be able to go swimming by then. I need to get a new swimsuit. I shredded the back of mine."

"I'll take you tomorrow to get one," Olivia promised. "I need to pick up a few things myself."

"Then I guess we're going boating on Saturday."

The well-fed and happy group headed home. Shannon and Simone were looking forward to being alone. "Simone, can we go for a walk on the beach by ourselves?"

"Of course, follow me." Simone quickly pulled Shannon out the back and down the beach path before anyone knew they were gone.

"Well done," Shannon chuckled as she followed Simone down the path.

"I wanted to be alone with you. I can't go another minute without touching you." Simone whirled and met Shannon with a kiss. Shannon moaned and met Simone's seeking lips with her own.

Shannon ran her hands down Simone's shoulders and back pulling her tightly against her body as they shared a loving kiss. "Simone, I thought I would go crazy at the restaurant. I wanted to hold you, to kiss you."

They kissed for several more minutes before they stopped to catch their breath, still wrapped in each other's arms. "Do you want to go for a walk on the beach?" Simone whispered as she breathed in Shannon's scent.

"I'd love to." Shannon wrapped her fingers around Simone's as they strolled slowly down the beach, content with the silence, except for the sound of the waves. That was the allure of Hawaii, the fragrant tropical scents, along with the heat that seeped into your body and the romantic sounds of the waves as they rolled on to the beach. If you shut your eyes you could almost hear the old Hawaiian chants as they welcomed their gods.

For several minutes, they walked along remaining quiet, while the half moon sparkled on the waves and lit their way. Shannon felt the emotion deep in her heart and shivered, unable to ignore her growing feelings for Simone. "I'm going to miss you tomorrow, I've kind of gotten used to being around you."

Simone's smile reassured Shannon as she turned to face her. "I'm going to take some time off next week so I can spend more time with you. I'm sorry I've got to go to work, I'd rather be with you."

"I'd like to see you at work." Shannon ran her fingers across Simone's cheek.

"Would you like to come in on Friday and have lunch with me? I can show you around the unit and you can see what I do."

"I'd love to."

"Good. Now, we'd better head back to the house. It's getting late."

They made the walk back to the now quiet house and entered Simone's bedroom. "You go ahead and use the bathroom; I'm going to get my clothes ready for work." Simone kissed Shannon gently.

Shannon became nervous as she prepared for bed. She wasn't at all sure that Simone wanted to make love, especially with Shannon looking they way she did, her back and legs still covered with bandages. It was bad enough that Simone was the sexiest woman she had ever met. Shannon was feeling a little less than spectacular with all of her injuries. How appealing could she be, covered with scabs and bandages. Shannon brushed her hair and slipped her tee shirt on. She wanted to make love with Simone. It was all she could think about.

Shannon entered the empty bedroom and crawled into bed. She reached for her journal intent on writing down her feelings. Shannon had been writing in a journal since she was a teenager. She found it relaxing. She expressed her innermost feelings as she wrote in her notebook. The only other hobby she had was her filming. Even when she wasn't working, Shannon's love for the camera and filming could be found in her video creation. She had a small studio in her home where she turned simple vacation videos into works of art.

Simone slipped quietly into the bedroom and watched while Shannon, unaware of Simone, wrote in her leather bound notebook. Simone wished she had a camera as she stared at the sexy woman in her bed. Simone wanted her there, and not just for a night. She wanted to spend her life finding out about all the things Shannon thought about. She wanted to know her dreams and wishes, but most of all Simone wanted to help make them come true. Nothing in Simone's life had prepared her for the overwhelming feelings that filled her mind and heart when she thought of Shannon.

Shannon slowly became aware of Simone watching her and raised her eyes to meet Simone's soft blue ones. Her breath caught her throat as she saw the naked longing on Simone's face. Shannon was mesmerized by the beautiful woman leaning against the door watching her with such obvious attraction.

"Are you ready for work?"

"Yes." Simone didn't move from where she was standing, she just continued to smile at Shannon.

"Are you coming to bed?"

"Yes." Simone didn't move.

"Tonight?" Shannon quirked her eyebrows at Simone as she watched her.

Simone bubbled with laughter as she headed for the bathroom. "I was just thinking how perfect you look sitting in bed. I love looking at you."

Shannon's mouth dropped open as Simone shut the bathroom door. In a few sentences, Simone had wrapped herself completely in Shannon's heart. There was only one problem and right now it loomed very large in front of the two of them. Shannon lived in Seattle and Simone in Hawaii. Would one of them be willing to move?

Simone finished preparing for bed and re-entered the bedroom. Shannon couldn't keep her eyes off Simone as she slid under the covers, her tee shirt as sexy as any negligee. Shannon put her journal away and went to turn the light off. Simone waited until Shannon turned to her and then spoke. "Shannon, we need to talk."

Shannon felt her heart drop to her toes. Simone was going to tell her she wasn't interested in a relationship. "Sure."

Simone's smile didn't alleviate Shannon's nervousness as she watched her with trepidation. "Shannon, look at me, please."

Simone gathered Shannon's hands in hers and lifted them up to her lips. "I need to tell you how I'm feeling even though I know you are still recuperating from yesterday. I want to make love with you and I want you to tell me now if you don't want that. If you aren't interested, you need to tell me."

Shannon brought Simone's hands to her mouth, placing soft kisses on her fingers. "I'm not just interested, Simone, I'm going crazy. I want you so much it hurts."

"Then will you tell me when you are healed enough so that we can make love?"

"I will." Shannon smiled at Simone as she leaned against her to kiss her. Their lips met in an open mouthed wet kiss that went on and on before Shannon pulled away long enough to whisper in Simone's ear. "Simone, I'm healed enough."

Simone didn't speak but her eyes sparkled as she met Shannon's mouth again. Her lips moved over Shannon's slowly as if tasting her for the first time. Shannon's hands shook as she stroked Simone's shoulders and back. Simone's mouth covered Shannon's, steeping her with passion. Shannon moaned as Simone's lips trailed down her neck, her tongue tasting in sips and nibbles. This was magic, pure and perfect loving magic.

"You're so beautiful. I love your eyes. They watch me with such intensity. And your curly blond hair, it's not blond, it's not brown, and it is full of streaks of sunlight."

Shannon covered Simone's face with soft kisses as she wooed her with the words that bubbled out of her heart. She needed to show Simone with her words as well as her actions that she was already committed to her.

"I love to watch you walk with so much authority, and when I saw you in your uniform, you looked so professional. And you were so gentle with me. You made me feel safe and protected." Shannon's hands stroked Simone's slim, well-shaped arms and shoulders, wanting to memorize every part of her body.

"I saw you kneeling at the beach, winded and exhausted, pale from loss of blood and your efforts in saving Justin, and all you asked me was how the boy was. I knew from that statement what kind of heart you had, and I felt an overwhelming need to take care of you. Shannon, right now I don't feel like taking care of you. I want to kiss every inch of your beautiful body and I want to see you tremble when I taste you for the very first time. I am going to make you melt with pleasure as my tongue teases you into orgasm after orgasm."

Shannon felt the rush of heat and moisture at Simone's words. "Simone, I want you so badly, it scares me."

"We'll be scared together," Simone whispered, her mouth meeting Shannon's in a promise, her hands sliding Shannon's tee shirt slowly up over her breasts and off of her arms. Simone moved away from Shannon and pulled her tee shirt off before wrapping her arms around Shannon, bringing them breast to naked breast. Shannon sighed as she felt Simone's breasts rub against her own.

"Please, let me know if your back and legs are uncomfortable."

"Honey, I'm fine." Shannon gently pushed Simone on to her back. "Especially when you are on the bottom." She grinned as she kissed Simone deeply.

Shannon tasted Simone's mouth completely, while her hands stroked Simone's breasts. They were full and firm and the nipples a deep rose just beckoning to Shannon. Shannon lips slid along Simone's fragrant skin finally surrounding her nipple, drawing it fully into her mouth. Her tongue lapped at her nipple as her fingers stroked both breasts. Simone cried out softly as Shannon moved to the other breast sucking sensuously before lightly nipping with her teeth. Simone's body arched toward her while Shannon bathed both breasts with kisses, her hot mouth pulling on Simone's nipples as her hands held Simone against her mouth. Shannon caught Simone's hands and stretched them over her head as she kissed her mouth again before returning to her breasts to feast. Simone's body became restless as Shannon teased her with her mouth and tongue. Her body ached as Shannon loved her slowly and thoroughly. Shannon rolled on top of Simone and settled her hips against Simone's as she once again kissed her deeply, her arms holding her with such gentleness and love that Simone was entranced. She softly caught Shannon's hands and kissed them as she rolled Shannon slowly on to her back. Simone's tongue swept through Shannon's mouth as Simone ran her hands over Shannon's stomach and covered her breasts. Stroking and teasing, her finger tips traced her nipples as her mouth left hot wet kisses lower and lower on Shannon's breasts. She licked her nipple as it hardened against her mouth and Shannon gasped loudly. Sliding her tongue around it she felt Shannon's body slide against hers in response. Her mouth surrounded Shannon's nipple as her hand stroked her stomach and hips. Simone slid Shannon's panties down her legs and off of her, her hands touching Shannon's calves and thighs. Shannon hips moved on the bed as Simone fingertips traced the skin of her inner thigh. Shannon's breath built in her chest as she waited for Simone to touch her.

"Oh, honey, you're so wet," Simone whispered as her fingers slid against Shannon gently. "And so soft."

"Oh God," Shannon cried out as Simone's fingers slid into Shannon slowly, tantalizing her. She stroked slowly, deeply, as Shannon hips pushed against Simone's fingers.

"That's it honey, open up to me." Simone's lips slid along Shannon's stomach, her tongue sliding slowly lower until she lapped at the moisture that welcomed her stroking fingers. Her tongue met the knob of tissue that pulsed and throbbed and she sucked heavily on Shannon while her fingers continued to move faster and deeper. Shannon began to shiver as she felt an orgasm well up in her body. Shannon's hands held Simone's head as her hips rose up to meet Simone's mouth. "Yes, Shannon, that's it, sweetie. Yes."

Shannon's body quaked as she tumbled straight into an orgasm that rolled from her head to her toes. Crying softly with pleasure, she stilled Simone's fingers, tugging her up into her arms. "I need to hold you," she gasped.

Simone slid up Shannon's body and pulled her over on top of her, being careful of her back as she gathered her closely to her. She kissed Shannon slowly and Shannon buried her face against Simone's while her body shivered and shook. "You're so beautiful," Simone whispered as her lips teased against her neck.

Shannon's eyes glistened with unshed tears as she kissed Simone gently, her fingers tracing over her face. Her hands ran gently over Simone's breasts again, caressing her slowly, thoroughly. Her hands removed Simone's panties and her scent made Shannon light headed as she rolled her hips on to Simone's spreading her legs around Shannon's hips. Shannon's mouth tasted her breasts as her hips moved erotically against Simone. Simone's hands gripped Shannon's buttocks tightly as she pushed up against her body wanting that perfect connection. Simone brought her legs up to bring Shannon's wetness against her as her head fell back in pleasure.

"Shannon, I need to kiss you," Simone whispered, her hips churning against Shannon's. Shannon mouth met Simone's silencing a moan as Shannon's fingers touched Simone between her legs. Shannon's fingers opened Simone's body, spreading her tightly against Shannon's wetness, her fingers teasing her, driving her closer as her body lost all substance. Simone's hands fell to her side as she gasped against Shannon's mouth.

Shannon smiled as Simone trembled in her arms while her fingers felt Simone's body pulse around them. She waited until Simone's body stilled before slowly stroking her again, as Simone gasped once more, her body again incandescent with passion so strong she could barely breathe. Shannon buried her face in Simone's neck as she lay on top of her, her hands clasping Simone's where they lay by her hips. Simone smiled as she threaded her fingers with Shannon's. Her face pressed against Shannon's as she recovered from her lovemaking. Shannon reached up and stroked Simone's cheek as she turned to stare at her.

"You are so beautiful." Smiling, she laid her hand against Simone's cheek. Simone turned and kissed her hand and wrapped her arms gently around Shannon.

Simone kissed Shannon slowly and than smiled back at the beautiful woman who looked at her with such complete trust. She stroked Shannon's long hair as she looked at her, her heart brimming with feelings she had never experienced before. She had made love before but not with a woman that made her feel so treasured and valued, it made her already full heart tumble.

"Is your back okay?" she whispered as she slid her hands down Shannon's ribs.

"My back is fine." Shannon grinned. "You need to get some sleep, honey. You're working tomorrow."

"Are you tired?" Simone asked, her hands moved slowly over Shannon's body, teasing her with the softest of touches.

"Not in the least." Shannon chuckled and Simone responded with a smile as she ran her hands down Simone's shoulders and bent to nuzzle her nipple. Simone's body tightened in response as she reacted to Shannon's attentions. Her body was enflamed with need that only Shannon could satisfy.

Simone didn't get much sleep as she and Shannon made love several more times until they were both limp with exhaustion. It was almost time for Simone to get up but she couldn't have been happier. She was in love and overwhelmed with a night of incredible lovemaking. "Go to sleep, honey," she whispered to Shannon, whose eyes were heavy lidded from lack of sleep.

"I'm afraid if I go to sleep this night will be over with and it will have been a dream," Shannon whispered as she snuggled against Simone.

"Shannon, look at me. I'm as overwhelmed by this night as you are. We have almost three weeks to figure this all out. Now, please go to sleep."

"Simone, I know you don't know me very well, but I don't sleep around. I haven't been with a woman in over a year."

"Shannon, I know you don't and neither do I. We'll work this out, I promise you."

"So if I told you I've fallen in love with you it wouldn't scare you away."

"Not any more than my telling you I've fallen in love with you. Does that scare you?"

"No, it makes me smile, it makes me happy, and it makes me think I am very, very lucky."

"Go to sleep, Shannon." Simone brushed her long hair over her shoulder.

"I love you, Simone." Shannon's voice drifted off as she fell asleep. She didn't have a chance to hear Simone's response.

"I love you, Shannon, and I'm going to love you for the rest of your life." Simone tucked the covers around the two of them and slid into sleep herself.

CHAPTER 5

"Shannon, sweetie I'll see you after work. I just wanted to kiss you goodbye."

Shannon opened her eyes to find Simone sitting on the side of her bed in uniform. She smiled at her as she sat up. "Did I tell you how sexy I think you are in your uniform?"

Simone smiled and kissed her. "Frankly, I think your being naked in my bed is a lot sexier." They shared a soft, long kiss. "Make sure you have Janice change your bandages."

"I will. Be careful today."

"I'll call you later on." Simone stood up, gazing down at Shannon. "I love you. Now, get some more sleep."

"Simone?"

"Yes."

"I love you."

Simone didn't respond, but her smile, and the twinkle in her soft blue eyes went right to Shannon's heart. With a wiggle of her fingers, Simone was gone. Shannon lay awake in bed reliving the unbelievable night of lovemaking she had spent with Simone. She needed to talk to someone about her feelings and soon.

Simone was thinking similar thoughts as she headed for work. She wasn't the least bit tired. But her mind was reeling with emotion as she tried to figure out what she and Shannon were doing. She needed to call her best friend as soon as she found out how work was going.

"So Shannon, spill the beans." Hanna teased her as they sat around the kitchen table drinking coffee.

"What do you mean spill the beans?" Shannon wasn't capable of keeping a secret from anyone, let alone her best friends, who could read her like a book.

"You and Simone slept together."

"We have been sleeping together for two nights."

"Shannon, quit stalling. You know you are going to tell us sooner or later."

Shannon's eyes filled with tears as she raised her head up to look at her friends. "I'm in love with her." She dropped her head on to the table.

"Tell us something we don't know."

"What am I going to do?"

"Move to Hawaii and marry her," Mel responded. All eyes turned in her direction.

"Excuse me?" Hanna responded with an incredulous look.

"You heard me. If Shannon has fallen in love with her, she should move here and live happily ever after."

"Don't you think it's a little premature to talk about moving?" Hanna questioned.

Shannon had yet to speak as her friends continued to discuss her fate. "It's never too early if you're in love with someone." Janice responded.

"They just met not two days ago." Olivia reminded them.

"So, what's that got to do with anything?" Mel asked the table of women.

"I agree if they are in love they should be together." Janice believed in happy endings.

"Excuse me, but don't you think this is between me and Simone?" Shannon inquired, interrupting the discussion, an amused look on her face.

"So how does Simone feel?" Mel asked as the other three watched Shannon's face.

Shannon smiled a huge, happy smile that left no doubt as to how Simone felt. "She loves me."

"What's not to love?"

"I'm serious, she really loves me."

"So why do you look so scared?"

"Because I'm frightened to death, we just met, and I can't think of not being with her. But I don't know if I could move."

"Shannon, you and Simone have two weeks to figure things out. Relax and let things happen," Hanna suggested, patting her hand.

"I'm trying to, but it's difficult when I remember I'm just on vacation."

"It seems to me that Simone took a big risk in inviting all of us into her home. She's taking a bigger risk by telling you she loves you."

"She's incredible." Shannon sighed. "She's so beautiful."

Shannon's friends smiled at their obvious besotted friend and then started discussing who was going to clean house. It was the least they could do. The telephone rang as they were arguing over the bathroom.

"Shannon, it's Simone."

"Hi."

"Hello, how is your morning going?"

"Good, Janice and Mel changed my bandages and we going to head out for some shopping. How's your day going?"

"Good, busy, I miss you."

"I miss you, too. When will you get home?"

"Five-thirty or so, unless we get a late run, but I'll call if I'm running late."

"Simone, I really miss you."

"That's a good thing, have a nice day, sweetie."

Shannon, Janice, and Mel headed for the shopping mall armed with Hanna's list of food and supplies, and Olivia's request for movies. After an hour and a half, Shannon was running out of steam, her back and legs itching from being chafed by the bandages. And she wanted to see Simone.

"Shannon, will you quit moping," Janice teased as they headed for the car.

"I'm not moping."

"Who are you kidding?"

"I'm just distracted."

"You're just thinking about Simone."

"I just can't help wondering what she does all day. There is so much I don't know about her, and I want to know everything."

"Honey, you just met, you have time to get to know her."

"But I don't Mel, I have two weeks."

"Honey, you don't have two weeks. If you and Simone love each other, you will figure out how to make everything work out."

"Shannon, even Mel and I don't know everything about each other. We're still learning what each other needs and how we can support each other."

"I know, but you guys are perfect together."

"Shannon, we're very good together, but we're not perfect. We work very hard to stay in tune with each other. And I would be the first one to admit, I'm not always good at paying attention," Janice admitted with a grimace.

"Honey, we take turns." Mel chuckled, hugging her girlfriend. "But she's right, Shannon. No one has a perfect relationship. It takes time to figure things out. We aren't the same people that moved in together after a month."

"Mel!"

"Well, it's the truth, Janice. We slept with each other that first night and we never stopped. We fell in love in an instant, but we figured out how to love each other in the years after."

"I want a chance to do that with Simone."

"Shannon, are you willing to give up your career in Seattle, and your home? Are you going to work harder than you've ever had to, to make a relationship work? And that isn't going to guarantee it's going to work out."

"I know I want to be with Simone, I know that much already. I know we are going to have to work at being together."

"Shannon, you have a career in Seattle that you have been working hard for since college. We know how important it is to you. You love your job."

"I do, but does that mean I can't have a relationship with Simone?"

"She lives here in Hawaii, and she loves her job. Her home is very important to her, and have you forgotten you have a condominium?"

"No, I haven't forgotten." Shannon's face showed her dismay. "But I can't be with her for a couple of weeks and just leave."

"Honey, that doesn't mean you and Simone aren't meant to be together. It just means you're going to have to work even harder to figure things out. It may take a lot of sacrifice on both of your parts," Mel responded. "I promise you, Janice and I will help you any way we can."

"I know you will, but I don't know if I can move away from you guys. Most of all I would miss all of you so much."

"Oh, honey. We would miss you. But if you and Simone decide to be together and your choice is to live in Hawaii, you wouldn't really leave us. We would always stay in contact. We'll always be friends."

Mel hugged Shannon tightly and then Janice hugged her. "I love you guys."

"We love you. Now, tell us, if you move to Hawaii can we come on vacation and stay with you whenever we want?" Mel asked with a grin.

Shannon cracked up as they climbed into the car. "I really love you guys."

"You say that to all the girls."

"Don't forget, we need to go to the grocery store for Hanna."

"Janice, you have the list."

"Yep."

"Does anyone know what fresh rosemary looks like?"

"No."

"Do you know what endive is?"

"What the hell is endive?" Mel asked as they pulled into the grocery store.

"I don't know, but I think Hanna wants us to buy some."

The grocery shopping was done with little incident, other than the three of them never located the endive or what ever Hanna had written on the list. Shannon was feeling a little bit better after spending a couple of hours with Janice and Mel. They could always make her laugh.

"Hey, guys, we're back."

"We're out on the patio. How was shopping?"

"Good, but can you explain what endive is?"

Hanna just grinned at the threesome. They never found everything on her lists. Olivia was the only one who could read her handwriting and find everything she needed. "Shannon, Christa is going to drop a copy of the interview off around four-thirty. She's bringing her girlfriend with her. She already talked to Simone."

"Great." Shannon's less than enthusiastic response caught Hanna's attention.

"Hey what's the problem?"

"Christa was Simone's first girlfriend." Shannon was intimidated by the very beautiful, professional woman.

"So what?"

"Christa is gorgeous."

"And you are beautiful."

"Hanna…"

"Shannon, who slept with Simone last night and the night before, and who called this morning, and this afternoon to talk to you?"

"Simone called again?"

"About an hour ago, and she said to say she'll be home around four-thirty. She told us Christa and her girlfriend were going to stop by. I told her I'd fix dinner for all of us."

"Hanna, you don't have to cook for everyone."

"Shannon, you know I love to cook, especially for a crowd of appreciative women." Hanna grinned. "So did you find a new swimsuit?"

"Yes, it's pretty skimpy," Shannon blushed.

"It's sexy," Janice grinned. "And she bought a bunch of clothes."

"I didn't buy a bunch," Shannon laughed. "I'm going to go put the groceries and my stuff away."

"You might think about resting a little bit."

"I'm fine, Olivia. I think I might take my video camera down to the beach and shoot some film."

"Good, Shannon. I have to tell you, Hanna and I are so proud of you."

Shannon's eyes filled with tears. "Thanks."

"Go put your clothes away." Hanna hugged her quickly, before gently nudging her toward the open sliding glass door. "And Shannon, Simone said I need to change your bandages and spread aloe vera on your back and legs. She said you can get it wet now."

"Good, I need to take a shower."

"I'll help with your bandages."

Shannon helped Mel and Janice put the groceries away, and then hung her new clothes up before taking a very short and extremely painful shower. Hanna spread gel over her back and legs and re-bandaged them before Shannon dressed in a pair of her new shorts and a shirt. She grabbed her video camera and headed for the beach. She needed to think, and filming was the best way she knew how to relax and figure out what was bothering her.

While Shannon did what she knew best, Mel and Janice joined Hanna and Olivia on the back porch to play pinochle. They humorously argued for over an hour as the four of them played cards until Hanna had to start dinner. She recruited Janice to do some of the preparation, while Mel and Olivia set the table and put out some snacks that Hanna had prepared earlier.

"Janice, I'm going to go change my clothes before dinner."

"Okay sweetie."

"Olivia, how's Shannon's back look?"

"Horrible, it's still very angry looking, and her legs and arms aren't much better. I'm going to talk to Simone about getting Shannon in to see a doctor."

"I think that's a good idea."

"Hello." Simone entered the kitchen.

"Hello how was work?" Janice hugged her.

"Busy, how was your day?"

"Heavenly, thanks."

"Where's Shannon?"

"She's down at the beach video taping. She does that all the time at home."

"How's she feeling?

"She says good, but I changed her bandages and I think her back and legs still look very angry. I want to get her in to see a doctor."

"I think that's a good idea. I'll call my doctor and make an appointment for her tomorrow."

"Good. Now, Hanna has made some incredible snacks for all of us. Do you want a glass of wine and some treats?"

"I'm going to get cleaned up and go find Shannon. I'm really glad you are all here." Simone hugged Hanna and Olivia.

"Go, Christa and her girlfriend are going to be here any minute."

Simone headed for the bedroom with a smile. She couldn't wait to see Shannon. After calling her doctor's office for an appointment, she changed out of her uniform into a pair of shorts and a blouse, ran a brush through her hair, washed her face, and headed back through the house. "Hi Mel."

"Hey Simone, what's up?" Mel grinned as she continued hugging Janice in the kitchen.

"Not bad, I'm going down to the beach. If Christa and Neely get here, call down."

"We will. Go find Shannon." Mel pushed Simone out the back door.

Simone hurried down the path a smile on her face. She had missed Shannon all day. Christa's telephone call earlier had triggered her insecurities and she needed to talk to Shannon. Christa had pointed out that they didn't know each other at all. Let alone the fact that Shannon was on vacation. Simone was having serious second thoughts. She reached the beach and looked south along the beach line, no Shannon. Looking north she caught Shannon's lone figure off in the distance, her back to Simone. Simone hurried along the beach, her heart pounding in her chest as she gained on Shannon.

"Shannon."

Shannon whirled around, a huge smile on her face as she threw herself into Simone's arms. Simone hugged her tightly as they swayed back and forth. Shannon reached up and touched Simone's cheek. "I've missed you so much."

"I missed you," Simone whispered, her lips capturing Shannon's in a passionate kiss that shook her right to her toes. The world around them dropped away as they shared kiss after wonderful kiss and all of Simone's questions evaporated.

It was several long minutes before they stopped kissing and just held each other tightly. "What were you filming?" Simone whispered as she enjoyed nuzzling Shannon's neck, memorizing her scent.

"This and that, I might be able to use some shots of the beach in a video of our vacation."

"I'd like to see some of your work."

Shannon was surprised by Simone's comment. She had never been with someone who took an active interest in her filming. In fact, her last girlfriend had complained to Shannon about her obsession with making videos. She hadn't liked it when Shannon worked in her studio. It became a bigger problem when Shannon grew more successful and needed to spend more time working. "I don't have any videos with me, but I can send you a couple when I get home."

Simone's face lost its smile as she thought of Shannon returning to her home in Seattle. "Simone, I'm sorry. We won't talk about my leaving."

"Shannon, we need to talk about it soon."

"We will, but not today, please." Simone couldn't have refused Shannon anything. She bent and kissed Shannon thoroughly, loving her with her mouth, needing that connection to push away all thoughts of losing her so soon after finding her. "Oh, God, Simone I love you."

"I love you, honey."

"Simone, Shannon!" Janice yelled down the beach. "Christa and Neely are here!"

Shannon groaned as she hugged Simone tightly. "I just want to be alone with you."

"Later, I promise you." Simone kissed Shannon softly.

They held hands as they walked back up to the house where they found all of the women seated on the patio with glasses of wine and loads of treats.

"Hi Christa, Neely how are you?" Simone went up to Neely and hugged her. "How's the law business?"

"Booming." Neely was a pleasant surprise to Shannon. She was short and stocky with wavy black hair liberally streaked with silver, pulled up on to the back of her head in a messy knot. Her glasses were perched on the end of her nose and she was wearing a tweed jacket and matching skirt. She looked friendly, smart, and comfortable. Not even close to the type of woman she thought Christa would be with. "Shannon, finally I get to meet you in person. Christa told me how you saved a young boy's life and injured yourself. I think that's truly amazing."

"I was the first one to get to him. Lots of other people were there."

"It's still important that you got involved. How are you feeling?"

"Fine, I'm good."

"Is that true, Simone?" Neely wasn't one to mince words and she had won Shannon's heart in a couple of minutes. As she stood talking to Shannon and Simone, she held both of their hands gently in her own. She was a gentle soul, as Hanna would say.

"She's pretty chewed up Neely. But she's healing."

"Good. Now tell me what you are going to do for the rest of your vacation after we get you both a glass of wine."

Shannon grinned at Simone as Olivia handed them a glass of wine. Simone winked in return as she pulled Shannon down next to her on the chaise lounge. Christa was visiting with Mel and Janice, while Hanna stood by the barbeque where something was sizzling away. Neely chatted with Shannon and Simone like an old friend. Simone sat back and pulled Shannon up against her, her arms surrounding her snuggly as she leaned back. Being held by her was as natural as breathing. It was a very pleasant way to spend an evening but she would have traded it all to spend the evening alone with Simone.

"Olivia, can you go grab the salad and the bread while I finish this? The fish is done and the vegetables are almost ready. The rest of you find a spot at the table and fill your wine glasses. Dinner is about to be served."

The women quickly found spots at the table as Hanna placed a platter of grilled vegetables and tuna on the table. Along with a salad of mixed greens and fresh Italian bread, dinner was served.

"Hanna, this is incredible." Christa raved while all of them dove into the meal. There was lots of conversation and laughter as the meal progressed. Hanna's gourmet meal was devoured quickly amid lots of appreciative comments.

"Neely, what kind of law do you practice?" Shannon inquired as she picked at her dinner.

"She does what ever her clients ask for and most of which they don't pay for," Christa shared, hugging Neely tightly. "She takes any cases that come to her office."

"Everyone deserves a good lawyer."

"Sounds like you love what you do."

"I do. Christa tells me you are a cameraperson for a sports network?"

"Yes, Fox Sports Network in Bellevue."

"Do you ever do any filming outside of work?"

"She films all the time and makes videos. They're incredible," Janice jumped in.

"I've got an idea, and you can say no if you aren't interested." Neely turned to Shannon as she spoke. "Simone has agreed to allow us to make a training video on what it's like to be a paramedic. We want to encourage high school students to look at different careers. Would you like to take a crack at it while you are here on vacation? We can't pay you; it would be strictly voluntary. Christa's network will provide the camera, the film, the editing time, and equipment. What do you say?"

Shannon's eyes had begun to twinkle as she listened to Neely's proposal. She already knew what she was going to say. "How long does the video have to be?"

"Minimum around thirty minutes, long enough to explain what it takes to become a paramedic and explain what happens on the job. It would require you to hang around the paramedics for a week or so to get some actual film of them working, maybe some interviews, but that's up to you. Simone has already agreed to allow someone to ride along with her medics."

"I'm only here for two and half weeks."

"You'd have to get started right away, then," Neely chuckled, as the rest of the women at the table grinned; they all knew Shannon was going to say yes.

"It sounds like fun. I'd love to do it." Shannon squeezed Simone's hand under the table.

"Shannon, before you start on the video I want you to do one thing for me," Janice requested.

"What?"

"I've asked Simone to make you a doctor's appointment to get your back and legs checked. It would relieve my worries if a doctor said you were healing."

"I made an appointment for two forty-five tomorrow afternoon," Simone responded. "I took the afternoon off and I'll come home and pick you up."

"Okay, I'll go. I can work on an outline tomorrow morning. When can I see the camera, so I know what I'll be working with?"

"Monday morning, you can come into the station and I'll have the equipment for you to choose from. I'll also introduce you to the editor who has volunteered to help. He can show you the editing room," Christa volunteered. "Let me know if I can do anything."

"Neely, how often do you need an update on the work?"

"You can call me at the end of the week and give me an update."

"You've got a cameraperson and a video. Can you tell me why you are doing this?"

"We have an overwhelming number of unemployed people on the Hawaiian Islands. Most of the kids who actually graduate from high school and don't go on to college end up working in the tourist industry, which is notoriously low paying. Of the kids that choose to go to college, many leave the island instead of looking for jobs here. We need to encourage our high school students to look at all careers. We need to retain our young on the islands. It will keep the islands strong."

"Neely volunteers her time at a local high school to help kids prepare to find work."

"That's very generous."

"Hey, when people work they commit fewer crimes. Fewer crimes means fewer hours for me, and more time with Christa." Neely was grinning as Christa kissed her gently, it was obvious to everyone how much they loved each other. Shannon watched the two women carefully. Her nervousness around Christa was lessening the more she saw of her.

Shannon turned and spoke softly to Simone. "Was this your idea?"

"I only mentioned to Neely that you were a cameraperson, Christa is the one who suggested you do the video." Simone smiled and hugged her. "I'm glad you want to do it. We'll be able to spend a lot more time together."

"I love that most of all." Shannon leaned against Simone and kissed her. "I love you."

Simone hugged Shannon and whispered in her ear. "How soon do think we can escape from all these people? I want to make love with you."

"Soon, I promise." Shannon's eyes promised everything as she gazed at Simone.

It was after nine-thirty before Christa and Neely left for home and the rest of the group started to settle down for the night. Olivia and Hanna decided to go on a moon lit walk on the beach and Janice and Mel were going to crawl in bed. They were going snorkeling in the morning and in the evening all of them were going to the movies. Shannon sent Simone in to get ready for bed as she and Mel finished cleaning up the kitchen. She needed to talk to Mel.

"Shanni, are you sure you are up to working on a video?"

"I can't wait, Mel. This is the real thing. I know I can make a good one."

"Honey, there's no question you will make a terrific video. I'm just concerned about your health."

"I'm fine. I'm going to the doctor tomorrow."

"You know, it was Simone who suggested to Christa that you do the video. She asked Janice and me if you would be interested. We told her how much you loved making video's. She really thought it would be something that would appeal to you."

Shannon smiled as she responded. "Then I'm going to have to make sure I thank her."

Mel just grinned at her friend. "You two are pretty cute."

"I think so."

"I like Christa and Neely."

"I do too, I was surprised by Neely. I wouldn't have pictured her as Christa's type but when you see them together they fit."

"Just like me and Janice."

"Exactly. Speaking about Janice, don't you think you had better join her in bed?"

"I'm on my way. Shannon, I really like Simone and I think the two of you are very nice together, but are you sure about this?"

"I'm very sure. I don't know how it's going to work out but I going to do everything I can to make it work."

"Okay sweetie. Well, I'm off to bed."

"So am I." Shannon walked down the dimly lit hall and entered the bedroom. Simone was still in the shower, so Shannon changed into her silk night shirt and sat on the bed, brushing her hair. She already had a plan shaping up in her head about the video and she closed her eyes as she worked it out in her mind.

Simone opened the bathroom door and stopped short as she felt the emotion fill her body at the sight of Shannon sitting on her bed. She was slowly brushing her hair and she looked incredibly lovely. Simone had been in love before but never like this. This was a full-blown romance, with all the trimmings. Simone walked slowly toward Shannon enjoying the quiet and her movements. She was elegant, her long hair shiny in the dim lights of the bedroom, and her slim shoulders covered with a turquoise silk shirt.

"I love you, Shannon." She spoke softly as she approached her.

Shannon's eyes opened to look up into Simone's beautiful blue ones. She melted under Simone's intense gaze. "I love you, Simone."

Simone bent to meet Shannon's upturned face, their lips sliding softly against each other's. The brush fell out of Shannon's hand as she and Simone fell back on to the bed, their kiss deepening and taking them both under. This wasn't the lovemaking from the night before; this was raw emotion and love. Shannon's arms wrapped around Simone's neck as she kissed her with all the passion that whirled through her body. Simone's fingers caught in Shannon's hair as she held her head while her lips opened to Shannon's questing tongue. They tasted each other as magic filled the room, weaving their lovemaking with an intensity that made them both tremble.

Shannon gently rolled Simone on to her back and trailed kisses along her neck and jaw, tasting her skin and nipping her with sexy little bites. Simone was overwhelmed at the raw emotion that radiated from Shannon. Shannon's hands stroked Simone's body unleashing a need that clamored to be fed. She moaned as Shannon stripped her of her nightshirt, as her mouth captured Simone's nipple, lapping at it with her tongue, first one breast and then the other as they swelled with Shannon's attentions.

"Simone, I love touching you and loving you. You are so beautiful, so gentle, and so sexy."

Shannon's hands slid over Simone's nakedness, kissing her way down her body. Simone's scent infused Shannon's senses as she settled herself between Simone's legs, her lips tasting the moisture that coated her tissue. Her tongue slid against Simone's slick lips as her hands cradled Simone's hips, bringing Simone tightly against her mouth. Her tongue slid into Simone slowly, deeply and withdrew, drawing a hiss from Simone. Slowly she entered Simone again, as her fingers found her pulsing clitoris. Shannon slid her tongue against Simone and pushed her fingers into her, as Simone's hips jumped off the bed. Shannon could barely hold on to Simone's hips as she rolled and bucked in response to their lovemaking. Shannon stroked Simone, her lips sucking deeply on her hardened bud, as an orgasm flooded Simone's body and she trembled and then stiffened before melting on to the bed.

Shannon moved up Simone's body and wrapped her arms around her as Simone shivered and shook her face tight against Shannon's neck. Shannon felt tears against her skin and turned Simone's face toward her.

"Honey, why the tears? Are you okay?"

"I'm fine, love, I'm just overwhelmed. I've never had anyone make love to me like you do. It's so perfect." She began to weep. "I can't believe I've fallen in love with someone who lives in Seattle."

"Honey, it is perfect, and I promise you we'll figure something out. Please believe me, I've never felt like this about anyone before. I want to be with you. I believe in fate and I know we're meant to be together. We met for a reason, and I think that was because we're supposed to fall in love."

Simone knew she was falling in love with Simone but Shannon's lovemaking moved her beyond falling to being in love. Time had nothing to do with it, when it was supposed to happen, it just happened. And it had.

Shannon was as overwhelmed as Simone. She held Simone as her fingers stroked her hips and thighs, sharing a mesmerizing kiss. Finding Simone still wet she slipped into her slowly stroking as her tongue mimicked the motion. Simone moaned as she was thrown immediately into another orgasm, heat enveloping her body as she tumbled. Stroking deeper and harder, Shannon drove Simone higher and farther as her body vibrated with pleasure. Shannon's mouth continued to cover Simone's with slow, wet kisses, as her stroking continued. Shannon felt the throbbing of Simone's body as if it was her own, and felt the exact moment when Simone's body dissolved. Simone's head fell back and Shannon watched as she gasped her pleasure. Shannon fell in love with Simone all over again as she melted with her own orgasm.

Shannon lay on top of Simone, her head resting on Simone's shoulder, their hands clasped tightly as they both caught their breath. Simone reached up and traced her fingers down Shannon's cheek before cupping her chin in her hand. "I love you, Shannon. You are an incredible lover."

"Only with you."

Simone's mouth captured Shannon's in a ravenous kiss as her hands slid down her arms before stroking her buttocks. Her legs slid between Shannon's and widened, opening Shannon's body against Simone's. Shannon ground her now trembling center against Simone's wetness as she arched against her. Simone forced Shannon's thighs even wider as she tightened her grip on Shannon's hips rotating her own to provide Shannon the connection she craved. Shannon's hips rocked faster and harder against Simone's as she tucked her face against her, her arms around Simone's neck.

Shannon cried out loudly as her body reacted to Simone's attentions. They had the closest of connections and Shannon found it overwhelming. She shook as her body reacted, then her hips stilled as she pressed her body against Simone's. "Oh, Simone," she gasped as she slid into ecstasy so quickly she could barely breathe.

Simone held Shannon tightly, their hips sealed as their mouths met again in a promise as emotional as the lovemaking they both enjoyed. Shannon placed her head on Simone's shoulder and just looked at her, memorizing the fine laugh lines around her eyes, the soft pale blue of them, and the way she smiled so beautifully whenever she looked at Shannon. Her blond hair curled wildly around her head like a golden crown around her stunning face. Shannon could look at her for the rest of her life and never get tired. Simone watched Shannon watch her and her heart swelled with feeling. This was a look she treasured above all else, pure love radiated from Shannon, there was no doubt in Simone's heart and mind that Shannon loved her. Shannon's brown eyes locked on Simone, her hair in a tangle, streaming down her back, her beautiful face relaxed after lovemaking.

"You need to go to sleep, honey. You're still healing," Simone whispered as she stroked Shannon's hair away from her face.

"And I need to thank you for convincing Christa to let me do the video for Neely."

"Honey, she didn't need any convincing. She checked on your work and asked me if you might be interested." Simone chuckled at the look on Shannon's face. "I think she said things like, innovative, talented, and incredibly hard working, were terms used to describe you by Fox News. She told them she was doing background on her interview. She shared your heroics with your boss and he requested a copy of the interview. He is going to have it run in Bellevue. He wasn't surprised that you saved someone and he was very complimentary of your extensive skills." Shannon flushed as she listened. "He said if you needed to take more time you should just call him."

"He's a nice man."

"He sounds like it. I want you to promise me if you start to feel exhausted or even a little under the weather that you'll slow down on the video production."

"I promise. So, I have an idea about that and before I suggest it to Christa I want to ask you if it's possible. When I ride along with your medics and film them at work, is it possible for me to interview them on video?"

Simone smiled as she responded. She had anticipated Shannon's request and had already sought permission from her boss and the Fire Chief. Their only demand was that they wanted to have the opportunity to see the video before being released. She already knew Christa had no problem with that request. Christa's job required her to understand all the city politics and keep the appropriate factions happy.

"I have already gotten permission for you to work with my medics with one condition. The video must be approved by my boss and the Fire Chief before it's released. Christa has already agreed if you are willing."

"I have no problem with that."

"Good. Now, go to sleep."

"I love you, Simone and I'm going to love working with you."

"I love you, Shannon and I am looking forward to watching you work."

"Goodnight sweetie."

Shannon snuggled up to Simone's body as she settle down to sleep, Simone's arms and legs wrapped securely around her as she slipped into slumber. Simone was quick to follow as she too fell into sleep.

CHAPTER 6

Simone slept soundly for over three hours before waking up and climbing out of her comfortable bed. She looked down at Shannon who slept undisturbed before putting her nightshirt back on, slipping quietly out of the bedroom, and padding down the hall to the kitchen. She poured herself a glass of water and stepped out on to the back patio. The evening was extremely warm but there was a slight breeze that provided Simone some relief. She stood looking out at the water deep in thought, unaware of Shannon coming up behind her until her arms snuck around her waist as Shannon snuggled up to her back.

"Is everything okay, Simone?" Shannon whispered.

The worry in Shannon's voice made Simone turn in her arms to reassure her. "Everything is fine, honey. I was just warm and needed to cool off."

"What were you thinking about?"

"I was thinking how, overnight my life has changed so much for the better. I woke up and realized that I didn't know what love was until I fell in love with you. I want you in my life; whatever it takes I will make sure we can be together."

"I promise you, I am going to be impossible to get rid of, Simone. I want to be with you. I can get a job here doing something, anything. We can be together I know we can work it out." Shannon's eyes glistened with unshed tears, her heart pounding.

"Shannon, I can be a paramedic anywhere. I can move to Seattle."

"But you have a home and a career here."

"You have one in Seattle."

"We'll figure it out together, okay?"

"Okay." They shared a soft, gentle kiss that grew quickly into passion as Shannon showed her commitment to Simone. She slid her hands underneath Simone's shirt finding her swollen breasts aching to be touched. Simone moaned against Shannon's mouth as she reacted to her touch.

"God, I love touching your body," Shannon admitted between kisses as her hands raced over Simone's hips and stomach. Her fingers slid between Simone's legs to find her dripping with welcome moisture. "You're so wet."

Simone slumped against Shannon as her body reacted to Shannon's attentions. Shannon slid quickly, deeply into Simone, tumbling her directly into an earth-shaking orgasm. She held on tightly to Shannon as she shook in her arms. Shannon fingers teased and pleasured Simone until she could no longer stand.

"Shannon, I can't stand," Simone gasped as she stumbled against Shannon's body. "I need to sit down."

Shannon pulled her over to a chaise lounge and sat down, pulling Simone down on her lap, her knees on either side of Shannon's hips. Shannon renewed her efforts as Simone wrapped herself around Shannon's body, their mouths meeting in a ravenous kiss. Simone's hips jerked one, twice and then stilled as Shannon held on to her tightly, kissing her tear filled eyes, her soft cheeks, and her beautiful mouth.

"I love you Simone. I will love you here in Hawaii, in Seattle, or anywhere else you want to go. I promise you, I will go anywhere with you."

Simone kissed Shannon, her hands cradling Shannon's head. "I love you, Shannon." Simone's fingers slowly unbuttoned Shannon's nightshirt until her breasts were exposed to Simone's mouth and she covered them with kisses, her tongue bathing first one nipple, than the other. Simone's hand moved between Shannon's legs and pressed against her, need welling up in Shannon quickly.

"Please," she whispered, her face pressed tightly against Simone's. Simone pushed two fingers into Shannon deeply, not moving as she felt Shannon's body contract around her. Shannon's hips rocked against Simone's hand as her head fell back in reaction. Simone's arm slid tightly around Shannon's hips as they churned against her.

"Simone," Shannon pleaded.

Simone smiled as Shannon's body softened against her and she quivered in her arms while her body tumbled over the edge. Crying softly against Simone's mouth, Shannon's arms locked around Simone's neck, as she tried to compose herself. They stayed securely in each other's arms for several minutes before either one spoke.

"Honey, we need to go crawl in bed. We both have a big day," Shannon suggested nuzzling Simone's neck.

"I think that's a good idea." Simone smiled and stood up, helping Shannon to her feet. "Oh, I like the way you look."

Simone reached out and ran her finger over Shannon's nipple watching it tighten in response. Both of Shannon's breasts stood proudly waiting for Simone's attentions. "Simone honey, I love it when you touch me but can we take this back inside?"

Shannon pulled her shirt closed as Simone chuckled quietly, before buttoning her own shirt. She gathered Shannon's hand in her own and they headed back into the house and to bed. Shannon and Simone stripped their shirts off as they slid into bed, where they wrapped their arms around each other and once again fell deeply asleep.

CHAPTER 7

Shannon slept through Simone's departure for work but was charmed by the note and flower left on the bathroom counter. "Have a good day and I'll be here by one-thirty to take you to the doctor's. Don't work too hard. Love, Simone."

Shannon tried to take Simone's advice but she was up and dressed by eight-thirty, with a cup of coffee and a tablet out on the back patio. She needed to get her outline done before Monday morning and have something to show Christa and Neely. She needed to sketch out her script and then run it by Simone before she fleshed it out. She wanted to make sure she was on track with her thoughts. She began to draw her scenes in order to clearly illustrate what she meant. She was still at it when Olivia joined her at the table.

"Hello, how are you doing this nice morning?" She sat down wearing her bathing suit and sipping a cup of coffee.

"I'm wonderful, how about you?"

"Terrific, fantastic, who wouldn't be staying in a place like this? Hanna and I are going for a morning swim and then we are going to lie on the beach and soak up some rays. With snorkeling on Saturday and sightseeing on Sunday, we decided to take it easy today. Besides, we have dinner and a movie tonight."

"Are you having a good vacation?"

"I'm having a wonderful one. How about you? You've had a rather difficult start."

"I wouldn't change a thing," Shannon grinned. "Well, maybe a little less of the pain."

"So are you working on your video?"

"Yes, can I run my ideas by you and see what you think?"

"Certainly."

A little while later Hanna joined them, followed shortly by Janice and Mel. The five women headed down to the beach for a couple of hours before pitching together and vacuuming the house and changing beds, washing laundry, and towels. Shannon was putting the finishing touches on her outline after she showered and changed in preparation for visiting the doctor. One section of her back was bothering her quite a bit and Janice told her it was angry, red, and puffy. She was glad she was going to the doctor. She sat at the kitchen table working quietly while the others played pinochle in the other room. She smiled as she listened to the banter back and forth. It was trash talk as Mel called it, designed to throw the other team off. They were quite entertaining to listen to. She finished her outline and began writing in her journal, recording her thoughts and feelings. She had a lot to write about.

Simone found her seated at the kitchen table, her head bent as she wrote rapidly, scribbling in her journal. She stood behind her watching for the longest time, just enjoying the sight of Shannon so intently writing. She finally went up behind her, bent over, and said hello. Shannon's head came up, her face beaming with a huge smile.

"Hi." Shannon hooked her arm around Simone's neck and kissed her sweetly, taking her time and enjoying the feeling she got every time she and Simone kissed.

"Hello." Simone stroked Shannon's hair as she gazed at her. "Are you ready to go to the doctor's?"

"I am. I'm having a little bit of a problem with one section of my back that doesn't seem to want to heal. I'm glad I'm going to the doctor."

"Good, than let's get going." Simone's look of concern touched Shannon.

"Don't worry honey, I'm fine. It's nothing."

But Simone wasn't so sure. Coral cuts could become quite infected. "We need to get going."

"Simone, Mel wanted to come with us. Is that okay?"

"Of course it is." Simone smiled as she stood up. Shannon reached out and grabbed her hand.

"Mel, are you ready?" Shannon called as she and Simone headed for the door.

"On my way."

"The house looks nice, thanks for cleaning," Simone commented as Mel joined her and Shannon in the hallway.

"It's the least we can do for you letting us invade you."

"Mel, I don't want any of you to think that you're invading me. I'm enjoying your company. I would like to think we're all becoming friends."

"We aren't becoming, we are. And friends don't take advantage of friends."

The three climbed into Simone's car and headed down the road toward town, Mel chatting away with Simone. Mel wanted to see and hear how the fire department was run. She had all sorts of questions for Simone as they made the twenty minute trip to town. Shannon sat quietly in the front seat, her hand on Simone's thigh. Periodically, Simone would reach down, squeeze her hand gently, and smile at her.

"Why don't you and Janice come down to the station and look around? I can set up some time with the Chief so you can talk to him."

"That would be great, Simone, thanks."

Shannon smiled as she turned to look at Simone. It amazed her how generous Simone was with everyone. She was innately good through and through and Shannon loved her even more because of it. She leaned over and whispered in her ear much to Simone's delight and Mel's amusement.

"I love you."

"Knock that off," Mel teased.

Simone just chuckled as she pulled into the medical center and parked. The three headed for the entrance and the doctor's office. Shannon filled out her insurance paperwork and then waiting impatiently to be called.

"Relax, honey." Simone slipped an arm around her shoulders.

"I hate this stuff," Shannon admitted as Mel grinned at her.

"We have to threaten to kidnap her to get her to go get a physical."

"I'm healthy I don't need to go to a doctor."

Simone just smiled as she watched her vulnerable lover fidget. She was still amazed that the beautiful woman seated next to her was her lover. She thought of the night before and flushed as she remembered how completely overwhelmed she was with Shannon's lovemaking.

"What are thinking about? You are so beautiful," Shannon whispered to Simone, making her blush even worse.

"I'll tell you later."

"Shannon Dunbar." The nurse called her name.

"Do you want either of us to come in with you?" Mel asked.

"No, I'll be fine." Shannon followed the nurse down a corridor and into an open room.

"I understand you were the young woman who saved a little boy's life the other day?" The nurse chatted as she had Shannon sit down on the table. "Let's check and see how your wounds are healing. Do you have any areas that are bothering you?"

"I have two spots on my middle back that are still very sore and my friends tell me they're pretty raw."

"Let's get you a gown to slip into so that the doctor can examine all of your scrapes. You can leave your underpants on. I'm going to take your blood pressure, temperature, and pulse. Are you still taking your antibiotics?"

"Yes, I have another week's worth."

"Okay, here's a gown. I'm going to step out and you can put this on."

Shannon quickly slipped out of her clothes and into the gown and popped back up on to the table. The nurse returned and went about getting all of her vitals. "Shannon, I need you to flop on to your stomach so I can remove all of your bandages."

"Okay."

Shannon rolled over and made herself comfortable on the padded table while the nurse began to gently remove all of her bandages. "Oh, honey you did get pretty banged up. I'm going to go get the doctor."

Shannon lay quietly as she waited for the doctor. She tried not to think about what her back looked like. She knew it was a mess.

"Hello, Shannon, I'm Doctor Farrell, how are you feeling?"

"Hello, Doctor, I'm fine."

"Let's take a look at your back. I'm going to touch it in a few places and you need to tell me if it stings when I touch." The first few times the doctor touched her she barely felt it but when he touched the area that had been bothering her, she hissed as pain radiated from her back.

"I'm sorry, I know this has got to hurt, but I need to know how far the infection has spread." He continued his probing and there were several more places on her back that were very painful, along with the back of one of her thighs. "Well, Shannon, you've got quite an infection on your back and part of your leg. I don't think it's very deep so I'm not terribly concerned. This is typical of a bad coral infection."

"Won't the antibiotic take care of it?"

"It goes a long way but we're going to have to clean your wounds and get some of this infection out. I'm not going to lie to you and tell you this isn't going to be very painful. The nurse will scrub the wound with an antibiotic wash and a scrub brush in order to remove the infected tissue. There isn't much I can do about the pain."

"Okay." Shannon took a couple of slow breaths.

"Do you want your friends in here to help you through it?"

"No thanks, but could someone tell them what you are going to do?"

"Of course, I'll go talk to them while the nurse prepares you."

"Thanks."

"Shannon, I'll be back in after the nurse finishes scrubbing your wounds to look at the cleaned tissue before we re-bandage you."

"Okay." Shannon lowered her head on to the table, close to tears. She couldn't believe this was happening.

The doctor checked with his nurse and then headed into the lobby and approached Simone. "Simone, how are you?" She stood up and hugged him. She had been going to Doctor Farrell for many years.

"Good, Doctor Farrell. How's Shannon? This is her friend, Mel."

"Hello, Mel. Shannon sent me out to talk to the two of you. She's got quite an infection in her lower back and the back of one thigh. We're going to scrub the wounds to remove the infection so they can heal."

"What do you mean scrub the wounds?" Mel asked as Simone winced. She knew what the doctor was talking about.

"The nurse is going to scrub her back, legs, and arms with an antibiotic wash and a scrub brush. It's very painful but necessary to get all the infection out."

"Can we be with her?"

"She asked me to have the two of you stay out here. She's going to be enduring a lot of pain and I don't think she wants you to see."

"Will someone come get us if she needs us?"

"Immediately."

"Thanks, Doctor."

Mel and Simone stared at one another as the doctor walked away. They felt ineffectual just sitting there. Mel got up and sat down next to Simone. "I hate that we can't be in there," she muttered as she grasped Simone's hand.

"I hate it, too." Simone felt sick to her stomach with worry. "She's going to be fine." But Simone knew what Shannon was dealing with and she was heartbroken she couldn't be there.

Shannon gripped the edge of the table as tightly as possible, her knuckles white as she kept herself from crying out loud. She breathed slowly and deeply, while tears streamed down her cheeks. The nurse was working diligently on her lower back and the pain was excruciating.

"Honey, I'm almost done with your back and then we can take a break. How're you holding up?"

"I'm okay," Shannon whispered as she tightened her hands on the edge of the table. There was nothing she could do but clench her teeth and wait for it to be over.

"You are doing more than okay, Shannon. Why don't you try to relax for a few minutes before I will come back and finish?"

"Thank you."

"Do you want me to stay with you?"

"No, I'll be okay."

The nurse left the room and Shannon laid her head down on the table and began to weep. She couldn't believe how much her back hurt. She felt a hand touch her cheek seconds before she heard Simone's voice.

"Shannon, I'm here." Simone bent over and wrapped her arms around Shannon's shoulders, her face tucked against Shannon's. "I'm here, sweetie."

Shannon turned her face into Simone's burying it in her shirt as she wept. Simone held her tightly, whispering softly to her as tears ran down Simone's cheeks. Shannon's weeping started to subside and her body unclenched while Simone tried to sooth her.

"I'm sorry," Shannon whispered against Simone's cheek.

"Shannon, you have nothing to apologize for. I'm going to stay with you, sweetie."

Shannon sighed and reached up to wipe her face clear of tears. "Thank you."

"Oh, honey, you don't need to thank me. I would have been in here earlier but you told the doctor you didn't care to have anyone here. Mel and I wanted to be with you. The nurse just came out and suggested one of us come back here and be with you. Do you want me to go get Mel?"

"No, but I am very glad you're here."

"I love you, Shannon." Simone leaned over and kissed Shannon softly.

"I love you."

Before Simone and Shannon could say another word to each other, the nurse re-entered the room. "Shannon, let's see if we can get this over with quickly. I have to clean the back of your thigh. Simone, why don't you stand over here by Shannon's head?"

The nurse touched the back of Shannon's leg and began to scrub quickly. Shannon's hands once again found the edge of the table to hang on to. She leaned her face tightly against Simone's shoulder, breathing deeply to keep from crying out.

Simone bent closer, placed her cheek next to Shannon's and whispered softly to her lover, words of love and comfort as she stroked the back of her head. She couldn't prevent her from feeling the pain but she could try and distract her enough to get through it. She winced as Shannon moaned; her eyes squeezed shut while tears slipped down her face. Simone began to cry as she tried to console Shannon to no avail. In the stark white clinic room, the nurse scrubbed vigorously while her lover underwent unbelievable anguish. Simone's hand shook as she stroked Shannon's head unable to do anything more to help Shannon.

The nurse stood up and stopped scrubbing. "Shannon, I am going to go get the doctor and have him look at your cleaned back and legs before we re-bandage. It will only take a few minutes."

"Okay." Shannon sighed loudly as she relinquished her hold on the table. Simone reached out and gathered Shannon's hand in her own gently massaging her fingers. Shannon turned her face into Simone's, her lips sliding against Simone's cheek. "I need to kiss you."

Simone understood what Shannon needed and met her lips with a kiss that rocked both of them. She met her seeking mouth, passion and need racing through the two of them. Simone's could feel the moisture from Shannon's tears and it overwhelmed her. She felt a yearning deep in her soul to take care of Shannon, to watch over her and protect her, and to love her with every fiber of her being.

The door started to open and Simone and Shannon broke apart but Simone still held on to her fingers, her other hand stroking the back of Shannon's head. "Hi Simone. Shannon, how are you doing?"

"Okay."

"I'm going to take a look at your back. It looks like it is free of the infected tissue, so does the back of your thighs. I am going to have the nurse spread some antibiotic ointment on all of the scrapes and then bandage you. I want you to keep it clean and dry tonight and tomorrow. You can take the bandages off after tomorrow and replace them. After tomorrow, you can take a shower or get in the salt water. If you have any more signs of infection I want you to come in immediately."

"I will."

"Now, I want you to go home and get some sleep. Do you want me to prescribe a pain killer for you?"

"I can take Ibuprofen."

"I think I'll prescribe something just in case. Shannon, ice bags will help take the sting out until it settles down."

"Thank you."

"You're welcome. I'm sorry you were so badly injured and I'm certainly glad you saved that young man's life. Now, I'm going to have the nurse finish up and get you out of here."

"Thank you, again." Shannon just wanted to go home and crawl into bed.

"Simone, it's good to see you."

"Thanks, Doctor, thank you for getting Shannon in so quickly."

"No problem. You both take care."

It wasn't very long before the nurse re-entered the room and finished her work. Shannon was exhausted and laid silently on the table, her face still tucked against Simone's shoulder. "Okay, Shannon, you're done. Let's help you up off the table. You might be a little dizzy."

Shannon slowly rolled off and stood up, the paper gown hanging haphazardly off of her shoulders. She moved slowly over to her clothes that were hanging on the back of the door. "Here, let me help." Simone held on to Shannon's arm as she walked.

"I'll leave you two. The doctor has a prescription for you at the desk. Shannon, take care of yourself."

"Thank you, I will." Shannon waited for the nurse to leave and then turned to Simone. Her eyes were glazed with pain, dark circles under them. "Simone, can I have a hug?"

It wasn't just the words that turned painfully in Simone's heart. It was the plea in Shannon's voice that hurt the most. She gently wrapped her arms around Shannon, pulling her against her body. Shannon's head rested on Simone's shoulder, her fingers twisted through Simone's curls as she clutched Simone to her. Not a word was said but Simone could feel Shannon's body gradually relax She could feel the tension release from her body. Simone gently stroked her shoulders and Shannon was content to be held by her lover.

"Let's get out of here," Shannon whispered.

"Good idea."

Shannon gingerly slid into her tee shirt and shorts and than she and Simone left the room and approached the nurse's station. "Shannon, here is a prescription for more antibiotics and some pain pills. I really want you to take the pain pills tonight otherwise you are going to be very uncomfortable," the doctor instructed her.

"Okay, Doctor." Shannon leaned against Simone as she turned to walk into the lobby to meet Mel. Mel stood up immediately, alarmed at Shannon's pallor and her obvious distress.

"Hi, honey." Mel met them halfway across the room and guarded Shannon's other side. "Let's get you out of here."

Shannon was too tired and miserable to respond as she walked slowly to the Rover. "Mel, can you sit in the back with Shannon and make sure she is comfortable?" Simone just wanted to get her home and as quickly as possible.

The drive to the house was done as rapidly as Simone could accomplish on a Friday afternoon. They stopped once at the pharmacy and then headed straight home. She practically threw herself out of the car and assisted Shannon to the door with Mel. They didn't stop as they entered the house but went straight to the bedroom.

"Shannon, just crawl in bed, I'm going to get an ice bag and a glass of water, so you can take your pill."

"Simone, I'm not going to be able to go to the movies tonight." Shannon started to cry.

Simone smiled at her girlfriend as she wrapped her arms around her and hugged her. "I don't need to go to the movies to spend time with you. I am content to stay here next to you in bed while you sleep. I love you Shannon, and that means you and I don't have to do anything but be together."

"But…"

"No buts, crawl in bed, please?"

"I love you, Simone."

"I love you, Shannon." They shared a soft, slow kiss, more of a promise than a show of love.

Shannon slid her shorts off and struggled with her bra, before climbing into bed and lying flat on her stomach. It was the only position that would keep her off of her injuries. Simone went to the kitchen and grabbed an ice bag and a glass of water. She returned and placed the bag on Shannon's back and then waited for Shannon to take her pain pill.

"Go to sleep, I'll be back in a little bit to check on you." Shannon closed her eyes as Simone stroked her head.

A few moments later Simone joined the rest of the women out on the patio. "How is she, Simone?" Hanna inquired.

"She's hurting quite a bit, but her pain pill will kick in soon and probably knock her out for most of the afternoon. Why don't you all go out tonight as we planned? I can stay here with Shannon. She'll probably sleep all evening."

"We shouldn't go out while she's hurt."

"Shannon would want you to go out. She feels bad enough that your vacation has been disrupted by her injuries. She would feel even worse if she thought you were staying home because of her."

"Are you sure you don't need some help?"

"I'm sure. Now, I know all of you love her very much and she loves all of you. She would want you to have a good time on your vacation. Besides, I love her too." Simone blushed as she spoke to Shannon's friends. "I know you find this hard to believe, but I love Shannon."

Janice responded to Simone as the others smiled. "We don't doubt you love her, Simone. And we know Shannon loves you. We like the two of you together and we know you'll take good care of her. We just feel bad about having a good time when she's hurting so badly."

"I'm hoping that she starts to heal and can spend the rest of her vacation enjoying herself."

"Simone, what are you and Shannon going to do when the vacation is over with?"

Simone's face lost its smile as she sat down next Hanna. "I honestly don't know, but I'm hoping we can figure out how to be together. I can always get a job as a paramedic in Seattle."

"You would move from your home and job?"

"If that's what it took to be together."

"Wow, I think Shannon is very lucky to have met you."

Simone smiled at the group as she responded. "I think I am the lucky one. I met Shannon and all of you."

The four women grinned in reply. They liked Simone an awful lot. They took her advice and decided not to change their plans. The four of them headed off to dinner before seeing a movie. Simone spent the early part of her evening finishing some paperwork she hadn't gotten to earlier in the day. She periodically checked on Shannon, who slept soundly in the bedroom. Simone took a quick shower before she started to prepare something to eat. Standing in her nightshirt in her kitchen, she thought about her earlier conversation with Shannon's friends. She had meant when she said; she could move to Seattle. She loved her home and job in Hawaii. But she wanted a relationship with Shannon and if that meant moving she would do it. This was the kind of love she had waited for all of her life.

"Hi, can I join you?" Shannon had slipped up behind her while she waited for her soup to heat up. Shannon's arms wrapped around her waist as her lips placed a brief kiss on Simone's neck.

"Of course, I'm fixing some soup and sandwiches for dinner. I'm not the chef Hanna is. Are you up to eating anything?"

"I'm a little hungry, can I help?"

"Yes, you can stay right where you are and hug me, that's all the help I need," Simone grinned.

"I can do that. I love you, Simone."

"You know what, Shannon, I love you and we are all alone in the house for the evening. How about a nice quiet dinner and then we crawl back in bed?"

"That sounds perfect. I want to thank you for helping me today at the doctors' office."

Simone turned around to face Shannon, her arms sliding around Shannon's neck. "Shannon, you need to quit thanking me. I went with you because I love you and I know you would do the same thing for me. Now, tell me, what kind of sandwich do you want, a BLT, tuna fish, or a grilled cheese?"

"I'd like tuna fish, please."

"Coming right up. How is the pain, do you need another pain pill?"

"It's manageable right now, so I think I'll wait awhile. The pain medication knocks me out."

"It's supposed to."

"I know, but I want to be coherent when I'm with you." Shannon grinned at her.

The two of them enjoyed the quiet as they shared their meal out on the patio in the nice warm, tropical night. It was as romantic an evening as the two of them had spent so far, sitting in the rapidly darkening night, the warm breeze swirling around them, as the waves pounded on the shore. Shannon sat between Simone's legs, gently leaning back against her on the chaise lounge as they sat in silence, their hands clasped together. They didn't have to talk; their feelings were as exposed as their hearts. There was no need to entertain, to do something other than touch each other. It was everything.

It grew late as they enjoyed each other's company and Simone was afraid that Shannon's back and legs were beginning to bother her. Besides, she needed her sleep, especially since Shannon had insisted on going with everyone on the boat in the morning. Simone had tried to talk her out of it but the one thing she had learned quickly about Shannon was she could be very stubborn.

CHAPTER 8

"Time to go in and take your pain pill and I suggest we go crawl in bed and get a good night's sleep."

The two of them prepared for bed together and it was like they had been living together for years. Both of them crawled in bed with Shannon on her stomach, an ice bag on her lower back, and Simone with a book to read next to her. She and Shannon had shared several loving kisses before she insisted Shannon lay down and go to sleep after taking her medication. Shannon's fingers were linked in Simone's nightshirt as she slid into slumber while Simone read next to her.

Two hours later, Simone was awakened from a sound sleep with lips sliding gently across her mouth in a slow, gentle kiss. Full, mesmerizing kisses that Simone wanted to continue for hours and hours. This was the kind of lovemaking that Simone had only dreamed about. Over and over they kissed, sampling the flavors of each other like a fine wine, as the need to make love burned steadily in Simone's body. While Shannon wooed her with passionate kisses, her hands slowly unbuttoned Simone's nightshirt to reveal the lush, beautiful body of her lover. Shannon would never get used to the overwhelming beauty of Simone. She gazed down at her full breasts and flat stomach, and her gaze traveled over the flare of her hips and long thighs. Shannon bent her head down and slid her tongue against Simone's nipple, teasing the hardening peak, while her fingers stroked her breasts. Shannon loved every inch of Simone's breasts as she lay between Simone's legs.

"I love your body," Shannon whispered as she left a path of kisses down Simone's flat stomach, hands sliding over her hips and thighs. "I'm going to show you how much."

Simone moaned as Shannon's tongue teased over her stomach, before sliding lower to nuzzle against the very center of her body. Simone's scent permeated the room as Shannon slid the flat of her tongue against Simone. Simone shivered with hunger as Shannon's tongue parted her, and she drank in the welcoming moisture that Simone's body released. Shannon's fingers joined her mouth as she stroked Simone deeper and faster, pressure building up in Simone's body. Simone arched up against Shannon's mouth as she cried out in gratification. Shannon stroked her faster and deeper while Simone's body twisted on the bed with uncontrollable pleasure. One huge shiver ran from Simone's head to her toes as she succumbed to Shannon's lovemaking and tumbled into an orgasm.

"Shannon, I love you," Simone gasped out as Shannon renewed her efforts, driving Simone crazy. "Oh my God!"

Shannon smiled as she kissed her way up Simone's body, her hands molding over her hips and breasts. She met Simone's lips in another slow, thrilling kiss, intoxicating Simone with the texture and flavor of her mouth.

"I want to make love with you, but I'm fearful of hurting your back or your legs," Simone shared as she held Shannon tightly against her body, enjoying the weight of her.

"I'll be okay if I stay on top." Shannon grinned down at Simone.

Simone smiled in return as she reached down to pull Shannon's tee shirt up and off of her body. The minute Shannon felt her breasts against Simone she moaned softly. Simone's hands stroked her breasts as she kissed Shannon's lips and her face. She worshiped Shannon with her mouth as Shannon's nipples ached in response to her attentions. Simone slipped her fingers between Shannon's legs and entered her abruptly, driving her immediately into an orgasm that wracked her body with intense pleasure. Shannon's head dropped on to Simone's shoulder as Simone's fingers played her perfectly. Shannon rocked her body against Simone's hand deriving even more pleasure from her lovemaking, before collapsing completely on top of Simone. She turned her face into Simone, her lips seeking Simone's mouth in a kiss, a deeply satisfying show of trust and love.

"I love what you do to me," Shannon breathed against Simone's mouth.

"You turn me inside out when you love me," Simone responded, tightening her arms around Shannon's neck. "I want to hold you like this all night."

Shannon smiled and settled against Simone's body, intimately joined at the hips. "I'll stay right here."

Simone stroked Shannon's hair as they both closed their eyes and slid back into sleep, the scent of their lovemaking still in the air. The night was full of magic, as they drifted off full of love.

CHAPTER 9

"Honey, are you sure you want to go today?" Simone asked Shannon again as Shannon groaned while sliding a tee shirt on.

"Yes, I'll be fine. I just need to get moving." Shannon's face didn't match her words as she grimaced in pain while bending to slip a pair of shorts on.

"Shannon, everyone would understand if you chose to stay home."

"I want to go. Besides, I want to see you diving." Shannon grinned and slid her arms around Simone's waist. "I can't wait to see you in your bathing suit."

Simone chuckled as she hugged Shannon. "You have already seen me totally naked."

"But seeing you in a bathing suit is different, it's a different kind of sexy. You're so beautiful, I love looking at you wearing anything."

"I actually like you wearing nothing but your earrings," Simone teased as she kissed Shannon. "We better get going if you want a cup of coffee before we have to leave."

"Aye, aye, captain." Shannon grinned as she slipped her feet into sandals and grabbed her pack.

They headed down the hallway into the kitchen where Hanna and Mel were sitting at the table drinking their own cup of coffee. "How are you feeling, Shannon?" Hanna inquired, standing up to hug her.

"Good. Are you guys ready to go diving?"

"Yep, I can't wait."

"Where are Janice and Olivia?"

"Janice is in getting dressed and Olivia is down on the beach."

"Is Olivia okay?"

"Yes, she just wanted to go for an early morning walk. I'll go get her. I'm glad you are feeling okay, Shannon." Hanna hugged Shannon again before she headed out the back door.

"I've packed our lunches in the ice chest, with a lot of water and juice. Here is the bag of chips and snacks." Mel pointed to the bag on the counter.

"Thanks Mel." Shannon tucked her arms around Mel's neck. "And thanks again for going with me yesterday. I really appreciate it."

"You're welcome, sweetie. Are you really feeling better?"

"I am a lot better than yesterday." Shannon smiled. "Now, shouldn't you go get your girlfriend so we can get going?"

"I can do that."

Simone slipped her arm around Shannon's neck. "You have wonderful friends."

"Yes, we do. They're your friends now."

Simone grinned at her girlfriend. "I think that's a pretty good deal."

"Are we ready?" Olivia and Hanna came in from the patio.

"Yep, last one out in the car is a rotten egg." Mel grabbed Janice's hand, the ice chest, and headed for the front door. "Hanna, grab the paper bag, please."

"Got it."

The six women climbed into Simone's Rover and headed down the road, all of them talking at once in anticipation of the day. Shannon reached out and placed her hand on Simone's thigh. Simone glanced at her and smiled. Shannon bent and whispered in her ear. "I love you."

"Hey you two, knock that stuff off!" Janice teased as they all laughed.

The teasing and the bantering went on for the whole trip. It took a little over forty-five minutes to get to the dock, where they were meeting Simone's friends.

"The boat's name is the *Windwalker* and it's a thirty-nine foot sailboat, white with a dark green stripe around the deck. Marcus and Leo are expecting us," Simone explained as they all climbed out of the car.

The women carried the ice chest and their things down to the dock trailing behind Simone and Shannon. Two very tan dark haired men in shorts, with the look of wind swept sailors, met Simone halfway down the dock.

"Hello gorgeous." One of the men gathered Simone up in a bear hug. "How are you, Simone?"

"Good Leo. Hi Marcus."

"Hello beautiful. Introduce us to your friends."

"This is Shannon, Mel, Janice, Hanna, and Olivia."

"Hello ladies." Marcus and Leo grinned at the group.

"This is Marcus and Leo, our hosts for the day."

"Thank you very much for letting us join you on your boat."

"You're welcome, we love taking people out on the boat. Besides, Simone promised to give me another diving lesson." The man named Marcus chuckled. He had curly, long black hair, tied back with a leather thong. He was obviously in good health as his body was a well-toned six feet. Leo was equally as healthy looking, with short, dark brown hair, a bushy mustache, and a cleft chin.

"Yes, I did," Simone agreed as she picked up her large duffle bag that contained her diving gear. "Did you pick up your diving gear this morning?"

"Yes Mom." Marcus grinned as he teased Simone. "Well, ladies let's get going and beat the crowd."

Shannon meanwhile, had taken her video camera out of her pack and was busily filming the dock, the boats, and her friends. She followed the group onto a very clean and ship shape boat.

"This is a beautiful boat," Olivia declared as she and Hanna stepped aboard.

"Thanks, we like it," Leo responded. "Come on. We can put your stuff away and I will show you around. Marcus, do you want to untie us and motor us away from the dock?"

Leo took all of the women on a tour below deck, showing them the galley, the head, and a bedroom to put their things in. Then they all trooped back on deck to watch Marcus skillfully navigate the marina and get them out into open water.

"Okay everyone, a few safety rules and then we are off. Under each of these seats are life jackets and there are more than enough for all of us. There are more in the cabin in the storage units. When moving around the boat, watch out for loose ropes and the boom. I will let you know when we swing the boom across. Also, if you are up on top, hang on to the rail because the boat deck can be very slippery. We'll be sailing for about an hour and then we will pull up anchor in a cove for some diving and snorkeling."

"Sounds great, where do you want us?"

"You can find a seat anywhere you want. Leo and I will set the sails and get us moving."

The women watched fascinated as the two men moved with precision in unfurling the sails and setting the course against the wind. Within minutes the boat was moving at a rapid clip through the water, the salt spray arching up on the sides of the deck. Simone took a seat next to Shannon and slipped her arm around her waist as Shannon filmed the men's movements, the sails, and the waves breaking around them. It was a scene right out of a movie, with the warm sun shining, and the beautiful boat knifing through the water.

"How long have you been sailing, Marcus?"

"Leo and I have been sailing for over twenty years but we just purchased the *Windwalker* a little over a year ago. It was our retirement to ourselves."

Mel looked startled at Marcus. "Retirement, neither one of you look old enough to retire."

"Leo is fifty-three and I am fifty-five. We both have worked hard most of our lives so we figured we owed ourselves an early retirement." Marcus grinned at Mel as he moved about the boat. Leo stood at the helm, correcting the ship's course as they were pushed along by the wind.

"What did the two of you do before retirement?"

"Leo was an investment banker and I ran a large hotel. What do you ladies do?"

"Janice and I are firemen, Hanna runs the kitchen of a large hotel, Olivia is a teacher, and Shannon is a cameraman."

"What a diverse group."

The two men were very friendly as they sailed along side the island. Shannon spent most of the time filming or snuggling next to Simone on the boat. It was a little shy of an hour before Marcus and Leo dropped the sails and the anchor inside a large bay on the other side of the island. Simone had taken them diving there several times and it was guaranteed to have turtles, manta rays, and dolphins if they were lucky.

"Alright everyone, it's okay to move about since we are anchored. I'm going to drop a ladder off of the back end to make it easier to get in and out of the water. Who's going diving?"

"Janice wants to dive, so it's you and I and Janice," Simone responded to Marcus' question. "We can put the dive buoy up over there."

Olivia, Mel, and Hanna were going to snorkel and Shannon had decided to stay on the boat. Her back and legs were too sore to expose to salt water. Besides, she was getting some great video.

"Marcus and Janice, let's check your equipment out." Simone was an experienced diver and safety always came first. Marcus was just learning and Janice had a little experience.

Mel, Olivia, and Hanna stripped into their bathing suits and quickly dropped into the water with their snorkel gear while Shannon filmed them. Twenty minutes later she grinned as first Janice and then Marcus flipped into the water, tanks on their backs, followed quickly by Simone after she shared a soft kiss with Shannon. Leo couldn't help but tease her.

"Leo, you can go swimming, I'll be fine."

"Shannon, if I wanted to go I would. Now, tell me when are you going to move here and make an honest woman out of Simone?" Leo's eyes twinkled at Shannon as he took a seat next to her.

"I don't know if I am moving here."

"What do you mean you aren't moving here? Of course you are, Simone loves you, and from what I can tell, the feeling is mutual."

"I'm from Seattle, Leo."

"They don't have moving companies there?"

Shannon grinned. "It's a little more complicated than that."

"Well, it wasn't so complicated for Marcus and me. He came to San Francisco for a week and came home with me."

"You're kidding?"

"No, and we have been together for over twenty years."

"Wow, that's wonderful."

"So tell me what is so complicated?"

"I have a condominium and a career in Seattle."

"So sell your condo, and can't you be a cameraman here?"

"I suppose so."

"So…"

"Simone has to want me to move here."

"Have you two talked about it?"

"A little."

"Maybe you should just tell her you are moving here."

"I can't do that, she has to want me to."

"Women, they always make things more complicated then they are." Leo sighed dramatically. "She wouldn't be with you if she didn't want you here. I've known Simone since I moved here and I've never seen the look on her face before. She loves you, Shannon."

Shannon's face softened into a gentle smile. "I love her."

"Then don't complicate things, move."

Shannon didn't respond, but she did think long and hard about Leo's suggestion. Maybe he was right. She should just take a chance and move. What was the worst that could happen?

"Shannon, look!"

Shannon turned and was surprised to see a school of fish swimming around the boat, sparkling in the water. They glimmered as they swam in a huge mass past the side of the boat.

"Wow, that's cool!" she exclaimed as she whipped her video camera around and began filming. "What are they?"

"It looks like a school of herring. Simone would know." Leo and she hung over the boat to watch. "She knows everything about the land, the water, and all of the animals. She loves Hawaii."

"She's an incredible woman."

"Yes, she's very talented. She seems to have good taste in girlfriends finally. I understand you didn't hesitate before going in the water to save that young boy."

Shannon ignored the comment about her heroism but jumped on the comment about Simone's girlfriends. "You didn't like her previous girlfriend?"

"Honey, there was nothing to like about her. She wanted Simone to be someone different than who she was, and I don't think you need to change perfection. For the longest time Simone just couldn't get away from her, hoping things would change. It wasn't a healthy relationship. Simone needs someone to accept her for who she is and value her incredible talents." Leo had also seen first hand how Liz had treated Simone in public. It had angered him that Simone allowed Liz to treat her with so little respect. When you loved someone you were proud to be with them.

"She's very special."

"Yes, she is. So tell me Shannon, what was your last girlfriend like?"

"She believed in open relationships, the kind that allowed her to sleep around, but also have someone at her beck and call."

"I take it you didn't agree to that."

"Not in the least! I think when you love someone you respect them, and you do that by committing yourself totally to their welfare. You're there for the good times and the bad, helping them fulfill their dreams, and loving them as they grow old."

Leo grinned at Shannon. "You feel pretty strongly do you?"

Shannon chuckled. "Let's say I prefer monogamous, loving relationships."

"Good for you. Now, I am going to get a cold pop, can I bring you anything?"

"Nope, I'm fine."

"Shannon, I am going to like you." Leo grinned as he headed into the cabin. Finally Simone had found a woman who would cherish her. Leo had no doubt Shannon would put Simone first.

Shannon couldn't help but smile in return. She liked Leo. He obviously wasn't shy about asking any questions. She turned to watch the water. Hawaii was an unbelievably beautiful place and she wanted very much to be with Simone. Would Simone want her to move in with her? She had a lot to think about. It was a huge step to move away from everything she was familiar with.

The group snorkeled and dove for over an hour before calling it quits for lunch. They happily chattered about what they saw as Shannon and Leo handed out sandwiches and drinks to everyone. It was a happy, contented group that sat around munching and visiting. Shannon slipped on to the bench next to Simone and was pleased when Simone turned and kissed her quickly. "Hi, how're you feeling?"

"Not bad, but I still don't think I can get in the water."

"You don't have to." Simone smiled at her gorgeous but frustrated girl-friend.

Shannon ran her eyes over Simone's scantily clad body still glistening with sea water and felt her body react. Simone was one beautiful, sexy woman. She leaned against Simone and whispered softly against her ear. "I want you so much I can taste you."

Simone turned to Shannon and kissed her before responding. "I've never been with someone I want as much as you. I love you."

"Simone, what are we going to do?" Shannon's quiet plea sent slivers of pain into Simone's heart.

"We are going to live together, whatever it takes," she pledged, her eyes large and full of love.

"You mean that?"

"With all my heart."

"So if I moved here could we live together?"

"Do you want to move here?"

"Simone, I want to be with you and I can get a job here, I know I can."

"Of course you can." Simone smiled and cupped Shannon's chin in her hand. "We will figure everything out. Now, eat your lunch."

Shannon smiled at her and forced her attention back to the group lounging around on the boat deck. She wouldn't let her worries ruin the day. Simone slid her hand over Shannon's and squeezed gently whispering one last time. "I love you, Shannon and I promise you we'll be together."

Shannon took her at her word and began to eat her lunch. One thing she had learned about Simone was she kept her word. When she promised Shannon they would be together, Shannon knew they would and it calmed her.

For forty-five minutes, the group hung around on deck relaxing and enjoying the sun and the conversation. The divers headed back into the water and Leo was going to go snorkeling with Hanna and Olivia. Mel, Janice, and Shannon stretched out on the deck enjoying the sun. Shannon had put her new bathing suit on after everyone headed into the water. She was a little shy about showing all of her bandages to two men she didn't know.

"Boy, Shannon that is a very cool bathing suit." Mel exclaimed as Janice grinned.

"You don't think it's a little too skimpy?"

Mel and Janice ran their eyes over their friend's body. Shannon may have been one of their dearest friends but she was also a very sexy woman, who had no clue as to how appealing she was. She had long slender legs and arms, her hips and stomach equally as slim, and her breasts were full and well displayed in the electric blue suit. Despite all the white bandages that covered most of her back and upper legs she was very appealing.

"Has Simone seen you in your suit?"

"Not yet?"

"Wait until she does, if she doesn't drag you downstairs, she's immune to a sexy woman," Janice chuckled.

Shannon raised her eyebrows to her two friends. "Excuse me?"

"Shannon, you could raise the dead in that suit," Mel teased as Shannon colored with embarrassment.

"Yea, me and my bandages."

"Believe me you don't notice the bandages when you are wearing that suit."

"That's the idea." Shannon grinned as she looked at her two best friends. "I don't want Simone looking at anyone other than me."

"Honey, you could wear a brown bag over your head and Simone would only look at you."

"I hope so."

"We know so. So when are you moving?"

"As soon as I can find a job."

"You are?" Both Janice and Mel stared at her with surprise.

"Yes, if I can get a job, I can move here."

"Shannon, are you really serious?"

"Completely."

"You should have no problem getting a job here, especially with your experience and your talent. Maybe your boss can help you."

"He might. He knows a lot of people in television and cable."

"You could talk to Christa."

"I don't know about that."

"Honey, Simone is in love with you. Christa is the last thing you need to worry about."

"I know, but I don't think I would feel comfortable talking to her about this."

"What does Simone think?"

"I haven't talked to her about all the details, just that I would be willing to move here."

"What did she say?"

"That we would live together and we'll figure everything out."

"We like her, Shannon."

"She's wonderful. I never thought I would find someone like her."

"It was meant to be."

"I really believe that."

The three of them settled down and dozed on the deck of the boat in the heat as the boat drifted on the water. Shannon fell sound asleep as she let the sound of the waves and the birds lull her to sleep.

CHAPTER 10

"Shannon, sweetie time to wake up." Soft lips slid against Shannon's and she slowly opened her eyes to find Simone leaning over her.

"Hi, honey. How was diving?"

"Good, Shannon, you look amazing in this suit." Simone's eyes gleamed as she looked at Shannon's body sensuously displayed in her brief suit. Her hands slid along Shannon's thighs as she leaned over her.

Shannon sighed as she looked up at Simone. She recognized the look on Simone's face and it made her flush with heat as she wrapped her arm around Simone's neck, pulling her down so she could kiss her. "I can't wait to get home so we can be alone."

Simone kissed her slowly, her lips tasting Shannon's, steeping her with passion and barely restrained hunger. "I love you," Simone whispered, kissing Shannon again.

Shannon's heart turned over in her chest as she reacted to Simone's words. She knew she loved Simone and at that moment she didn't care were they were or who saw them. She wanted Simone so much she was shaking. It was several moments before Simone sat up breathing heavy. The rest of the crowd was oblivious of the two of them on the front deck.

"Simone, I've never felt like this with anyone else," Shannon admitted as she sat up and took Simone's hand in hers. "I want you all the time."

Simone smiled at Shannon as she sat next to her. "The feeling is entirely mutual. I want to be with you, and I have never ever felt the way I feel with you. I know you don't know me very well, but I promise you I would never be with anyone else. I am quite a few years older than you, are you sure that doesn't bother you?"

"Simone, I wouldn't care if you were twenty years older than me. I want to make this work. I just need to make sure you are okay with me moving to Hawaii."

"Shannon, I want to live with you, but you will be leaving your home and friends, let alone your job."

"Do you want me to move here?" Shannon watched Simone carefully waiting for her answer.

"Shannon, I want you here, but I am willing to move to Seattle."

"I know you would, but it's easier if I move. I just need to find a job as a cameraperson. I can sell my condo."

"What about your friends?"

"I'll miss them but they can come to visit." Shannon leaned her head against Simone's shoulder, slipping her arm around her waist. "Simone, I've waited all my life to meet you."

Simone kissed Shannon's fingers as she listened. "Your friends can come and stay with us as often as they want, and I've waited all my life to meet you. I love you, Shannon."

"So are you going to marry me?" Shannon smiled as she slid her lips along Simone's jaw and cheek.

"Yes I am." Simone kissed Shannon and slowly let her words and her kiss work their magic.

"Look at those two," Olivia commented as she handed a pop to Leo. "I can't believe how perfect they are with each other."

"They are pretty cute," Leo commented. "I've never seen Simone so open before. She's usually pretty reserved. Her last girlfriend would barely be seen in public with her. It hurt Simone very much. She needs to feel like she's a priority in her relationships."

"Well Shannon will make sure she knows she's special. I have never met anyone who loves more deeply or more honestly then Shannon."

"So who's moving?"

"Shannon is thinking about moving to Hawaii, if she can find a job. That's if Simone wants her here."

"What do you think?" Leo poked Olivia and pointed at Simone and Shannon who were in a sexy embrace.

"I think Shannon is going to be moving," Olivia chuckled.

The rest of the afternoon flew by as everyone visited and enjoyed the afternoon. It was getting dark before they started the sail back to the dock. Simone had invited the two men over for dinner. Mel and Janice had volunteered to barbecue. It was a great day and everyone had lots of fun.

While Mel and Janice began dinner, Shannon and Olivia set the table and Hanna prepared dessert. Simone had to return several telephone calls from work. She reentered the kitchen with a serious look on her face.

"Is everything okay?" Shannon touched her arm.

"Everything is fine, I had a medic call in sick and it's been a very busy day."

"Do you need to go in?"

"Not yet." Simone kissed Shannon. "I may have to go in tomorrow for awhile."

Shannon wrapped her arms around Simone's shoulders and hugged her. "Can you tell everyone to go home so we can be alone?"

Simone chuckled against Shannon's neck. "I don't think so, but I promise you, you aren't going to get much sleep."

"I'm going to make you keep that promise."

The dinner was as pleasant as the rest of the day. The two men were a welcome addition to the group. As they lingered over dessert, they made plans for getting together the following week and going out for dinner and dancing.

"We had a wonderful time, but we need to head home." Marcus and Leo dispensed hugs to everyone before Simone walked them to the door.

"Thanks for the sailing today, we all enjoyed it very much." She hugged Leo and Marcus.

"We like you and Shannon together."

"So do I." Simone smiled at the two men.

"Take care."

"Goodnight." Simone turned to head back into the kitchen to finish cleaning up. Shannon met her coming out of the kitchen and she took Simone's hand and led her down the hall.

"You're coming with me," Shannon informed her as she tugged her toward the bedroom. Simone bubbled with laughter as she allowed herself to be dragged down the hall.

"Goodnight," Mel called with humor in her voice as she watched Shannon rush Simone into her bedroom. There was no doubt what Shannon had in mind.

"Shannon." Simone choked back laughter as she was pulled through the door. Shannon didn't wait. She slammed the door shut behind them and whirled around to face Simone.

"I couldn't wait one more minute to be alone with you." Shannon explained as she struggled to remove Simone's shirt and shorts. "I have been going crazy all night."

Simone grabbed Shannon's hands and stopped her movements. "I love you, Shannon." Simone smiled as she held Shannon's hands in her own.

Shannon gazed up at Simone as she stilled her movements. "I love you."

Simone let go of Shannon's hands and slid her hands around Shannon's face as she bent down to kiss her. "I love you and I want to touch you so badly it scares me."

Shannon smiled as she slowly began to remove her shirt and dropped it to the floor. She then removed her shorts and dropped them to the floor. She was still wearing her blue bathing suit and Simone's eyes slid over Shannon's body.

"You're gorgeous," Simone whispered as she traced her finger tip down Shannon's cleavage.

Shannon didn't respond other than to reach out and remove Simone's shorts, as they fell to the ground. Simone had changed earlier and was wearing a pale pink bra and matching underpants. Shannon stopped to admire her as she stood in front of her.

"You're so beautiful," she spoke softly as she ran her fingers over Simone's shoulders and arms. "So strong and so capable, I'm amazed at how talented you are."

Shannon leaned into Simone's body and kissed her on the shoulder slowly, breathing in the scent of sun, vanilla, and lilac that was so much a part of Simone. Her lips whispered across her upper chest and along her other shoulder as she tasted her skin over and over. Their fingers clasped each other's as Simone bent over and nuzzled the tops of Shannon's breasts. She had never been so fascinated by a woman's breasts as she was Shannon's, full and heavy and so responsive to her touch. Her mouth traced lower until she ran into the bathing suit top.

She released Shannon's hands and reached behind to unclasp her bathing suit as Shannon's breasts were released from the constraining top. "I think you're so beautiful."

She placed her face against Shannon's breasts as Shannon's arms circled her neck. She kissed one and then the other over and over before sucking on Shannon's nipple, teasing it with her lips and tongue. Shannon's arms tightened around Simone's neck as she encouraged her to continue. Simone bathed each nipple with her breath and her tongue as she tantalized Shannon with her love-making. Her hands slid the bathing suit bottoms off of Shannon's hips and dropped them to the floor so Shannon could step out of them. Simone hands clasped Shannon's hips and pulled her tightly against her body as they kissed, Shannon moaning as Simone's tongue slid between her lips.

Shannon loved the way Simone kissed, it was full of passion, sexy, and touched her like no one else. She reached behind Simone to unclasp her bra, pulling it from her body. She slid Simone's panties down her legs until they were both naked in each other's arms. Simone sighed with pleasure when Shannon's body slid against her own, her breasts rubbing against Shannon's, her hips clasped against hers. Simone's hands slid down over Shannon's naked buttocks and pulled her even more tightly against her body.

"Simone, look," Shannon whispered as she turned to catch their reflection in the mirror over the dresser. They stood in silhouette, two naked women clasped tightly in each other's arms, Shannon's long dark hair, loose and flowing over her shoulders, in direct contrast to Simone's blond curly hair crowning her head. Simone turned and her breath caught in her throat as she caught sight of the two of them. There was nothing more sensuous than two women's bodies entwined.

"We're beautiful together," she admitted turning back to Shannon who was watching Simone's reaction. "I wish we could take a picture of us just like this."

"I love you, Simone."

"Shannon, I can't tell you how much I love you. I don't care how long I've known you. I just know that I want you with me for the rest of my life."

"I want that too."

"I wish my parents were here so they would know I found my soul mate."

"Simone, they know." Shannon placed her hand on Simone's cheek. "They know, honey."

Simone's eyes glittered with tears as she bent to kiss Shannon. Kisses that touched Shannon's very heart and soul. "Come to bed." Simone pulled Shannon over to the bed side. "Shannon, do you have any objections to using a vibrator?"

Shannon grinned up at Simone as she pulled her on to the bed next to her. "No, I just didn't bring mine with me."

Simone chuckled as she reached over to open the bedside stand. "Then it's very lucky that I have one of my own."

Simone pulled it out of the drawer and Shannon grinned again. "We have twin vibrators."

"Good, than I won't have to explain how to use it." Simone soft blue eyes twinkled at Shannon. "But I am out of practice so why don't you go first and then if I miss anything you can show me how it's done."

Shannon reached for the vibrator as she rolled on top of Simone. Her mouth immediately found Simone's nipple and sucked heavily on it as she flipped the switch on the vibrator. Slowly, she rolled it against Simone's breast as she continued to suckle first one breast and then the other, as Simone lay back and enjoyed Shannon's attentions. Shannon's legs slipped between Simone's and her knees pushed Simone's legs open until Shannon's hips were tight against the very center of her. As she continued to slide the vibrator against Simone's nipples over and over, her lips left a trail of kisses down her stomach. Slowly Shannon rolled the vibrator over Simone's flat stomach as Simone's hips began to push against Shannon's middle. Shannon could feel how wet she was as she pressed her stomach against Simone's very center. Shannon slid even lower until her face was even with Simone's strong thighs. The scent of Simone was drawing her as she stared at her lover's glistening swollen lips; Shannon kissed her softly, tasting her. Simone groaned and shifted her hips against Shannon wanting her to continue. Sliding the vibrator against Simone lengthways, she coated it with Simone's moisture as she teased her. Back and forth, she moved it as Simone moaned loudly. She barely entered Simone and stopped as the vibrator hummed against the very sensitive mound.

"Shannon, you're killing me," Simone gasped half laughing, half begging.

Shannon just smiled as her lips kissed Simone's drenched lips and she lapped at her with her tongue. Sliding the vibrator in a little more, Shannon's other hand touched her, opening her up to Shannon's wonderful mouth. She felt Simone's orgasm begin and she moved the vibrator deeper into her body. Then stroking her with it, she erotically drove Simone crazy. Simone pulled a pillow over her face, screaming into it to muffle the sound.

Simone's body was uncontrollable as she twisted back and forth, Shannon continuing her lovemaking until Simone was exhausted and limp on the bed. Slowly Shannon withdrew the vibrator and kissed Simone thoroughly, her lips loving her one last time.

Shannon placed kiss after kiss up Simone's body as she slowly moved back up to find Simone's face still under the pillow. She grinned arrogantly as she pulled it off of her lover. "I know I need practice so will you tell me what I need to improve on?"

"Are you always this smug after lovemaking?" Simone grinned back as she glanced up at Shannon, too limp to move.

"Who's smug?" Shannon chuckled as she leaned over Simone. "Do you always scream into a pillow?"

Simone pulled Shannon over on top of her, grinning the whole time. "No, that's a first for me. I didn't think you wanted all your friends to hear me scream with pleasure."

"No, that's only for me to hear." Shannon's face grew serious as she stroked Simone's cheek with her fingers. "I'm the only one that gets to hear that from now on."

"The only one," Simone promised as she pulled Shannon's face down to kiss her.

Slowly Simone rolled Shannon over onto her back as she once again kissed her, deep sensuous kisses that Shannon craved. Over and over, Simone's mouth covered Shannon's as her hands slid over Shannon's body gently memorizing every single place she could touch.

"I love your body. You have such beautiful, large breasts. I love how your nipples swell when I kiss them," Simone admitted as she kissed both nipples and teased them with her fingers. "And I love the way your hips fit so perfectly against mine, and they way you slide them against me." Simone wedged her hips between Shannon's thighs as Shannon rolled her hips against her.

"Honey, I want to feel you against me," Shannon asked as she looked up into Simone's eyes.

Simone bent down and kissed Shannon before reaching for the vibrator that lay quiet on the bed. Turning it on, she reached down with her other hand and slid it between Shannon's legs, parting her lips. Simone lifted her hips until she was over Shannon with her own. She slid her wet core slowly against Shannon, her fingers parting her lips until they were perfectly joined.

Shannon cried out as Simone rubbed her body intimately against Shannon's wetness. Lifting her body slightly away from Shannon's, she moved the vibrator between the two of them and very slowly began to slide it up and down.

"Oh, God." Shannon gasped as she jerked against Simone, her legs wrapping around Simone's thighs.

Shannon's hips began to move quickly faster and harder as Simone held the vibrator tightly between them. Pumping against Simone, Shannon began to pant as she felt her body tremble just seconds away from an orgasm. Simone lifted up and slid the vibrator deeply into Shannon, driving her quickly into an orgasm that ripped through her body. Simone held on as Shannon twisted frantically against her, overwhelmed by her body's response. She just began to settle down when Simone moved the vibrator slowly stroking her as Shannon cried out again, while her body was thrown once more into throbbing pleasure. Her hips ground against Simone's as she found herself inundated with passion. Simone removed the vibrator and turned it off before running her fingers once again against Shannon, opening her so that Simone could press herself intimately against her. Simone slid herself tightly against Shannon as Shannon grasped her hips pushing up and into Simone. Faster Simone's hips worked against Shannon's until she cried out and slumped against Shannon's still quaking body. Shannon wrapped her arms around Simone's neck holding her tightly as she shivered and shook on top of Shannon. Simone turned to find Shannon's lips as she kissed her gently before settling her face against her shoulder gasping for breath.

"I guess we don't need any lessons," Simone whispered, still trying to catch her breath.

Shannon couldn't help but giggle. "No, but I think my friends may have figured out what we are doing in here. We weren't exactly quiet."

"Sorry." Simone didn't look the least bit sorry as she turned to look at Shannon. She looked very pleased with herself.

"I'm not sorry," Shannon laughed. "I'm overwhelmed, but I'm not sorry."

"I love how we are together," Simone admitted playing with Shannon's long hair. "I don't seem to have any inhibitions with you."

"Simone, our lovemaking is what pleases the two of us and is no one else's business. I enjoy making love with you and I think it's an important part of a relationship."

"I do too. I've just never had it like this. You're incredible"

"I think it's because we're good together. So do you have any fantasies that you keep hidden away?"

"I've always wanted to make love at night in the ocean and on the beach."

"What about you?"

"I've always wanted to make love somewhere public where you might get caught."

"Interesting," Simone chuckled. "Where do you have in mind?"

"I don't know, but you will be the first one I tell." Shannon promised. "You had better go to sleep in case you have to work tomorrow."

"I'm not tired. In fact, I want to hear more about this fantasy of yours."

"It's nothing, I just think it might be a little exciting to make love with my lover somewhere others might be able to catch us."

"Have you ever done this before?"

"No, I've never loved or trusted someone enough to tell them about my fantasy let alone do something about it."

Simone smiled as she absorbed Shannon's comments. "So you trust me?"

"Simone, I trust you with my heart, let alone my body," Shannon pledged as she kissed Simone.

"I trust you Shannon with everything. And I promise we'll make your fantasy come true."

"What about yours, can we make that come true?"

"I think we can do that," Simone grinned as she snuggled up against Shannon in preparation for going to sleep. "I love you."

"I absolutely love you." Shannon tucked herself up against Simone and closed her eyes. She felt unbelievably blessed that not only were she and Simone compatible in bed but they could talk about sex without any reservations.

CHAPTER 11

"So tell me Shannon, did you get any sleep last night?" Hanna teased as she helped Shannon change the bed.

Shannon colored with embarrassment but she couldn't help but grin at her friend. "Enough."

"So you and Simone are getting along well?"

"Perfectly."

"When are you moving?"

"As soon as I have a job and can sell my condo."

"You really are moving here?"

"Yes, and Simone and I are going to live together."

"You're really sure about this?"

Shannon stopped folding the sheet and looked up at Hanna. "I am very sure about this. It's like it was meant to be. I feel like I have known Simone forever. We can talk about anything."

"And I take it you two are happy with the sex part?" Hanna grinned at her friend.

Shannon giggled as she continued to make the bed. "That part is perfect. I've never been with anyone like Simone before. I can't explain it to you, other than it is perfect."

Hanna gazed at her friend and smiled as she listened. "You don't have to explain it, Shannon. Olivia and I are like that with each other."

"I'm going to miss all of you when I move. That's the only hard part about it."

"We'll visit as much as possible and Olivia and I have talked about looking for a retirement place over here. Maybe we'll join you."

"You're kidding?"

"No, we love this part of Hawaii and you know we're both planning on retiring early. You and Simone could help us find a place."

"That would be wonderful, Hanna."

"We even talked about a bed and breakfast. I love to take care of people and Olivia loves to cook."

"You guys would be perfect with a bed and breakfast! So we need to work on Mel and Janice and get them to move here too."

"That might be a little more difficult." Hanna admitted. "But not impossible."

"Cool."

Shannon happily finished making the bed. Simone had gotten a call and gone in to work early that morning. She expected to be gone most of the day. Shannon spruced up the house and then had plans to work on her video script since she wanted it complete before the meeting the following morning with Christa. Janice, Mel, Hanna, and Olivia were off to do some sightseeing for the day.

Shannon worked most of the early afternoon before taking a lunch break and heading for the beach with her video camera. She loved Hawaii and especially the beaches. She could walk for hours and never get bored. Shannon felt connected with the islands, their mysterious spirituality called to her spirit, let alone their rugged beauty. She had tape after tape of scenery to weave into her vacation video and she was looking forward to working on it.

Simone pulled up into the shopping mall after leaving work. She had an errand she needed to complete before heading home to Shannon. Going home to Shannon felt so right to her, she was so happy with her life. For the first time she felt content, things were happening the way they were supposed to happen. She laughed softly as she entered the jewelry store, remembering her conversation with Christa earlier.

"You're going to marry Shannon?" Christa couldn't keep the disbelief out of her voice. "Don't you think it is a little early to make that kind of plan?"

"Christa, you know me, I don't make spontaneous decisions. But this is right."

"But Simone, you just met!"

"This from a woman who moved in with her lover the first week they met."

"But I am spontaneous."

"Christa, I love her, and she loves me. Why would we not want to live together or have a commitment ceremony?"

"Honey, that isn't my point. She doesn't even live here. Don't you think you should wait until she moves here?"

"We will, I'm just telling you we are getting married."

Christa heard the sincerity in Simone's voice and she couldn't help but respond. "I'm glad for you, Simone. I like Shannon."

"She just needs to find a job here, and that's where you can help. You know the industry and where there are job openings. You could give Shannon some guidance."

"Simone, I can do more than give her guidance. Her reputation in Seattle is more than solid. If the video she is working on is as good as her boss claims she is, there will be no shortage of job offers here."

"You think so?"

"I know so. We're always looking for good cameramen. But don't say anything to Shannon yet. Let's let her finish the video first. We will deal with the job after that."

"Good. Christa, I don't know how to thank you."

"Simone, how long have we been friends?"

"Twenty-three years."

"Do you think you need to thank me, when more than anything I want to see you happy?"

Simone's eyes filled with tears. Very few people knew how loving Christa was. She kept her emotions well hidden except to those who counted in her life. Simone was lucky enough to be one of them. "I am happy."

"I know. Now, go home to your girlfriend. You don't want her to figure out you're a workaholic yet, do you?"

"She already knows."

"Go home and say hello to everyone. Tell Shannon I'll see her bright and early tomorrow morning. Are we still going out Thursday night?"

"Yes, dinner and dancing, Leo and Marcus are coming."

"Terrific. Love you."

Simone roused herself as she swung through the doors. She needed to find the perfect gift for Shannon. She wanted to celebrate their commitment to each other. She passed by the rings heading for the necklaces. It was too early for rings, besides that would be something both she and Shannon could pick out together. She needed something personal and meaningful now to give Shannon.

"Hey Simone, how are you? We haven't seen you for quite awhile."

"Hey Toby, I'm fine. How're you doing?"

"Great, can I help you with something?"

"I need a necklace, something feminine and sexy."

Toby grinned at her as he pulled out a tray and laid it on the counter. "There is nothing sexier than a good diamond necklace."

Simone had to agree. The diamond pendant stood out from the other necklaces, glittering white hot against the warm gold that surrounded it. "This is beautiful, Toby."

"Thanks, I just finished it." Toby was a well-known jewelry designer on the islands. His designs were inspired by the beautiful nature around him, as he created waves in gold to hold pearls and other beautiful stones. The diamond appeared to float on top of the delicate gold froth. "The diamond is first rate and point four nine carats."

"Does the necklace come with it?"

"It will for you," Toby responded. He had known Simone practically all his life. She was an islander, just like him.

"I'll take it. Now tell me what it will cost me." Simone grinned at him. She knew he would charge her a pretty penny.

After a little discussion, Toby took Simone's credit card and ran it through before polishing the pendant one last time and putting it in a beautiful tiny wooden jewelry box, a signature of his store *The Wooden Jewelry Box*. "Do you want me to wrap it?"

"No, I think the box is perfect the way it is."

"Well, whoever you are giving this to is a very lucky woman." Toby smiled knowingly.

"Yes, she is," Simone chuckled as she waved goodbye and headed for her car.

She was in a very good mood as she walked through the open front door of her home. Olivia was puttering around in the kitchen and Janice and Mel were visiting on the back patio while sitting in the sun. "Hi Olivia, how was sight seeing?"

"Wonderful, we took hundreds of pictures. You're right, those churches are incredible." Simone had given them directions to some of the oldest churches on the island. They had spent hours wandering through them.

"Where's Hanna?"

"She's lying down. She's got really bad cramps, so I put her to bed with a Motrin."

"I've got a heating pad if she needs one."

"Thanks, I think she's okay for now. How was work?"

"Not bad, I just had to cover for half the shift and it was a pretty light one. Where's Shannon?"

"She's down on the beach."

"How's she feeling?"

"She says fine. I haven't seen her back without the bandages so I don't know if she's healing."

"I'll get her to change them and check."

"Good, I've got a cold fruit salad, chicken breasts, and roasted potatoes for dinner."

"Olivia, you and Hanna are going to put weight on me."

"No I won't, you work too hard." Olivia laughed. "Go find your girlfriend, she's been moping around all afternoon."

Simone just grinned as she dropped her bag off in her bedroom and headed for the back door. The necklace was all but burning a hole in her pocket.

"Hi Simone."

"Hello ladies, how was your day?"

"Wonderful. Shannon is down there." They both pointed to the left.

"Thanks." Simone hurried down the path, her fingers holding the necklace box tightly. She saw Shannon way down the beach, her video camera pointed off into the distance as she filmed. Simone was halfway to her when Shannon turned and saw her. Dropping her camera on the strap, Shannon started to run toward Simone. Simone laughed as she too began to run, picking Shannon up in her arms as Shannon threw herself at her.

"Whoa your camera." Simone laughed as she struggled to move the camera from between them.

"I missed you," Shannon admitted as she kissed Simone rapidly all over her face.

"I missed you." Simone put Shannon down to kiss her. It was the perfect kiss, full, soft, and so gentle. It went on and on as Shannon held Simone tightly to her.

"Look at that." Mel and Janice pointed as Olivia joined them on the patio. The three women watched as Simone and Shannon embraced on the beach, the sun setting behind them. Janice picked up her camera and began to snap pictures. It was a beautiful scene, one that would grace any romance movie.

Simone and Shannon stopped kissing but remained wrapped in each other's arms, content to stand on the beach together as long as possible. Shannon ran her fingers slowly over Simone's cheek before stepping back and gazing up at her. "How was work?"

"Good, how was your day?"

"Good, except that I missed you terribly."

Simone smiled down at her beautiful girlfriend. "I like your hair."

Shannon had French braided it to keep it out of her face. "Thanks, sometimes it gets in my way when I video."

"I've never seen it up like this. It shows off your beautiful face." Simone's hands cupped Shannon's face. "I love your face."

"I love you."

"I got you something." Simone hugged Shannon.

"When did you have the time?"

"After work and I wanted to give you something to remind you of me when you go home after your vacation is up. It will make you think of me as you prepare to move here."

Shannon felt the pinch of emotion to her heart as she thought about having to leave Simone. "I don't need anything to remind me of you. I love you Simone, and I'm going to live with you for the rest of our lives."

"I know. But I still want to give you something, so you'll know I mean what I say when I'm committed to you."

"I'll take it as long as you let me give you something to remind you of me."

"It's a deal." Simone bent her head close to Shannon's as she pulled the box out of her pocket. "Here."

Shannon took the beautiful wooden box from Simone and leaned into her brushing a kiss upon her lips. She slowly flipped the lid back and gasped as she saw the diamond pendant nestled against navy blue velvet. "Oh my God, this is too much, Simone."

Simone just smiled at her and pulled it out of the box. "No, it's not. Turn around so I can put it on your neck."

Shannon turned and held her braid up while Simone placed the necklace on her neck and fastened it. She kissed Shannon's neck before turning her back around. "It's perfect." She whispered as she bent and kissed the pendant were it lay nestled in Shannon's cleavage.

"I don't know what to say." Shannon appeared shocked.

"Thank you would work." Simone teased her as she took her hand.

"Thank you, but this must have been very expensive."

"Shannon, I'm not a pauper, I can afford to give my girlfriend a nice gift."

Shannon picked the pendant up in her fingers. "This is the most beautiful necklace I have ever seen."

"I'm glad you like it. Olivia said dinner is in an hour so will you come back with me so I can change your bandages and check your back? I want to make sure you're healing."

"Simone, thank you." Shannon slid into Simone's arms, hugging her tightly.

"I love you, Shannon."

"I love you."

They walked hand in hand back up the beach to the house, Shannon still overwhelmed by the gift and Simone pleased that she had surprised her. As they headed up the path below the patio, Mel called to Simone.

"You have a telephone call, Simone."

"Thanks Mel, I'm on my way." Simone kissed Shannon quickly and then hurried up the path taking the telephone from Mel as she met her on the patio. She took the telephone into the house while Shannon took a seat next to Janice at the table.

"Shannon, I took some beautiful pictures of you and Simone kissing on the beach," Janice shared, as she looked at her friend.

"You did, when?" Shannon was still a little stunned by Simone's gift.

"Shannon, are you okay?" Mel asked as she watched Shannon.

"I'm fine, I'm very fine." Shannon smiled as she fingered the necklace. "Simone just gave me a gift and I am still a little surprised." She held the pendant out so her friends could see.

"Wow, that's incredible." Janice all but leaped out of her chair as the three of them crowded around.

"That's so beautiful." Olivia admitted. "I've never seen anything like it."

"It's special isn't it?"

"Yes, it is. She must like you or something," Mel commented, poking Shannon in the arm.

"She loves me," Shannon responded with laughter as she poked Mel back.

"Yes, I do." Simone joined them, chuckling at their teasing.

"Simone this is a beautiful necklace," Janice commented.

"I thought so. It sure looks beautiful on Shannon." Simone bent over to brush a kiss across her lips. "I need to borrow you for a few moments so we can change your bandages before dinner."

"Okay."

"Do you need any help?" Mel asked.

"Yes, I want a second opinion on whether her back and legs are healing."

"Okay." Mel followed the two of them into the house. Hanna was just coming out of the bedroom.

"How are you feeling, Hanna?"

"Better, now that I'm on drugs," she sighed. "The trials and tribulations of being a woman."

"Don't I know it?" Mel agreed as she hugged her and then followed Simone and Shannon into the bedroom. "Okay Shannon, take your clothes off."

Shannon just chuckled at Mel as she slipped out of her shorts and top and lay down on top of the bed.

"Shannon, tell me if I cause you any pain at all," Simone requested as she bent over her back and began to gently pull the bandages away.

"Ouch," Shannon cried as the bandage stuck to her back.

"Honey, I am going to have to soak the bandages off. They're stuck to your scabs. It might sting a little."

"Okay, can I take a shower after they are removed?"

"If they look like they are healing you can. If there's any sign of infection you're going back to the doctor." Shannon knew what that meant, more scrubbing, and that was the last thing in the world she wanted.

"Hey, you okay," Mel whispered, sitting next to Shannon's head.

"Is there anything less sexy than having your new girlfriend peel bandages off of your body?" Shannon dropped her head down on the pillow, tears sliding down her cheeks.

Simone heard the comment and approached Shannon, standing next to Mel. "Shannon, I love you. There is nothing in this world that would make you any less sexy than I already find you. If you hadn't been hurt, we never would have met. I'm sorry for the pain it caused you, but I am infinitely grateful to have found you."

"I guess she told you," Mel responded with a grin.

Shannon's muffled laughter came from the pillow. "Okay, I'm ready."

"I am going to get a bowl of warm water and a washcloth."

"Okay."

Simone left the bedroom and Mel stroked the back of Shannon's head. "She's right, if you hadn't been so brave and jumped in to save the boy, you two wouldn't have found each other."

"I think that was my lucky day."

"That and the day you met me and Janice."

Shannon laughed against her pillow. Leave it to Mel to make her laugh. "You're absolutely right."

"Okay, sweetie, I'm going to place a hot washcloth on your back and then pull the bandage off. I'll apologize in advance for hurting you."

"It's okay. I'm ready." Shannon buried her face in the pillow, gripping tightly with her hands.

Mel and Simone both knew that Shannon was undergoing a lot of pain. Her back was tense, her hands white, as they gripped her pillow while Simone placed the hot washcloth on each bandage to soften the scab.

"Shannon, I am going to peel the bandage off now. I'm sorry."

"It's okay."

Simone's heart hurt as she pulled the bandage from Shannon's raw back. She continued to work in complete silence as Mel sat next to Shannon, her hand on Shannon's shoulder in comfort. Shannon didn't utter a peep while Simone worked quickly. Hanna had come to the door of the room but stopped when she saw what Simone was doing. Shannon's back was raw and sore. Hanna couldn't prevent the tears from forming. Janice and Olivia crowded in the doorway with her and were also moved to tears as they watched. Shannon remained completely silent until Simone removed the bandage from her left thigh. It was still angry and red after the gauze was removed and she cried out in pain when Simone pulled on the bandage. Hanna turned away and buried her face in Olivia's shoulder. She had seen and heard enough.

Simone's hand shook as she pulled the last bandage off of Shannon's leg. She could take care of fatalities, she could comfort badly wounded strangers, but when it came to Shannon, Simone couldn't handle hurting her. Simone stood up, went to the other side of Mel and bent over Shannon, her fingers pushing the hair away from Shannon's face.

"I'm sorry, sweetie," Simone spoke softly, her face inches from Shannon's. Shannon turned until she was looking at Simone, the tears evident on her face.

"I know. I love you, Simone."

Simone sighed as she looked at her girlfriend, love radiating from her. "I love you." Simone kissed her softly, wishing she could take the pain away with a kiss.

Simone stood up and went to look at Shannon's back. She needed to make sure there were no signs of infection anywhere. She and Mel looked it over several times and checked out both thighs. They were raw and angry but clear of any problems. Both Simone and Mel breathed a sigh of relief.

"Honey, your back and legs are healing and there is no sign of infection. I am going to put some aloe vera gel on them and fresh bandages. The aloe will feel nice and cool when I put it on."

"Okay."

"Mel, do you want to help me?"

"Sure, tell me what to do."

"Spread this gel over Shannon's legs, it is a slight analgesic and will help dull the pain."

"Okay. Shannon, I'm sorry if this hurts."

"Mel, it doesn't hurt since the bandages were taken off."

The three women in the doorway flooded into the room to sit on either side of Shannon while Simone and Mel worked. They chattered quietly with each other entertaining Shannon with their quirkiness. They loved her and that's what counted. She had the most wonderful friends and a new incredible girlfriend. She was very, very lucky.

"That feels nice." she commented as Mel and Simone finished covering all of her wounds with gel.

"It should give you a little relief. I will cover them up with new bandages and then we are going to bundle you up on the patio for dinner."

Shannon smiled as she listened to Simone and Mel visit with the others as they re-bandaged her. Simone was as much a part of the group as she was, and that was important to her. She'd hit the jackpot. She touched the diamond pendant around her neck and sighed. She had never received anything so beautiful or so expensive before.

"We're done, honey." Simone bent over and spoke softly to Shannon. There were still tear tracks down her cheeks and Simone wanted more than anything to kiss them away. The others quietly left the room as Simone crawled on to the bed next to Shannon and gathered her into her arms. Shannon tucked her face against Simone's neck as the tears started once again. She had kept them bottled up inside and she could no longer hold them back. She sobbed on Simone's shoulder as pain and frustration bubbled out of her. Simone stroked her head and whispered softly to her as she comforted her. It was several minutes before Shannon stopped her sobbing and settled against Simone's shoulder breathing deeply.

"I'm sorry I got your uniform shirt all wet," Shannon mumbled.

"Shannon," Simone put her hand under Shannon's chin and lifted her face up so they were eye to eye. "You have every reason to cry. The last thing I'm going to worry about is a uniform shirt."

Shannon's eyes filled with tears again as they slid down her cheeks. "I love you, Simone so much."

"I love you." Simone kissed Shannon gently, full of love and a heart that wanted more than anything to protect her as much as possible from any more pain and suffering.

Shannon whimpered as she kissed Simone back, opening her lips to Simone, her tongue slipping into Simone's mouth. Shannon kissed Simone fully, as much with passion as emotion. It pulled Simone under as she loved Shannon with her kisses, cradling her in her arms. Shannon's kisses were full of need and hunger for the woman that she needed physically and emotionally beyond life. Simone gentled the kisses until Shannon was once again resting softly against her, content to be held in Simone's arms.

"Ladies, dinner is ready. Would you like us to bring it in here?" Hanna called from the doorway.

"No, I'm getting up," Shannon responded hugging Simone once more. "Do you want to hop in the shower before you eat?"

"Yes, I'm filthy from work."

Shannon watched Simone as she stood up and then Shannon slowly rolled on to her thighs expecting some pain. She was surprised when she didn't feel any discomfort. "Have I told you how much I like looking at you in your uniform?"

Simone was just heading for the bathroom when Shannon spoke and she turned with a grin on her face. "You like me in my dirty uniform?"

"Yes, I do." Shannon grinned at her surprised girlfriend. "I like that you're a paramedic and that you help people every day. I also like the fact that you train new ones, because you can teach them the heart side of the job. The person I first met at the beach was gentle and competent and made me feel safe. I felt protected immediately. I am so proud of who you are."

Simone stood silently just outside of the bathroom staring back at Shannon, her blue eyes large and sparkling with unshed tears. "I think that's the most amazing thing anyone has ever said to me."

Shannon slowly walked over to Simone and slid her hands around her waist. "Yea, well get used to hearing it because I'm going to tell you at least once a week for the rest of your life."

Simone was without a response as she looked down at Shannon, her emotions too jumbled to do anything other than to hold Shannon.

"Go take your shower." Shannon gently pushed her toward the bathroom. "I'll be out with the girls."

Simone shut the bathroom door and sat down on the toilet, her head in her hands. She was completely overwhelmed by Shannon's comments. She'd waited all her life to find a woman that understood her and respected the fact that she was a good paramedic. In less than a week, Shannon had not only figured it out, it was what she liked about Simone. Simone shook her head and grinned as she stood up. Boy was she a lucky woman.

Shannon stepped out on to the patio where all of the women were seated at the table. She slipped up behind Mel and hugged her. "Thanks."

Mel pulled on her arms and looked up at her friend. "You're welcome, how're you feeling?"

"Better."

"Is Simone getting cleaned up?"

"Yes, she'll be out shortly."

"She's a nice woman, Shannon."

"I know. I think I'm very lucky."

"So are you hungry?" Hanna asked as she stood up.

"Yep, can we wait until Simone joins us?"

"You bet. I have some snacks we can munch on and a wonderful bottle of wine."

Shannon sat slowly on a chair. "That sounds perfect."

"Can I see your necklace again?" Janice asked as she sat down next to Shannon.

She and Shannon visited as Janice looked at the very beautiful necklace while Olivia, Hanna, and Mel munched on treats. In less than ten minutes, Simone joined them on the patio, wearing a pair of shorts and a tank top, her feet bare. She bent over and nuzzled Shannon's neck before finding a chair next to Mel and sipping on her own glass of wine.

"So Shannon, are you ready for your meeting tomorrow?"

"Yes, I have a story board completed and a tentative script to show Christa."

"Do you want to walk it by us?"

"No, I want to wait until I have talked with Christa before I do that."

"I'm going to drive you to the meeting," Mel announced as she handed the plate of goodies to her girlfriend.

"I can drive, Mel."

"I know you can, but you aren't going to tomorrow. I'll bring a book with me."

"Mel…"

"I'm not going to change my mind," Mel interrupted Shannon. "Don't even try."

Shannon and Mel glared at each other until Shannon started to smile. "You are the most stubborn woman I have ever met."

"Ha." Mel just laughed and sipped her wine. The rest of the group laughed at the two of them. They all knew Shannon was equally as stubborn.

"Time for dinner," Janice announced. "Come on Mel, help me serve."

Mel looked a little sheepish when she headed into the house behind Janice. Janice was probably going to talk to her about being a little more subtle with Shannon. Janice turned to face Mel and she braced herself for a tongue-lashing. She was totally surprised when Janice slipped her arms around Mel's neck and kissed her.

"Have I told you how much I love you today?" Janice asked as she looked at her very startled girlfriend. "That was very nice of you to drive Shannon tomorrow. She still isn't in great shape and none of us wanted her to go alone."

"I thought you were going to tell me I wasn't very subtle."

"You weren't, but it was warranted. I love you, Mel."

"I love you, Janice. So do you want to look for a retirement place over here?"

"I'd love to. I would go anywhere with you."

"Are you still going to make me serve dinner?" Mel teased as she kissed her girlfriend.

"Yep, but I guarantee that you are going to be a very lucky woman tonight," Janice promised with a glint in her eye.

"Tell me what to do." Mel grinned at her.

"I thought you'd like that. Grab the salad out of the refrigerator."

The dinner was full of pleasant conversation, good food, and lots of laughter. Shannon had refrained from drinking any wine and about two hours after dinner she began to feel her legs and back ache. Simone had been watching Shannon closely and knew when she started to get uncomfortable.

"Shannon let's get you into bed with some ice on your back and legs. It will dull the pain," Simone suggested to her.

"I think that's a good idea." Shannon stood up slowly. She bent over and hugged first Hanna and then Olivia, before kissing Janice on her cheek. "I'll see you all in the morning. You have to get up early, Mel," she teased hugging her best friend.

"I'll be up. You get some sleep."

"Thanks, I will." Shannon took hold of Simone's hand and headed into the house. Simone stopped her long enough to grab an ice bag and then the two of them headed for the bedroom.

"Simone, you don't have to go to bed yet. I'll be fine."

"I know you will. I thought I would crawl in bed next to you and do a little paperwork. Will that bother you?"

"No, I would love your company."

The two of then changed into tee shirts and both washed up before climbing into bed together. Shannon kissed Simone goodnight before flipping on to her stomach, the ice bag on her right shoulder. She was beginning to hurt quite a bit and needed to go to sleep.

"Goodnight."

Simone gazed at her girlfriend on the bed and placed her hand on her arm. "Goodnight, honey."

Within minutes, Shannon was sound asleep and Simone settled down with her briefcase from work. She was awfully glad Shannon was able to sleep. She needed it to heal. Simone worked for several hours, periodically switching out the ice bag for a fresh one. She was returning from the kitchen with a new ice bag when she ran into Hanna.

"Simone, how is she?"

"Sound asleep."

Hanna reached out and placed her hand on Simone's arm. "I am very glad she met you, Simone."

"Hanna, I am extremely glad to have met all of you, and I will be thanking God every day for letting me find Shannon."

"Shannon is just as lucky to have found you." Hanna smiled at the woman she liked very much.

"Are you guys going to swim with the dolphins tomorrow?"

"Yep, and I wish Shannon could go in the water."

"She'll enjoy filming the whole thing."

"You know her well."

"I'm starting to."

"I think you know her better than her last girlfriend ever did. Filming is what keeps Shannon's creative spirit going. She loves it almost as much as she loves you. She would die if she couldn't create her videos."

"I guarantee you Shannon will always be able to make her films. In fact, I was thinking that she might need a studio to work in. I was going to look into putting one in on the left side of the patio. What do you think?"

"I think that would be perfect." Hanna smiled at the obviously besotted woman. "I would talk to Shannon before you plan anything. She's pretty particular about the type of equipment she uses."

"I will, Hanna, thanks."

"Go to sleep, sweetie. You have a long day tomorrow."

"Goodnight."

Simone entered the darkened bedroom and closed the door. Shannon still slept heavily on the bed as she crawled under the covers. Simone placed the ice bag against her back and Shannon stirred. Simone lay down and prepared to go to sleep. Shannon turned into her, sliding her arm around Simone's waist, her head resting on Simone's shoulder. Simone smiled and turned into Shannon, tucking her even tighter against her body as she closed her eyes. Shannon was a snuggler and Simone loved it that she turned to her in her sleep. Simone placed a kiss on Shannon's forehead and allowed herself to relax as she too slipped into sleep.

Shannon woke up slowly, her body draped on Simone's, their legs intertwined, their faces tucked against one another's. She stared at Simone's sleeping face for the longest time admiring her beauty as she slept next to Shannon. Shannon checked the clock and was amazed to see it was almost time for Simone to wake up for work. She had slept heavily throughout the night and was surprised at how much better she felt. She lay quietly enjoying the feeling of waking up with Simone next to her. Even in sleep, Simone's well-toned body was impressive as Shannon ran her eyes down Simone's uncovered legs. She loved the look of her when she put her shorts and uniform shirt on. She looked so professional and so capable. Shannon laid there for almost thirty minutes, listening to the sounds of the ocean and her lover sleeping next to her. She didn't notice Simone had woken up until Simone's lips whispered against her cheek before kissing her.

"Good morning."

"Good morning to you. How did you sleep?"

"Wonderfully, I was next to you." Shannon smiled as she hugged Simone. "You need to get up in ten minutes."

"I know but I need to give you a good morning kiss." Before Shannon could respond, Simone rolled her on top of her body and kissed her thoroughly, driving every thought out of Shannon's head.

"Wow that was some good morning kiss." Shannon responded as she leaned up on her elbows to look down at Simone who held her firmly on top of her.

"It's going to have to keep you going for the next eight or nine hours until I see you again."

"Do you think I could get one more for the road?"

"You bet." Simone grinned as she did what Shannon asked.

"I'm going to miss you today," Shannon volunteered as she slid off of Simone so she could get out of bed.

"I'll miss you, but I expect you will be busy with the video most of the morning and you're going with the girls to take pictures of them swimming with the dolphins."

"And you will be out saving lives and training paramedics."

"I don't know about the saving lives but I have a ride along today so if you need or want to talk to me, call me on my cell phone."

"It's okay if I call you at work?"

"Of course it is." Simone smiled as she headed for the bathroom. "How else will you be able to tell me you love me during the day?"

"Good point." Shannon climbed out of bed. "I'm going to get you a cup of coffee."

Shannon headed down the hall in her tee shirt intent on grabbing two fresh cups of coffee but Olivia and Hanna had beat her to it.

"Nice outfit," Olivia commented as she sat in the living room with Hanna sipping coffee. "This is the best coffee."

"It's Kona Gold. You can buy it in Seattle."

"In Starbucks country, are you nuts? That would be sacrilegious," Hanna teased her.

"What are you two doing up so early?"

"Enjoying the day, it's so beautiful here we hate to miss a single moment."

"I know the feeling."

"Is Simone getting ready for work?"

"Yep, I'm going to bring her a cup of coffee." Shannon headed back down the hall with two full cups in her hands.

"Fresh coffee for my girlfriend," she announced as she entered the bedroom.

"Thanks." Simone was just starting to put a clean uniform on.

Shannon sat down on the bed and watched her as she sipped her coffee. "You have an incredible body," she commented.

Simone's eyebrows lifted as she sat down on the bed to put her shoes on. "Are you trying to make me late?"

"No, I just made a comment. Besides, I told you I love you in uniform."

Simone just grinned as she put her other shoe on. "Maybe tonight you will have to show me how much you love me in uniform."

Shannon's eyes lit up with pleasure as she responded. "I can do that."

"I thought you were up to the challenge." Simone stood up and grabbed her briefcase, strapped her cell phone on her belt, and stood in front of Shannon. "Good luck this morning at your meeting."

"Thanks, I'll call you when it's over and give you an update."

"I'd like that." Simone remained standing in front of Shannon.

"Can I do anything else for you?" Shannon asked a sexy smile on her face.

"Do you think you could wrap that beautiful body around me in a goodbye kiss?"

"I believe I can do that." Shannon stood up and slowly moved within inches of Simone. "I really do love you in uniform."

"Keep that in your thoughts until this evening, please." Simone and Shannon kissed, Shannon's arms snaking around Simone's neck as she did as Simone requested, wrapping her scantily clad body tightly against Simone's.

"Have a good day," Shannon whispered against Simone's lips as Simone stepped away from her.

"You too." Shannon walked with Simone to the front door, her hand held tightly in Simone's free one.

Simone turned to Shannon and bent to kiss her stopping inches from her lips to speak. "I love you naked in our bed." She covered Shannon's lip in a kiss meant to knock her socks off if she'd been wearing any.

Shannon stayed at the door until Simone pulled down the driveway and drove out of sight. When she shut the door and turned around intent on going back into the bedroom to get dressed, she saw the humorous look on Hanna and Olivia's face.

"What?"

"Do you and Simone always kiss like that?"

"What do you mean?"

"You kissed each other like you were going to eat each other up."

Shannon grinned as she sailed by the two of them. "Yes, we always kiss like that." She couldn't help but hear Hanna and Olivia chuckle as she entered the bedroom.

"Do we kiss like that?" Hanna asked Olivia as she turned to face her.

"Honey, Simone and Shannon are amateurs compared to us. We could show them a thing or two."

"You're absolutely right." Hanna grinned and then proceeded to kiss her girlfriend breathless.

CHAPTER 12

"Shannon, I like your story board and outline. This whole idea of tracking a paramedic through their training all the way until they are certified is a great idea. But how are you going to do it in less than two weeks?"

"Well, I know Simone has four medics in training right now, and she has two that are just ready to be certified. By filming and interviewing the six different medics, we should be able to get enough information and video to put it together. With that, and interviews with veteran medics, there should be more than enough stories and action. Since the video is only going to be thirty minutes in length, the problem will be in getting the right cuts to solidify the message, not a lack of information. I figure it will take me this week, and the following Monday and Tuesday of next week to complete the videotaping and the interviews, at the longest. That leaves Wednesday, Thursday, and Friday to edit and do the voice-overs. I don't leave until a week from Sunday night."

"Are you sure you want to spend all of your vacation working."

"It's not working, Christa."

"Okay, I'm all for it. What do you think, Art and Susan? You're going to be helping Shannon edit this piece."

"I like her outline. I can start pulling together any other video we have in archives about the medics. We probably have some good clips." Susan Clemens responded. "What do you think, Art?"

"It works, and I like it. I've seen your work, Shannon. I'm looking forward to working with you. I think we have the perfect camera for this work. You want the hand held look, right?"

"Yes, I want the viewer to know we were actually there with them and not in some studio."

"Good. Come on let's get you outfitted with the camera and a bunch of film. Susie will scour the archives and I will take a look at your script. Since we are on a tight time table it would be nice to get the voice-overs recorded in advance so we can be ready to pull it all together."

"Great idea, Art."

"Well, it looks like you're in capable hands, Shannon," Christa almost laughed. Art and Susan had all but adopted her and they were not pushovers. She knew that Art had looked at Shannon's camera work and he was very impressed. Art was not one to be easily awed. Even if this was a voluntary project, he took it very seriously. "I'll catch up with you later in the week."

"Okay, Christa. Thanks."

Christa watched Shannon follow Art and Susan to the equipment room with a smile on her face. If she wasn't mistaken the three of them were going to create video magic, and Christa was rarely wrong. Art and Susan would work their tails off, and Shannon was a surprise. According to Art, she was in hot demand by anyone who wanted to do action video. She was quite a well-known videographer, especially for athletes wanting to make a video to showcase their talents. She had no doubt that Shannon would be offered a job with her network, especially after she completed the video. She picked up her telephone to call Neely.

"Hi honey, got a minute?"

"Just one."

"Shannon just left here with Art and Susan to pick up her camera."

"What do you think?"

"I think we're in for some filmmaking magic. Shannon wooed Susan and Art. The three of them clicked immediately. She should have no problem getting a job with the network, especially if Art recommends her."

"Good, I like Shannon."

"So do I."

"But you have reservations because of Simone."

"I just don't want to see Simone get hurt again. She just got over Doctor Bitch."

"Christa…"

"I know, mind my own business."

"No, I think you should be protective of your best friend, but with an open mind. Now, I have to go. I have a paying client in my waiting room."

"Thanks honey."

"I love you, Christa."

"I love you."

If anyone in Christa's office were to hear her talking to her girlfriend, they wouldn't recognize the soft loving woman that melted at the sound of her girl-friend's voice. Christa was known at work as a very tough, all business news reporter. But in her private life, Christa was a romantic, loving woman, who loved nothing better than going home, and spending the evening with her partner. Very few people at work knew that Christa was gay, those that did understood that Christa valued her privacy and her relationship above all else.

Christa settled down to work, but not without a little trepidation about Simone and Shannon. Christa was one of a few people who knew how much Simone had grieved over her relationship with Liz. Christa had never liked Liz and she certainly hadn't trusted her. Even Neely, who loved everyone, disliked Liz, and resisted spending time with her when she and Simone were dating. She didn't like the way Liz treated Simone.

Shannon meanwhile was hard at work learning her equipment. She had been fully outfitted with a camera, plenty of tape, and a carrying case. She, Art, and Susan had made plans to get together later on in the week and review any video she had filmed. She liked Art. He was blunt, articulate, and interesting. Susan seemed to be nice, but reserved. She was looking forward to working with them. She smiled as she worked the camera controls. She knew this kind of camera very well. She loaded her bag, pinned her temporary badge on her shirt, and prepared to leave the building. She had things to do for the rest of the day with her friends, because starting Tuesday morning, Shannon was working.

CHAPTER 13

"Way to go, Mel!" Shannon yelled as she continued to video tape her friends as they swam with dolphins. Simone had made one telephone call and Mel's dream of a lifetime had come true. Mel grinned from ear to ear as the dolphins allowed her to hold on to them as they towed her through the water. Shannon would have some great film to share with her friends.

They spent three hours swimming and lying on the beach, laughing and just enjoying each other's company. Even Shannon spent some time in the water. She waded up to her lower thighs to cool off. She wanted to take her bandages off and go swimming but she didn't dare.

They all piled into the rental car and headed back to Simone's about five in the afternoon. Shannon was anxious to see Simone. She had plans. They had stopped at the shopping mall on their way home so that Olivia could pick up a few things for dinner and Shannon purchased some surprises for Simone. She started preparing everything immediately. She wanted the evening to be perfect.

"Okay guys, you need to stay off of the beach tonight," Shannon reminded them as she re-entered the house.

"We will," Janice promised as the other three grinned at Shannon.

Shannon went into the bedroom and rapidly changed into a clean pair of shorts and a tee shirt, washed her face, and splashed a little perfume on. She was just finishing when she heard Simone's voice talking to her friends.

She slipped up behind her in the kitchen wrapping her arms around her waist. "Welcome home."

"Hi, how was your day?" Simone turned in her arms, bending to kiss Shannon hello.

"Excellent and it just got better. Come with me please." Shannon took Simone by the hand and led her to the bedroom. "I need you to put your brief-case down and then follow me. I have a surprise for you."

"A surprise?" Simone snagged Shannon by the hand and pulled her against her body. "You have a surprise for me?"

Shannon smiled up at her lover and placed her hand against her cheek. "Yes, I have a small surprise for you. I love you, Simone."

Simone turned her face and placed a kiss on Shannon's palm. "I love you, Shannon." They shared a kiss, a slow, softly intoxicating kiss that filled them both with emotion. They stayed locked in each other's arms for several long moments.

"Sweetie, follow me, please." Shannon took Simone by the hand and tugged her out of the bedroom down the hallway and past the grinning women seated in the living room. They had their orders. They were to stay far away from the beach.

Shannon stopped in the kitchen and picked up her already prepared box of goodies and turned to Simone who was watching her carefully. "Come with me."

Simone did as she was asked and followed Shannon out on to the patio and down the path to the beach. She turned right, and straight in front of her was a blanket spread out on the sand. A chaise lounge sat next to it and there were candles stuck in the sand every few feet.

"Have a seat, please." Simone sat on the chaise and watched in silence as Shannon unloaded her box. She pulled out a bottle of wine and two wine glasses, along with a corkscrew. "Could you open this?"

"I would be happy to." Simone took the bottle and the corkscrew from her. Simone removed the cork and looked at Shannon before she poured the wine. "Are we having a picnic on the beach?"

"Yes, we are, all by ourselves." Shannon grinned at her pleased girlfriend. "And then I am going to do my very best to show you how much I love you in your uniform."

Simone felt the stirring of passion as she reacted to Shannon's words. It was amazing that with only a look or a few words, Shannon could make her yearn to be touched by her. She leaned over and kissed Shannon with just a brush of her lips in promise.

"Will you pour the wine while I get our dinner ready?"

"I'd love to."

Shannon, with Olivia's help, had prepared two full plates of cheese, fruit, and sliced meats. There was a loaf of French bread, and a bowl of fresh raspberries and strawberries. She placed the plates on the blanket and pulled out a book of matches and lit the candles. When she was done setting the stage she took a glass of wine from Simone and sat down in front of her. Simone couldn't help but smile at Shannon. She looked so beautiful sitting on the blanket, her hair pulled back into a knot at the base of her neck, her pale yellow tee shirt accentuating her tan skin, and her pale blue shorts showed off her long slender legs. She had never been more beautiful than she was at that moment. Simone fell in love with her all over again.

"Simone, I need to tell you something and I wanted to do it here on the beach."

Simone took a big deep breath, she had no idea what to expect. Simone sat completely still as Shannon put her wine glass down and took Simone's hand in her own.

"Simone, I love you. I have never loved anyone like I love you. I know we haven't known each other for even a week but if you feel anything like what I feel for you, time doesn't matter. I want to be with you, I want to live the rest of my life loving you and being loved by you. I promise you that I will always be there for you, no matter what."

Shannon stopped speaking and waited for Simone to respond. This was the most important conversation she would ever have. Simone relaxed as she listened to Shannon and saw the tears form in her eyes.

"Shannon, I don't care how long I have known you. I would have married you the first day I met you. I love you and I want to be with you." Simone slipped to her knees in front of Shannon. "I promise you, I will love you for the rest of our lives."

Shannon began to cry as she held Simone's hands in hers. "So will you marry me?"

"Yes."

"I will always love you, Simone."

"For ever and ever."

"Do you know how much I like you in your uniform?" Shannon's eyes lit up with humor as her fingers fumbled with the buttons on Simone's shirt.

"Honey, we're on the beach in plain sight."

"No one can see us and I really like you in this uniform." Shannon ran her hands down Simone's strong thighs and around to her backend. "You're so sexy in your shorts."

Simone all but melted when Shannon's hands slid tightly over her and pulled her snug against her body. Their mouths met in a kiss that turned them both inside out as they tasted each other completely. Simone was no longer aware of the fact that they were on the beach. She just wanted to make love with Shannon, here and now. Shannon quickly opened Simone's shirt, her hands covering her breasts as her mouth nuzzled between them. Her tongue slid along the edge of her lace bra as her fingers teased her nipples. Simone moaned as Shannon unhooked her bra and pushed it out of the way to suck on her nipples, first one and then the other was pulled into her hot mouth. The rush of hunger was overwhelming, the heat pooling between Simone's legs.

Shannon fingers unzipped Simone's shorts and slipped her hand under her panties and rapidly entered Simone. Simone's reaction was instantaneous, she tumbled directly into an orgasm, her body quaking around Shannon's as Shannon kissed her, prolonging the pleasure. Simone held on to Shannon as her body shook and trembled, her body inundated with waves of emotion and pleasure. Shannon knew her lover well and her talented fingers teased Simone into another orgasm so huge it engulfed Simone's senses to the point that she could barely breathe. Gasping, she tightened her arms around Shannon's shoulders, tucking her face against her neck.

"Shannon, Shannon," Simone gasped as she struggled to stay on her knees, her body had lost all strength, and her bones had dissolved with Shannon's attentions.

Shannon removed her hand and steadied Simone against her, kissing her slowly, deeply, before speaking, "I told you, I love you in uniform, and out."

Simone could only sigh as she looked into the eyes of her very sexy lover. She was swamped with passion, it throbbed throughout her body.

Shannon zipped her pants and buttoned her shirt as she placed small, quick kisses all over Simone's face. "That was just the start to our evening."

"But, what about you, I want to make love with you." Simone reached for Shannon as she moved away from Simone.

"You will get the opportunity, but I want you to sit back and enjoy your dinner. I am going to go rinse off in the surf and join you."

Simone's eyes followed Shannon as she went into the surf and washed. Her eyes didn't leave her figure as she returned to the blanket and sat down next to Simone. "Shannon, I need to kiss you."

"My pleasure." Shannon leaned against Simone and turned her face up to meet Simone's as she bent to kiss her. The kiss was sweet, soft, and so perfect. "Now, eat this wonderful picnic."

The two of them visited as they shared their plates of treats and fed each other raspberries and strawberries, while sipping glasses of wine. It was a quiet, romantic meal and Simone was very grateful that Shannon had planned it.

"So your meeting went well this morning?"

"It went perfectly. Are you ready for me to go to work with you?"

"I am, but I've never been around a lover while I work. It's going to be hard to concentrate with you around." Simone chuckled as she tucked Shannon next to her on the blanket. They were both lying on the blanket watching the sun drop in the sky.

"I won't be around you that much since I'll be riding with your medics. Did you talk to them today?"

"I did, and they only grumbled a little bit," Simone teased. "Actually, they are very excited. And I have scheduled you to ride Thursday during the grave-yard crew as you requested."

"Good, I hope it will only take one night. I might have to go back Friday night."

"You're going to make me sleep alone for two nights?" Simone couldn't help but remind her.

"I'll make sure you don't miss me."

"I'll always miss you when you aren't around," Simone promised as she ran her lips down Shannon's neck.

"Am I going to get to interview you in your office?"

"Wherever you want to do the interview, my office isn't very big though."

"I can't wait to see where you work; it's such a huge part of who you are."

"Shannon, do you have a video studio at home?"

"A small one, I do most of my videos on my computer or I edit them at work. Why?"

"I thought we could put a studio in at the house to the left of the patio. It wouldn't take too long to build and you could put whatever equipment you need in there."

"I don't need a studio."

"Of course you do. It's what you do for your heart. You make videos, and you need your own space."

"Don't you want to wait until I move here? And we haven't even talked about finances?"

"Shannon, do you love me?"

"You know I do."

"Do you want to live here with me?"

"More than anything."

"I own the house and make a fair amount of money. There is no problem with the finances."

"Simone, I won't live with you if you don't allow me to contribute. I'll get a job here and I have quite a bit saved. I can also sell my condo."

"We'll figure all this out, but I still want to put in a studio for you. It will make this your home."

"It will be my home as long as you are in it."

"So when are you going to move?"

"As soon as I can sell my condo, pack, and quit my job."

"So I can start building the studio?"

"Honey, I need to sell my condo before I can give you some money."

"I'm still going to get started. It will provide you an even stronger incentive to hurry back here."

"I don't need any other incentive I want to be with you."

"Good, because that's what I want, you with me." Simone rolled Shannon on to her back and kissed her, her hands holding Shannon's face as she pleasured her with her mouth. There was nothing that could intrude on their world when Simone kissed Shannon. She tugged Simone on top of her, wanting the weight and the intimacy of her body on her own.

She wrapped her legs around Simone's hips, her arms around her back as she and Simone kissed over and over. The sun had set as they submerged each other with a power that shook them both. Not everyone was lucky enough to find the passion and the love that they had found with each other, it was rare and to be treasured. Their mouths feasted as they let passion move slowly through their bodies. There was no need to hurry, they had all their lives, and that made their lovemaking even more poignant. Simone's fingers trailed down her arms and then back up her ribs as she went to push Shannon's tee shirt up and off her body. Shannon was not wearing a bra and her full breasts and nipples distended the front of her shirt, just begging for Simone to touch.

"Honey, its dark out and I thought we could continue this in the water." Shannon drew Simone's hands up to kiss her fingers. "I think we need to fulfill your fantasy about making love in the water."

"What about your back and legs."

"I'll be fine, they're healing, and I had Janice pull the bandages off and replace some of them with large band aids. Besides, I'll be with you."

"I don't know about this?"

"I do. It's dark out and no one will see us." Shannon began to unbutton Simone's shirt and pull it out of her shorts. She dropped it on to the blanket and began to unzip her shorts. "Besides, I want to see you naked in the water."

Simone wasn't going to say no to Shannon. She went to work, quickly removing Shannon's tee shirt and pulled her shorts off of her hips, pushing them down her legs. Shannon stood in front of Simone wearing only a pair of pale blue thong underwear, her tan, slender body beckoning to Simone.

"You're so beautiful." Simone unclasped her bra and stood in her own underwear.

"So are you." Shannon moved close to her. "But you are still over dressed.

"I like this underwear." Simone stroked her buttocks as she smiled down at Shannon.

"I though you would. Now, let's get naked and get in the water."

The two of them stripped quickly and Shannon took Simone's hand as they walked to the water. Slowly they moved out into the surf, Simone watching Shannon carefully for any sign of discomfort. Shannon expected it to sting but was not going to let on to Simone. She held her breath as the salt water met the wounds on her legs and back, ignoring the pain as she turned to Simone. There was only one thing that could distract her and that was Simone. She moved into Simone, placing her arms on her neck as she turned her face up to kiss her.

"Simone, kiss me, please?" Simone's hands clasped Shannon's hips bringing her tightly against her as she nibbled on Shannon's lower lip, her tongue tasting her as she did as Shannon asked.

Dripping with warm salt water and lust for each other they kissed in the surf that splashed against their shoulders. Shannon mouth tasted Simone's shoulders, her tongue lapping at her skin as her fingers teased her nipples, twisting and pinching them just enough to make them harden in response. Simone found Shannon's breasts with her mouth, her tongue flicking against her nipple before surrounding it with her mouth. Shannon arched against her holding Simone's head to her chest. Simone reached down and lifted Shannon up in the water.

"Put your legs around my waist."

Shannon did as Simone asked, locking her arms around her neck as Simone once again suckled on her breasts. She sucked heavily on Shannon's nipples as Shannon pushed her hips into Simone's body. She wanted Simone inside her. Simone knew what she wanted and she slipped her hand between them, sliding into Shannon as she held her hips tightly wedged against her own. Shannon's hips slammed against Simone's over and over, mindless pleasure her only thought. Simone stroked her until Shannon began to shake.

"Honey, lay back in the water." Shannon did as Simone asked as Simone parted her legs and raised her hips so that her mouth could reach Shannon. She ran her tongue inside of Shannon, who could barely stay afloat.

"Enough, Simone, I'm going to drown."

Simone lifted her up until she was once again wrapped around Simone's waist with her legs, her head on Simone's shoulder. Shannon ran her hands down Simone's torso until she found Simone's very center. She slid her fingers against Simone as she rubbed against her body. Slowly she stretched Simone's body with her fingers deep inside her. Simone rippled around her as Shannon drove her quickly into an orgasm. Even her wildest fantasy hadn't come close to this as she completely dissolved. Simone stumbled in the water as she came and Shannon slid her legs down Simone's body and wrapped her arms around her.

"Oh God." Simone shivered as Shannon held her tightly, kissing her over and over. "I need to sit down."

"Come on, sweetie. I have towels with our things."

Shannon supported Simone as they headed for the blanket in the moonlight. Simone allowed Shannon to towel her off, completely undone by their time in the waves. She sat quietly on the blanket as Shannon wrapped a towel around her before beginning to towel her own body off. Simone snagged the towel out of Shannon's hands and rolled her on to her back. In one move she was between Shannon's legs her tongue inside her. She tasted the salt and her lover's unique flavors as her fingertip found her sensitive nub. Shannon began to pant as Simone felt her body flood with welcoming moisture.

"Right there, yes…"

Shannon's body froze with a thundering orgasm that moved up her body. She tugged on Simone's shoulder to pull her up so that she could hold her. Simone rolled onto her back taking Shannon with her so she could protect her back. Pulling the blanket up, she covered their bodies as Shannon clutched onto Simone, too exhausted to do anything, other than lay draped on her body. Shannon's fingers twisted with Simone's as she closed her eyes content to remain exactly where she was. Simone tucked her face against Shannon's and closed her own eyes as she slid into a satisfied nap.

"Honey, wake up." Shannon's voice roused Simone from a dead sleep.

"What time is it?"

"It's after eleven. We fell asleep. Here's your bathrobe. I've already taken everything up to the house but the blanket. Come on, and we'll pop into the shower and crawl into bed."

Simone stood up and slipped her bathrobe on as Shannon shook the blanket and folded it up.

"Shannon?"

"Yes, honey."

"This was a perfect night, thank you." Simone slipped her arms around Shannon's neck.

"It was, and I think I'm as thankful as you are. I hope it came close to your fantasy."

"Close, it is so much more. What makes it perfect is that you are the biggest part of it. I love you."

"I love you." Shannon kissed Simone gently. "Come on, sweetie. We working girls need a good night's sleep.

CHAPTER 14

Sleep was slightly delayed as Simone talked Shannon into showering with her. Simone lathered the front of Shannon's body and rinsed her before turning her around and carefully washing her back and thighs. It was Simone's lips on her backend that drew a groan from Shannon. She planted her hands on the shower wall as Simone slid her legs apart, her tongue sliding between her cheeks as her finger played with Shannon's anus. Shannon bit her lip as Simone's fingers found her clitoris and squeezed just enough to entice her. Simone's fingers slid into Shannon as she ran her tongue back and forth between her cheeks. Shannon couldn't stand it and she cried out loudly reaching back for Simone.

"I need to hold you." Simone gathered her into her arms as Shannon tried to catch her breath.

Simone rinsed her off and then gently pulled her out of the shower, toweling her dry. "Go crawl in bed, honey. I'll be right there."

Simone sent her off with a kiss and a gentle shove. Shannon didn't argue with her, she was suddenly very tired.

Simone dried off and wiped up the bathroom. Turning the light out, she headed for the bed. She stopped short as she caught sight of Shannon curled on her side, already sound asleep. Simone went up and stood next to her, watching her slumber. Her damp hair was loose and waving around her face and shoulders. Her hands were tucked under her pillow, the covers tossed haphazardly over her legs to her waist. Her face was relaxed as she breathed deeply, her skin pink from exposure to the sun. Simone reached out and pushed the fine strands of hair away from Shannon's forehead. Simone knew that when she met the woman of her dreams she would fall in love forever but she had never comprehended how deeply she would fall until this evening. Simone leaned over and kissed Shannon softly on her cheek and then rounded the bed and crawled under her own covers. She turned out the light and rolled over, tucking up against Shannon's back, slipping her arms around Shannon's waist. Shannon murmured in her sleep and moved back against Simone, her hand clasping Simone's arm at her waist. Simone slid quickly into slumber, dreaming of many more nights with Shannon.

Simone never heard the alarm, and it was Shannon who woke her up with a delicious kiss and a full cup of coffee. "Time to get up, honey."

"What time is it?"

"Six-thirty, and you need to get up."

"Can I have another kiss first?"

"Yes, you may."

They shared a gentle kiss before Simone climbed out of bed. Shannon was already fully dressed and sitting on the edge of the bed brushing her hair. "Did I thank you for last night?"

"Several times." Shannon grinned as she gazed up at Simone's naked body. "You'd better cover up that gorgeous body. I find it almost impossible to resist you."

Simone chuckled as she headed into the bathroom. "Almost, I see I have some work to do."

Shannon laughed at her as she began to braid her hair. She didn't want it in the way when she worked the camera. She was excited and nervous to begin her filming.

Simone and Shannon were right on time as they pulled into the parking lot of the main fire department in downtown Kona. Simone's office was in the building along with the Fire Chief. It also housed fire unit number six and her paramedics on shift. There were two fire trucks in the garage, three medical response vans, and two marked fire units. Most of the administration work for the fire department was run out of this building even though there were seven other houses located around the island.

"So I guess it wouldn't be wise for me to kiss you before we go into the building?" Shannon teased as she collected her things.

"They already know I am gay and if you feel the urge to, I wouldn't stop you."

"I think we will keep our kissing between the two of us. Now, let's go see your office. I want to see where my lover works."

Simone felt warm all over as she looked at Shannon seated next to her in her Rover. It was so amazing to have a girlfriend who thought her being a paramedic was special. "I love you, Shannon."

"I love you, Lieutenant."

"Come on," Simone laughed at her darling girlfriend. "Let's go so you can make a movie."

"A good movie, about my girlfriend and her medics." Shannon grinned as she followed her into the building, her camera bag on her arm.

It didn't take Shannon long to ingratiate herself with the firemen and the medics. She had all of them telling stories about each other and generally sharing their work life. The fact that Shannon was pointing a camera at them didn't seem to faze them; it just seemed to be a part of Shannon. Even the Chief managed to get in a few good tales about his experiences. The plan was for Shannon to go along with the first unit to be called out as a ride along. She would then tag along with them for the rest of their shift.

Simone left Shannon with the crew and headed back to her office. She had work to do and so did Shannon. She smiled as she heard the crew already teasing Shannon. Shannon returned the favor, eliciting laughter from the group. Shannon had a talent, and that was bringing people out of their shell and sharing their thoughts on tape. Simone already knew the video was going to be great.

Shannon was out most of the day and Simone spent the bulk of her time with scheduling and budget issues. As usual, budgets determined the level of resources she could deploy and it was always contracting. Her radio crackled on her hip as she entered the firehouse.

"What's up guys?"

"Not too much, it's been a calm day as far as fires goes, but a lot of medical calls. We just had another call with a potential heart attack at the shopping center. That makes twenty-three calls today."

"Wow that is a busy shift."

"Shannon is getting a lot of good footage. She showed us a couple of her tapes at lunch. She's good."

"Yes, she is. She is very well known for her sports videos in Seattle."

"Is she just here to do the video?"

"Actually, Shannon is going to be moving here."

"Cool, I like her."

Simone refrained from announcing that Shannon was going to be living with her, even though that was her inclination. She wanted everyone to know about her and Shannon, but announcing it at work was probably not a good idea.

"Where are Seth and Mike?"

"Just finishing up with the car accident out on the highway, Shannon is going to be exhausted after the day she's spent with those two. They should be back soon. They called when they were just leaving the hospital. Can Shannon go with us tomorrow?"

"Sorry guys, but Shannon is just going out with the medics this time around."

"That's too bad."

"I'm going to be in my office, can you tell Shannon?"

"Yep Simone, when are you going to go out with us again?"

"Don't know, Rich, can I get back to you on that?"

"Sure, but we're all going out next week for some Mexican food."

"I'll check my schedule." Simone headed back into her office intent on getting some more work done as she waited for Shannon to return.

Thirty minutes later, Shannon came bursting into Simone's office, full of energy and enthusiasm. "I got so much great film today I can't wait to show you."

"I'm glad. Are you ready to head home or do you need to stay a little longer?"

"Nope, I'm done for the day. I'm sorry you had to stay late."

"Honey, I stay late all the time. Before last week, I had nothing to come home to."

"Well, you have someone to go home to and with. Are you ready?"

"I am."

"So, how was your day?"

"Good, not as interesting as yours, mostly paperwork."

"I got all sorts of stories about your rescues from your crew!" Shannon grinned at her as she climbed into the Rover.

"I thought you were getting stories on the medics' training?" Simone smiled back at her.

"I am. You wouldn't believe how good they all are. You've got such a talented group of people and they give all the credit to you. Every one of them swears you are responsible for their success."

"They're responsible for their own success."

"I think you've had an enormous influence on all of them. They respect you, Simone, your skills, your honesty, and your affection for all of them. I'm not surprised at all by their attitude. You're incredible."

"I appreciate that, but every one of them worked extremely hard to become a medic. They're all very talented and dedicated."

"They said you would say that." Shannon chuckled as she took Simone's hand in hers as they pulled out of the parking lot. "I'm so proud of you, Simone. You train very good people and medics."

"I love you, Shannon."

"You know what? I love you more and more every day."

"So what do you say to a quiet dinner and an early night? You have a very long day tomorrow."

"Sounds very nice, I'm a little tired."

They arrived home to find the other four women already seated at the table eating a dinner of fresh fruit and cracked crab. They had been sightseeing all day long at the volcano and were planning on another hike in the morning around the Waikeloa lava fields. The six women visited for several hours and then Shannon's eyes began to droop. After a suggestion from Mel, she headed off to bed as Simone helped Mel and Janice wash the dishes.

"Simone, how're you doing?"

"Terrific, how about you guys. How's the vacation going?"

"Excellent, we love it here. Janice and I are going to look for retirement property here."

"Good. I might be able to help you with that."

"You have done enough for all of us, Simone."

"That's what friends do." Simone smiled as she put the last plate away. "You know Mel and Janice, both of you could get jobs here as firemen if you wanted to. We're always looking for good, trained firemen."

"I think we are going to try and get our twenty years in where we are. Mel will be there in six years, I will be there in eleven. But that doesn't mean we can't come visit as often as possible, especially since we can visit you and Shannon. Shannon is going to move here, isn't she?"

"Yes, as soon as she sells her condo, and moves her things."

"Good, we think you're perfect together."

"So do I." Simone put the last of the pans away. "Well ladies, I'm going to go crawl in bed. Have a good time tomorrow."

"Hey Simone, how was your picnic last night?"

Simone colored as she responded to Janice's question. "It was wonderful."

Mel and Janice chuckled at her embarrassment. "Shannon threatened us with death if we even came out on to the patio."

"It was beautiful, and quite a surprise."

"I've never known Shannon to go through such efforts to impress a girlfriend. She loves you, Simone."

"The feeling is entirely mutual. Goodnight." Simone hugged them both.

"Goodnight."

Janice and Mel watched as Simone headed down the hall to her bedroom. "I sure like that woman," Mel commented.

"So do I, she's just as nice as a person could be. And I like the way she treats Shannon."

"So, what do you think of a late night swim?" Janice suggested as she snuggled up to Mel.

"With or without suits?"

"I think its dark enough for us to go without. What do you think?"

"I think that's a great idea. I'll go grab some towels."

Simone entered the bedroom expecting to find Shannon asleep. She was surprised to find Shannon sitting up in bed, a tablet on her lap. She had obviously been working on her project.

"Hi, honey."

"I thought you were going to sleep?"

"I couldn't without you."

"Ha, you can't fool me, you were working."

"I was, but only until you came to bed."

"Give me a minute to clean up and I'll join you."

Shannon stuffed her tablet in her bag and put her things away before climbing back into bed. She was exhausted, but a little wired after having a successful day filming.

"Did you know all four want to find a retirement place here?"

"I did, they love it in Hawaii."

"I'm going to introduce them to a friend of mine that sells real estate."

"I've decided that you always take care of everyone. It's so much a part of you that it's automatic," Shannon responded as Simone climbed into bed. "I love that about you. You are so generous."

"I'm no different than you and your friends."

Shannon decided to let it drop as she snuggled up to Simone. "I love you just the way you are."

"I love you." Simone turned and kissed Shannon slowly, drawing it out as she tasted the one woman she desired above anything. They kissed for several minutes before settling down for a night of sleep, both tired and very comfortable with sleeping together. Shannon threw her leg over Simone's hips, her head next to Simone's on the pillow. Simone tucked her fingers in Shannon's and slid into a deep slumber.

CHAPTER 15

By Friday morning, Shannon was exhausted and very satisfied with her filming. She had a short meeting with Art and Susan and then she was going home for a nap. She'd been up for over eighteen hours filming and interviewing the medics while her friends had gone out dancing.

"Hi Christa, I didn't know you were going to be here. Want to see some film?"

"I'd love to. How's it going?"

"Excellent."

"You look tired, Shannon. How is your back?" Christa kept her question quiet, but she was a little concerned.

"I'm fine, Christa. It's just been a long night."

"Hey, Shannon, Susan said you've got some film for us," Art commented as he entered the editing room.

"I do. I ran out of tape this morning so it was perfect timing. Let's set this up and see what you think."

Despite Shannon's exhaustion, she was pumped with adrenaline when it came to her videos. An hour later so were Christa, Art, and Susan, and they'd only seen a third of her tapes.

"Shannon, this is good," Art commented as he watched. "You have a lot of good tape and we only need thirty minutes. It'll be hard to trim it down."

"I just have a little bit more to get to finish it. I've got a killer ending." Shannon shared excitement in her voice. "I should be done by Monday evening, will that work?"

"What do you think Susan, Christa?"

"I don't think we need any more tape, but if Shannon wants to film a little more, I'd say great. I can begin wading through this and matching it up to our script and our voice-overs," Susan responded.

"I'd say we are creating a winner," Christa volunteered. She was surprisingly impressed with the quality of Shannon's work. Not only was the camera work first rate, the interviewing was extremely well done.

"Good. Art, I need some more blanks, please."

"No problem, Shannon. I'll load you up." Art began to stuff Shannon's camera bag full of blank tapes. "How's the camera working?"

"Like a dream."

"Good."

"Well, guys, I am going to get out of here. I'll be back first thing Tuesday morning with the rest of the film, if that's okay?"

"Works for us, see you Tuesday, and get some rest, Shannon."

"I will. See you." Shannon was busting out of the door when Christa touched her on the arm.

"Can I speak with you for one minute?"

"Certainly." Shannon followed Christa into her office. "Is everything okay?"

"Relax, Shannon. Everything is fine. First, I want to tell you that I am very impressed with your work. Your camera work is spectacular and your interview skills are equally as good. Why aren't you doing more reporting?"

"I don't like to do interviews, I really like being behind the camera."

"I've been in this business a long time, and I have rarely seen such talent in a cameraman. I want you to know that I'll recommend to the network that they offer you a job."

"Thanks, I appreciate that, but I want to make sure any job I get will be because of my skills as a cameraman."

Christa wanted to grin but she schooled her reactions while she prepared her response. "Shannon, if I'm not mistaken, Art has been in the news director's office since you left the editing room to show him your work. Art will tell him to hire you before someone else does. I'll bet you ten bucks that he'll bring up the offer on Tuesday morning. Art is in charge of all editors, but he has a huge influence over our camera crew." Shannon was too surprised to respond as she absorbed Christa's words. She was tired, shocked, and unable to respond. "Oh, and by the way, I wouldn't offer a recommendation if I didn't think you had the talent."

"Thank you, I appreciate it very much."

"Shannon, I really do want to see you and Simone make it."

"And if I hurt Simone a little bit you'll kill me." Shannon grinned at her.

"That too." Christa laughed at Shannon's comment. "But I'm not worried about that."

"Either am I."

"Good, get out of here, you need to get some sleep. Is your back really okay?"

"Yes, it's healing and just itches. I'm fine, other than I don't know how the medics and firemen do what they do all night long. It's exhausting, and I am more impressed than ever by all of them."

"Your video shows that. I think Simone and her medics are going to be very pleased with what you've done."

Shannon's eyes filled with tears due to exhaustion and emotion. "I hope so, it's very important that the respect they have for each other, and the unbelievable job Simone does training them, comes across."

Christa smiled at the obviously emotional woman. "I think it will more than come across. Now go. Neely and I will see all of you Saturday night at the luau."

"See you." Shannon strode out of Christa office and down the hallway.

Christa was still smiling when she picked up her telephone. "Honey, it's me. You were right."

"Of course I was, about what specifically?"

"Shannon and Simone."

"What happened?"

"I just saw Shannon's film. Neely, it's incredible. When I offered to give her a job recommendation she all but refused it. She wants to make sure she gets a job on her talent and experience."

"Wouldn't you?"

"Of course I would. When I told her I thought she'd done a wonderful job, she became teary, worried that she hadn't gotten across the fact that the medics were good because Simone had trained them. Neely, she has done that and more."

"Good for her."

"You're going to be amazed."

"I'm not surprised."

"I like her, Neely. And I like her and Simone together, they fit."

"They do."

"Like us."

"Just like us. What do you think about a little sushi and an early night?"

"How about sushi in bed?"

"Even better, see you later."

"Bye honey." Christa grabbed her jacket and her briefcase and sailed out of her office. She had work to do.

Shannon was dragging as she entered the empty house and headed straight back for the bedroom. All she wanted to do was flop on the bed and sleep for hours, and that was exactly what she did.

CHAPTER 16

She was sound asleep at three o'clock when her friends came back from tour-ing art galleries and she was still sleeping when Simone walked through the door at four.

"Hello," she called as she passed them in the kitchen. "Is Shannon still sleep-ing?" Simone had called earlier and spoken to Mel.

"Yes, she's sound asleep. We keep checking on her, but she's out like a light."

"She's had a long week."

"How did the videotaping go?"

"I haven't seen any of it. Shannon won't show it to me. But Christa called this afternoon and she's seen most of it. She says it's fantastic." Simone grinned at the foursome. "And Christa doesn't say that unless she means it."

"Shannon's very talented."

"Yes, she is. I think I'm going to go wake her up."

"Take your time we're going to barbeque around six."

"Great, what can I do?"

"Go spend some time with your girlfriend, we have it covered."

Simone didn't have to be told twice. She entered the bedroom and shut the door. Turning to Shannon, she almost laughed when she saw her girlfriend. Shannon had obviously gotten warm because she was in the middle of the bed, the covers thrown on the floor, her tee shirt wadded up next to them. She was face down. The only thing she was wearing was a pair of pale yellow thong underwear. Simone felt the infusion of heat as she watched her girlfriend sleep. She really liked how comfortable Shannon was with her body. Simone dropped her briefcase and began to shed her clothes. She was going to wake Shannon up very carefully. Simone slid on to the bed and bent over Shannon's body, her lips softly drifting over her shoulders.

"Mm, that feels good." Shannon's muffled voice rose from the pillow.

"Don't move it's going to feel much better in a minute."

Simone let her lips drift over the still healing back and legs of her lover, and spent most of her time kissing the firm backside that had somehow avoided being injured. Her hands slowly slipped the underwear down Shannon's legs as her lips followed down each calf and thigh. Simone covered every inch of Shannon as she teased her with faint touches, the trail of her tongue, and the soft, sensuous feel of her lips. This was lovemaking that lulled Shannon into a haze of pleasure so acute she couldn't move. She could barely moan as Simone wooed her. The sound of the vibrator made her body shiver as Simone touched her buttocks rolling the vibrator against her skin. Shannon's breathing became labored as anticipation built rapidly. The vibrator slid between her cheeks and Shannon almost shot off the bed, her hands gripping the pillow. Slowly Simone slid up and down getting closer and closer to Shannon's quivering, wet center.

"Simone, please!" Shannon cried out as she trembled with a need so huge it made her ache.

Simone rolled her body between Shannon's legs and slid the vibrator against her slick lips as her fingers spread her wide open. She entered Shannon slowly, prolonging the pleasure as long as possible. Stroking deeply, while Shannon's hips pushed against her, she brought Shannon to an orgasm that shook the bed. Simone removed the vibrator and turned it off before lying down next to Shannon, who lay panting on the bed.

Shannon rolled over and turned to her, pulling Simone's face closer, capturing her in a kiss that tugged at Simone's toes.

"Come here," Shannon demanded, rolling Simone's body on top of hers.

Spreading Simone's legs she settled Simone against her lower body, which still tingled with pleasure. Reaching for the silent vibrator on the bed, Shannon turned it on and using her fingers she opened Simone's lips and slid the vibrator between the two of them.

"Kneel over my hips."

Simone did as Shannon asked, her body sealed tightly against Shannon and the vibrator. Shannon sat up and wrapped her arm around Simone's hips pulling her even tighter against her body. Simone's arms were around Shannon's neck as she began to shiver. The feel of the vibrator and Shannon's body so intimately joined to hers was overwhelming as her hips began to move.

Simone's head dropped on to Shannon's shoulder as she slammed her hips against Shannon's in a dance as old as time. An orgasm began to move through her body in waves and Shannon felt it radiate from Simone. She removed the vibrator and shoved her fingers deep inside of Simone.

"Shannon!"

Simone cried out as she slumped against her, her body no longer able to contain the desire that she was feeling. Her hips continued to pound against Shannon's and she reached own to slide her own fingers against Shannon before entering her. Shannon and Simone's body were in a frenzy of pleasure and sex, mindless physical gratification. Simone began to cry on Shannon's shoulder no longer able to contain her feelings or the extraordinary reactions she was having. Shannon followed rapidly, her body dissolving into a quivering mass as she lay back on the bed, bringing Simone's body with her. Both of them lay panting on the bed, exhausted, overwhelmed, and completely surprised at the intensity of their lovemaking.

They drifted off, close to sleep, in the netherworld of satisfied lovers who don't want the world to intrude for a little bit longer. Floating on their feelings, they stayed intimately joined at their hips, their faces tight against one another's.

Shannon was the first to stir as she stroked down Simone's back leisurely enjoying her lover's lean, strong body. "Do you always wake your lovers like that?"

Simone heard the humor in Shannon's voice and smiled. "Never before today."

"It was overwhelming and perfect."

"Yes, it was. Shannon, I am amazed at how perfect making love with you is, every time it is so much more than I have ever dreamed of."

Shannon turned to face Simone, her eyes still heavy lidded from passion. "It's the same for me but I think that's because we're in love with each other. It makes it even more special and meaningful."

Simone's finger traced down Shannon's nose and over her lips. "You mean it has nothing to do with the fact that you're beautiful and have a fantastic body."

"Not any more than that you're the sexiest woman alive," Shannon grinned at her.

"I'm not the one who wears these," Simone teased as she held up Shannon's thong underwear.

"They're very comfortable."

"And sexy."

"I'm glad you like them. Maybe I can talk you into putting your uniform back on. It has the same effect on me."

Simone's heart filled with emotion at Shannon's comment. All her life she had wanted to be with a woman who recognized her love of being a paramedic, and in one week Shannon had made it clear that that was a big part of her attraction.

"I love you."

"I love you, I need you, and I can't keep my hands off of you."

"Good, I love your hands on me." Simone smiled at her lover. "We'd better get up. Dinner is being planned as we speak. We're barbequing."

"Sounds perfect, dinner on the patio, a nice warm night, and my lover in my arms, what more could I want."

"Christa called me this afternoon."

"Was she reporting on me?" Shannon voice had a little edge of irritation.

Simone heard it and understood. "No, actually she called to brag. She is taking credit for asking you to make the video. She said the film work was in her words, incredible. She's very excited."

"It is good."

"I have no doubts, my girlfriend is extremely talented."

"You haven't seen anything I've done."

"I don't have to see it, I saw how you work. There wasn't a person at the station who didn't respond to you, even the Chief."

"He's a pushover."

"Shannon, he's a crusty, old nut who thinks you're a doll."

"I like him."

"So do I. Now, when do I get to see the video?"

"This coming week when we get done editing it, we'll show you and Neely first, and then you can show the Chief and the guys at the station. I would say by mid-week."

"Good, I can't wait."

"It has been so much fun to do this."

"Maybe when you move here you could do more videos like this? There is always some group who needs this kind of thing."

"Maybe, what do you say to a shower with me?"

"I'd say I'd love to."

The two of them took their time showering and Shannon washed her hair. She was just getting dressed into a pair of shorts and a tank top when Janice knocked on the door. "Shannon, you have a telephone call."

"Okay, Janice. Thanks." Shannon picked up the telephone as Simone finished getting dressed and straightening the bed. "Hello."

"Shannon, Art here. Could you come to the station in the morning around nine?"

"Yes, what's up Art? Is there something wrong?"

"Not at all, everything's fine. My boss wants to meet with you and tomorrow is the best time."

"Why does your boss want to meet with me?"

"He wants to offer you a job."

Shannon dropped to the bed in surprise. "You're kidding?"

"Shannon, do you think I'm a kidder? He saw your work and was impressed. Nine o'clock at the station, and don't dress up. He said beach casual."

"I'll be there, Art. Thanks."

"No thanks needed. I like your work too."

Shannon sat on the bed, the receiver still in her hand. She didn't know what to think. This was such a surprise. She knew she was good with a camera, but this was unexpected.

"Shannon, is everything okay?" Simone approached her, concern on her face.

"Everything is perfect, just perfect!" Shannon threw the telephone down and grabbed Simone pulling her on to the bed. "I'm meeting with Art's boss in the morning. He wants to offer me a job! Can you believe it? He wants to talk to me about a job!"

"Oh, Shannon, that's wonderful. I'm not surprised, that's so cool! When do you have to be there?"

"Nine in the morning, and I'm to dress beach casual."

"Would you want to work for that station?"

"Simone, it's the largest and most well known on the islands. It would give me so many opportunities, but they haven't offered it to me yet. Let's not say anything until after tomorrow's meeting. I don't want to nix it."

"But your friends would want to know, they have been your biggest supporters."

"Not yet, please. What if it doesn't work out, or he doesn't like me. I don't want to tell anyone until after tomorrow."

"Okay." Simone was surprised to see the hidden insecurities that Shannon had. She was so confident and competent while she worked, and Simone knew that Shannon took her work very seriously. Simone would pray that the meeting was successful. Not just that it would make Shannon's move easier but it would validate her talents as a cameraman. Simone understood how important Shannon's work was to her. "Come on, let's go eat."

Dinner was laid back and just what they all needed as the six women sat on the patio until late in the night, talking and enjoying the breeze off the water. One more week of paradise and they were all back to their jobs in Seattle. Despite Shannon's earlier injuries, the vacation was more than a huge success. It was after eleven before Simone and Shannon said goodnight and turned in. Shannon and Simone rolled together in the middle of the bed, and holding each other tightly, dropped into heavy sleep. Simone was going to take Shannon to her interview in the morning while the rest of the group was going for a little early morning snorkeling with Marcus and Leo before the luau. The luau was on the other end of the island, put on by Neely's family, and they were all looking forward to it.

CHAPTER 17

"Well, Shannon, what do you think? Do you want to work for us? We have plenty of opportunities for someone with your talents." Jim Shaw was the head of the Hawaiian television news network. He had worked for many years as a news anchor in Los Angeles for one of the major networks, before coming to Hawaii. He knew the business well. He also knew talent when he saw it. Art had provided him with tapes of Shannon's work and her work history. She had plenty of talent and Jim always made room in the network for talented people. It's what made his network successful.

"It sounds very nice, Mr. Shaw. Could I think about it and call you back in a couple of hours?"

"Shannon, call me Jim. That would be fine. Take the package with you and review it. Here's my cell phone number in case you have any questions regarding anything in the offer. Working in Hawaii is different than anywhere else, Shannon. We're very good and run a well-regarded network but we aren't quite as structured as you might find in other networks. We still want talent working for us and from what I have seen, you're very talented. We would like to see you work here."

"The offer is very nice and I know your network is award winning. I would be honored to work for you. I just need to talk it over with my partner before taking the job."

"That's very smart," Jim smiled. "My wife would kill me if I made such a big decision without discussing it with her."

Shannon had told Jim she was a lesbian so that there would be no misunderstandings. He had smiled and said that it was a non-issue. Shannon believed him. "I'll let you know by this afternoon."

"I appreciate that. Now, get out of here and go make your decision. The day is too beautiful to stay inside. I am going to take my girls out on the boat."

"I'm going. Thanks again, Jim."

"Thank me by taking the job." Jim stood up and shook Shannon's hand. "I'd really like to see you work for us."

"I would too." Shannon grinned as she turned to leave. The offer was more than fair and she couldn't wait to tell Simone.

"Well?" Art stood in the hallway.

"It's a great offer, Art. I just need to talk to Simone about it before I accept."

"You are going to aren't you?"

"I can't see why not," Shannon laughed. "Art, thanks. I know you had everything to do with it."

"Hey, it makes my life easier if we have competent people behind the camera, and you're competent."

"Thanks, I think." Shannon grinned at the gruff man, who hid a huge heart. "I'll see you Tuesday morning."

"Early."

"I'll be here." Shannon all but floated out of the building and raced across the parking lot to where Simone sat in the car with a book.

"They offered me a job?" Shannon blurted out as she flung the car door open.

"A good one?" Simone grinned at her very excited girlfriend.

"A great one, they even offered to pick up some of the relocation expenses, and the salary is a lot more than I make now. They're offering me a senior cameraman position."

"What's that mean?" Simone couldn't help but smile at her lover. She was all over the seat, bubbling with emotion.

"It means I get to pick my stories, and I get to work on specials and things, not just news items."

"Did you take the job?"

"Not yet. I told Jim Shaw I needed to talk to my partner first. I told him I'm gay and that I have a lover."

Simone felt her heart swell in her chest. She'd always wanted a lover who considered her as important as her job. She didn't want to be kept in the background. "So do you want the job?"

Shannon turned to Simone and grasped her hands. "I do, if you still want me to move here. It's important that you be a part of the decision. I would work odd hours and be on call. I would be out all times of the day and night, depending on the work."

"Shannon, do you want the job?" Simone smiled as she repeated her question.

"Yes, I do."

Simone gathered Shannon to her and hugged her. "Then I suggest you tell them you want it."

"Really?"

"Shannon, you'll be here with me, that's all I care about. I want you to take the job. It sounds perfect."

"Let me show you the salary and benefits before I call Jim and accept. I may have missed something and we can get it clarified before I take it." Shannon shoved the packet at Simone, who calmly took it.

"I'm proud of you, Shannon." Simone bent to kiss her.

Shannon's arms slid around Simone's neck and she responded, kissing Simone slowly. "It was my lucky day when I met you on the beach."

"Now, let's look at the offer." Simone opened the folder as Shannon hung over her arm. Simone was more than impressed with the job package. The salary was considerably more than she was making, there were full healthcare benefits, a bonus and retirement package, and a substantial relocation sum. She couldn't see anything wrong with it. The only problem she saw was that they wanted Shannon to report to work a month from this coming Monday and that didn't leave her much time to move.

"Shannon, you would need to be here in a month. That only leaves you two weeks to be packed and moved."

"I know, but I think I can do it. They have a moving company I'm supposed to call. They will even move my car. They also have a real estate agent for me to contact to sell my condo. All I need to do is give notice at work and pack. They'll take care of everything else."

Simone looked up at Shannon and placed her hand against her cheek. "Than I think you should go home and tell your friends about it and then call and accept the offer."

"Simone, it's incredible. It's like my life is some amazing dream with everything I've ever wanted coming true." Shannon started to cry. "I'm afraid I'll wake up and it will all be over with."

"This is as real as it gets, honey." Simone picked her hand up and kissed her fingers. "Now, we need to head home so you can tell your friends and I can start planning the studio. You're going to need one. Besides, with what you are making, we can afford it."

Shannon giggled as Simone started the car. "Do you think I should sell my car and get a new one? I have a two door Miata. I think I would rather have a jeep or something like the Rover."

"I think we can afford a new car. It's pretty expensive to move the car so it's probably smarter to sell it. How about if we stop at the car dealership next week and look around?"

"This is so cool."

Simone agreed with Shannon, it was very cool. They stopped at the grocery store for a few things and then the two of them spent the rest of the morning on the beach. All the girls showed up at the house around two with Marcus and Leo in tow, and Shannon told them about the job. It was unanimous that she take it, and with Simone standing right next to her, Shannon called Jim Shaw and accepted.

"Well that's it. I start work one month from next Monday here in Hawaii. I'll call my boss on Monday morning and give him verbal notice."

"I have a suggestion." Simone took Shannon by the hand and tugged her into the living room to sit on the couch. "Why don't I fly back with you in a week and I can help pack and take care of things. I have the vacation time and can get at least a week off."

"I would love that." Shannon slid her arms around Simone's waist. "I don't want to be away from you any longer than I have to."

"I'll juggle my schedule next week and see what I can do. Meanwhile, I want you to write down everything you want in a studio, and I mean everything. I want you to draw it out exactly the way you would like it."

"I can do that."

"Good, now I'm going to go clean up before the party."

"Can I join you?"

"No, because I'll never get cleaned up, we'll just end up in bed," Simone teased as she kissed her. "Go share your good news with your friends, I'll be out shortly."

"I love you, Simone."

"You know what Shannon? I love you, and I'm very proud of you. You got the job on your talents and I can't wait to see what you will do here in Hawaii."

Shannon's eyes filled with tears as she watched her girlfriend head down the hallway to the bedroom. She sat on the couch, overwhelmed by her good fortune.

"Shannon, are you okay?" Hanna joined her on the couch, her eyes full of concern.

"I'm wonderful, Hanna. It's just so amazing to have everything you've every wanted in life handed to you. I feel so incredibly lucky."

"Shannon, nothing has been handed to you. You have worked amazingly long hours to be a great cameraman. You work harder than anyone I know. You earned your job."

"But I also found Simone."

"And she found you. Do you think that it's going to be easy to make your relationship work? This is just the beginning. You and Simone will have to put out a lot of effort to make your life together successful. You both have been given a wonderful opportunity and I am glad you're taking advantage of it."

"Thanks, Hanna. I'm going to miss you."

"Shannon, we can e-mail and talk on the telephone, and you know we'll visit as often as possible."

Shannon and Hanna hugged tightly; Shannon was extremely emotional. "Hey guys, what's up?"

"Hey, Mel, I'm just a little weepy."

"Well, knock it off we have a party to attend."

"You're right I'm going to go change my clothes. I'll be right back."

"Is she okay, Hanna?"

"She's fine, a little overwhelmed at everything that's going on."

"The job offer is her perfect job."

"I know, and Simone is her dream partner."

"It's about time."

"Yes, it is."

Shannon slipped out of her shorts and blouse and into a short sundress. Thin sleeves, with no bra and a slit on the side to her hip, it was cool and light and just perfect for an afternoon at a luau. She stuffed her swimming suit in her beach bag along with a towel and her video camera.

"You look amazing." Simone came out of the bathroom and saw Shannon twisting her hair into a knot. She was going to wear it up and off of her neck for the night.

Shannon turned and looked at Simone. "So do you." And she meant it. Simone was wearing a pair of navy shorts and a white tank top. She looked healthy, athletic, and very sexy. "I love you."

"I love you." Simone touched the necklace sparkling against Shannon's cleavage. "This looks very nice on you."

Shannon slid her arms around Simone's waist, looking up at her. "My girl-friend bought it for me."

"She must like you very much."

"She adores me and I adore her."

"Yes, she does." Simone bent and kissed Shannon, her hands sliding over Shannon's hips and under her dress. "Oh my, what are you wearing?"

"A pair of underwear." Shannon looked through her eyelashes at Simone.

"A pair of thong underwear." Simone ran her hands over Shannon's naked backside.

"We don't have time for this, honey." Shannon ran her lips down Simone's throat.

"I know." Simone sighed and stepped away from Shannon.

Shannon grinned and took her girlfriend by the hand. "Come on, sweetie, we have a party to go to. But I promise you when we get back, we'll have all the time in the world."

Simone moaned, taking Shannon's bag from her as they walked down the hall. "You're killing me wearing that underwear."

"Good, you can think about me all night."

The party was in full swing by the time they all got there. There were over fifty men and women visiting and sitting on blankets on the beach, two men playing the drums, and one strumming on a guitar. There was a fire pit with a grill over it, full of sizzling meat and chicken, along with vegetables. Two large ice buckets were overflowing with beer and pop. Mel and Janice placed their ice chest down next to them, while Hanna and Olivia pulled out their bowls of salad. Everyone who came brought something, which made it a huge banquet of wonderful food. Christa was standing talking to some women and Shannon did a double take when she saw Neely. Neely's hair was loose and flowing over her shoulders down to her waist. She had a bathing suit top on and it revealed full breasts and a very muscular body. She had a lava lava low around her hips with a flower strand around her ankles and wrists, her feet bare. She looked very Hawaiian and very sexy.

"Wow, look at Neely," Janice whispered.

"Simone, is she Hawaiian?" Shannon asked, surprised at the transforma-tion.

"No, she's Samoan. Wait until you see her dance. She does the hula and tra-ditional Tahitian dances."

"She's beautiful."

"Yes she is, inside and out. Those are her brothers on the drums and the guitar. They all take their heritage very seriously."

"That's very cool."

"Yes, it is." Simone took Shannon's hand and started in the direction of Neely and Christa. "Let's go tell them about your job."

"I'm sure Christa already knows."

"Maybe, but you hadn't accepted it yet."

While Simone and Shannon visited with Christa and Neely, the rest of the women were introduced around by Marcus and Leo. It was a friendly group who welcomed the women from Seattle as they settled down to enjoy the afternoon. By dusk, everyone had eaten their fill and the dancing began, starting with a soft, romantic hula. Christa sat next to Simone and Shannon as they watched several women including Neely, dance to the soft strumming of the guitar. They were all mesmerized by the movements and the ancient story telling. Shannon pulled Simone's arms tighter around her as she leaned up and kissed her.

"This is so beautiful, Simone. I can't wait to live here."

"Soon, honey, very soon."

"Look at Christa." Simone and Shannon turned and watched Christa whose eyes were locked on her girlfriend. The love and attraction were evident in her expression as she watched Neely. No one would question their commitment to each other.

"She's beautiful, Christa." Shannon touched Christa on the arm.

"I fell in love with her the first time I saw her dance. It's so much a part of her and her family. It's so important to preserve the history and language. She works so hard to keep Hawaii's legacy."

"Can I help?"

"You already have." Christa turned to Shannon and Simone. "Your video will help us attract and keep our youngsters from leaving the islands, and will encourage them to look for different jobs other than tourism. The more jobs we have available, the healthier the islands become."

"If there are other things I can do, please ask," Shannon requested as Simone smiled at her comment.

Christa had already decided she liked Shannon, she knew she was a very generous and honest woman. "I'll certainly do that, and Neely will appreciate your offer. She doesn't turn anyone down."

The beat of the drum moved from a hula to a much faster more sensuous beat and Christa grinned. "Watch this."

Shannon turned and all but gasped. Neely and the other women were dancing what was a traditional Tahitian dance where their hips moved in a blur.
Two men joined them as the drums pounded faster and their hips gyrated. "Oh
my God, that's incredible!"

The whole crowd grew silent as the pounding of the drums grew louder and
the dancers continued their frenzied movements. One by one they dropped
out until Neely and her cousin were the only ones left. Sweat poured down the
naked chest of the man as the two of them stood face to face, their hips moving
rapidly as their feet pounded the sand. With a loud cry, they both stopped and
hugged each other, laughing as they grinned at the applause that thundered
around them. Neely was thrown a towel and she caught it and toweled her face
as she walked over to Christa who stood up to greet her.

"I'm getting old. I used to be able to beat Loua at dancing," she chuckled as
she sat down on the chair that Christa had vacated.

"Neely, that was unbelievable. The hula was so beautiful but that was amazing. How do you do it?"

"I grew up dancing. You should see my mother. She's the best."

"Aren't you exhausted?"

"A little, but I'll get my second wind."

"Who are you kidding? She can dance all night," Christa interrupted, taking
the towel from her girlfriend and drying her shoulders and back off. "I've seen
her and her family dance for days. Don't let her fool you, she can out dance,
out surf, and out work any of us."

"Come here." Neely tugged Christa down to kiss her.

Shannon turned to Simone and whispered in her ear, "I like the two of
them."

"So do I. Can I talk you into a walk?"

"Sure." Shannon stood up and pulled Simone out of her chair and took her
hand. "I'd love to go on a walk in the moonlight with my girlfriend."

The crowd was so busy no one noticed when Shannon and Simone headed
down the beach. It was empty and they strolled along the water's edge, enjoying the quiet, and the light breeze that came from the ocean. Just out of earshot
and eyesight, Simone turned into Shannon and wrapped her arms around her.
Shannon's face turned up to Simone's as they kissed, Shannon's tongue sliding
through Simone's mouth as their lips meshed. They kissed as the breeze ruffled
around them, the moonlight glowing off the water. They broke apart and continued walking along the shore back toward the party. Standing at the outskirts

behind everyone Shannon stood in front of Simone, Simone's arms around her shoulders.

"Shannon, stay right in front of me," Simone whispered as one of her hands slid under her dress in the back and ran over her backside.

"Simone, what…" Shannon moaned as Simone's fingers drove into her.

Simone held her tightly with one arm as she stroked her deeply bringing her quickly to an orgasm five feet from the crowd. Shannon shivered as she bit her lip to keep from crying out. The combination of getting caught and the rush of lust that raced through her body almost brought Shannon to her knees. Simone leaned into her, holding her tightly against her body, her lips sliding along her bare shoulders and neck. Shannon raised an arm up and wrapped it around Simone's neck, leaning back into her as she was rocked with an orgasm. She turned her face into Simone's neck, smothering her moans while Simone continued to pleasure her. Over and over, Simone slid inside her body while Shannon was completely enthralled with her lovemaking. Shannon began to tremble as her body could no longer contain the assault on her senses. She stiffened and then slumped against Simone as Simone wrapped her arms around her holding her tightly while she shivered and shook.

"I love you, Shannon. I love your body, the way you smell, the way you taste, and the way you melt when I love you. I will never grow tired of touching you." Simone ran her lips along Shannon's neck as she whispered softly in her ear. "No one saw or heard you but me."

Shannon turned in her lover's arms as she locked her arms around her neck, a slight smile on her face. "You wanted my fantasy to come true."

"Only with me." Simone breathed against her mouth before loving her with her kiss. "Always with me."

Shannon melted against Simone as she shared another toe curling kiss, her body still throbbing with pleasure. "I can't believe what you do to me."

"Did you enjoy it?"

"What do you think?" Shannon's smiled up at her lover.

Simone licked her fingers as she watched Shannon's face flush again with passion. "I know I enjoyed it."

"Simone…" Shannon rubbed her body against Simone's. "You're making me crazy here. Wait until we get home."

"I'm looking forward to it." Simone hugged her once more. "I'm going to find the bathroom."

"I'll go find the girls."

Simone headed up the path as Shannon walked over to where Mel and Janice were seated talking to Leo. "Hey guys, how are you doing?"

"Good, how about you."

"Great, this party has been a blast. We've met so many nice people."

"Where's Simone?"

"She went to the bathroom. Have you seen Hanna and Olivia?"

"Yep, over there with Neely and Christa. Neely's brother was teaching them the hula."

"Boy, I have to see this!" Shannon grinned as she looked around for the group. She caught sight of Neely and Olivia moving in the dark and headed over to where they were, in time to see Olivia finish a hula dance with Neely and her brother.

"Nice job." Shannon clapped as she approached them.

"Thanks, Neely and her brother are teaching me."

"Very beautiful."

"Shannon, you haven't met my brother, Tio. Tio, this is Shannon. She's the woman who saved that young boy from drowning last week."

"Hello, Shannon, it's nice to meet you. You're also making a video about paramedic training, right?"

"I'm helping with it."

"Don't let her fool you, she's a very talented cameraman," Christa stated as she stepped up to the group.

"Would you be interested in helping with a video to record the history of the hula?"

"I would, very much."

"Great. Neely, we can get Mom and Aunt Leoni to help us."

"I think we should let Shannon get moved and settled in her new job before we ask her to take on another video."

"Okay, but once you have some time, let Neely know." Tio grinned, hugging his sister. He was huge, well over six feet, with a massive chest and arms, his thighs all but splitting the lava lava wrapped around his waist, Neely looked tiny being hugged by him. He turned to pick Christa up in a bear hug that made her laugh before setting her on her feet. "I've got to go. I've got a group to take out tomorrow."

"Be careful, Tio."

"Aloha." He slipped away in the crowd, a gentle giant moving gracefully on the balls of his feet.

"He's wonderful, Neely."

"Yes, he is. He works way too hard."

"What does he do?"

"He runs his own contractor's firm during the week, and on weeknights and weekends he takes tour groups around the island to show tourists the sacred areas."

"Does he have a family?"

"Tio, he's too busy to settle down." Neely chuckled as she responded. "But we have hope."

"How big is your family?"

"I have four brothers and one sister. My sister and three brothers are all married, and at last count there were fifteen nieces and nephews."

"Wow that is a big family."

Christa burst into laughter. "That's only her brothers and sisters. Her cousins number in the hundreds. The last family party we went to there were over two hundred relatives before I lost count."

Neely grinned as she hugged Christa to her. "They all came to see our wedding, honey."

Christa and Neely shared a sweet kiss, as Simone joined them. "I ran into Mel and Janice and they're ready to head home."

"So are we," Hanna announced as she took Olivia by the hand. "We're going to go back to the house and practice our hula dancing."

"Neely and Christa, thanks for inviting us. We had a wonderful time."

"You're very welcome, and congratulations on your new job."

"Thank you."

"By the way Shannon, don't you owe me ten dollars?" Christa grinned at her. She couldn't help but remind Shannon of her earlier bet.

"I do, and I'll gladly pay it." Shannon grinned at Christa.

The ladies gathered all their things and climbed into the Rover. Within minutes they were headed for home. The six women were silent as they made the twenty-five minute drive back to the house, Shannon snuggled up to Simone. Sunday was going to be a lazy day of sun and swimming in Simone's backyard.

"Simone, thanks for driving tonight."

"You're welcome."

'You have wonderful friends."

"I do, I'm very lucky to have all of you."

"So Hanna and Olivia, are you going to show us how to hula in the morning?" Mel teased her friends.

"I don't think we'll be ready for a show by tomorrow," Hanna chuckled as she and Olivia snuggled in the backseat next to Mel and Janice.

Simone parked the Rover and they all piled out of the car and entered the house. Shannon tucked her fingers in Simone's as they walked down the hall and into their bedroom. Simone shut the door and turned to face Shannon who stood at the foot of the bed.

"Simone."

"Yes."

"Come here, please."

Simone stood in front of Shannon and gathered her hands in her own. "Did you have a good time tonight?"

"I had a wonderful time, especially when you made love to me with everyone standing within ear shot. You made my fantasy come true."

"I love you, Shannon."

"I know you do." Shannon slowly slid Simone's shirt up off of her body and dropped it on the floor. Even slower she unzipped Simone's shorts and slid them down her legs to remove them. She unclasped Simone's bra and stood gazing at her near naked lover. "You're so beautiful."

Shannon pulled Simone over to the bed and gently pushed her to a seat. She kicked off her sandals and lifted the dress up over her head before dropping it on a chair. She moved up to Simone and parted her legs so she could stand between them. She ran her finger down Simone's breast and lower down her flat stomach, stopping just above the waistband of her panties. Simone's soft blue eyes never left Shannon's face as her skin rippled from Shannon's touch.

"Lay back on the bed, honey."

Simone slid back and lay flat as she watched Shannon carefully. Shannon slowly removed Simone's panties and then her own before climbing on to the bed and rolling on top of her, she propped herself up to look into Simone's face. "God, I think you're so beautiful."

Simone started to reach up for Shannon but Shannon gently surrounded Simone's wrists with her fingers. Shannon stretched Simone's arms up over her head as she smiled down at her. "I want you to hold on to the railing and not let go."

"Shannon…"

"Trust me honey, I'm just going to love you until you scream, like I promised."

Simone moaned as Shannon's mouth surrounded Simone's nipple, sucking on it as she massaged her breasts. Over and over, Shannon's lips and tongue teased Simone's nipples as Simone struggled to keep from grabbing Shannon. Shannon's knees spread Simone's legs wide until she was resting against her, her stomach sealed against Simone's wet lips. Simone rolled her hips as she groaned in anticipation.

"I need to touch you."

"Not yet, honey."

Shannon's lips traveled over Simone's stomach kissing and placing small bites along her hipbones and down the tops of her thighs. Simone cried out with pleasure as her hips rolled back and forth on the bed. Shannon's mouth traveled down both of Simone's legs and she nuzzled behind Simone's knee, along her calf, and kissed the arch of her foot. Simone was ready to explode from Shannon's attentions as she tossed and turned.

Shannon pushed Simone's legs up until they were bent, her feet even with her hips. Shannon's hands traced down Simone's thighs and stopped at the juncture of her legs. Shannon bent her head and lightly touched Simone's glistening moist lips with her tongue. Simone cried out as she jerked against Shannon's mouth. Slowly Shannon ran her tongue against her as Simone shook. Shannon smiled as Simone's body flooded with moisture just beckoning Shannon to taste her. Pink and swollen, Simone's body begged for Shannon's mouth to cover her, but Shannon had other plans. Moving up on her knees, Shannon straddled Simone's thigh placing her wet center directly against Simone's and pressed her body tightly against her. Moving slowly, she rubbed against Simone, both of their bodies fused at the center.

"Oh God!" Simone choked on a scream as Shannon rubbed harder and faster, pushing one of Simone's legs up to open her even wider. No two women could be closer and Shannon knew Simone needed that connection. She felt the instant Simone's body began to spiral and her fingers entered her deeply, driving her totally over the edge. Simone could no longer stay still as she sat up still intimately connected to Shannon and wrapped her arms around Shannon's hips pulling her even tighter against her body as her hips pounded against Shannon's. Shannon pulled her fingers from Simone and grabbed her hips as they slid against each other, faster and harder until they both slumped together in the middle of the bed, panting.

"Jesus, Shannon." Simone gasped as she lay across Shannon's stomach trying to catch her breath. Shannon was unable to respond as she lay on the bed still shaken by her own orgasm. Shannon reached for Simone's hands and grasped them tightly, barely able to move, her body limp. They fell asleep on top of the bed, still entangled as their bodies relaxed and their hearts stopped pounding. Sometime during the night, Shannon pulled the blanket over the two of them as they slept in the middle of the bed, still connected with each other, unwilling to let go.

Simone woke up early and smiled as she looked at Shannon asleep next to her. She filled with heat as she thought of their evening of lovemaking. She ran her hand down Shannon's naked back as she thought of her inhibited response the night before.

Simone slid out of bed and gathered their clothes up with a chuckle. Her bedroom looked like a bomb went off. She went into the bathroom and washed up, putting her bathrobe on. She'd let Shannon sleep awhile longer, she'd had a pretty busy week. Simone headed for the coffeemaker, pleased to see it was full of freshly brewed Kona Gold. Grabbing her favorite mug Simone headed out her back door and took a seat on the chaise lounge. She lay back and sipped her coffee enjoying the clear morning sunshine and the sound of the surf.

She was drinking her second cup of coffee when Shannon slipped up behind her. "Can I join you?"

"Of course." Simone pulled her down next to her on the lounge. "Good morning."

"Good morning. Is everything okay?"

Simone kissed Shannon, answering her without a word. Simone wrapped her arms around Shannon as they lay quietly on the chaise. "Shannon, I love you."

"Honey, I love you to death. Do you think when we get married we can have the ceremony here on the beach at the house?"

"I don't know why not." Simone kissed her girlfriend.

For another hour they were alone on the patio, half asleep as they enjoyed their time together. Janice was the first to slip out of the house, and then Hanna, joining the two of them for a cup of coffee.

The rest of the day, they all enjoyed the beach, swimming and sleeping. It was a perfect day, one that they all would remember. Shannon videotaped as they played and visited, before they all headed in for an early night of sleep.

CHAPTER 18

Monday flew by for both Simone and Shannon. For over an hour Shannon interviewed Simone while taping her for the video. Simone was pleasantly surprised at how professional and charming Shannon was while she interviewed Simone. She asked all sorts of probing questions, but Simone didn't feel intruded upon as she answered them. At the close of the interview once Shannon turned the camera off, she had to chuckle when Shannon looked her straight in the eye and spoke. "I can't wait to get home. I want to kiss you so much."

Simone had promised to make it worth her while as Shannon grinned at her before darting out of her office heading back to the break room to complete her work. She then did some final shots with the medics and called it a wrap around three. She spent the rest of the day helping to clean the station and visiting with the firemen and medics on duty. She had gotten to know them fairly well and they didn't have a problem including her in their activities. Simone came and found her at five and the two of them drove home. Simone followed through with her promise and kissed Shannon's breath away in the driveway, much to Shannon's delight.

Tuesday morning began early for Shannon. She was at the studio as planned and she, Art, and Susan began work immediately editing the tapes. By mid-day they had whittled it down to forty minutes.

"We need to cut another ten minutes out of the tape."

"I don't think we should. Let's bring Christa in and get her opinion," Art suggested. "I think if we take another ten minutes out we'll ruin it."

"But Christa said it should be thirty minutes." Shannon wanted the video to be perfect.

"I'll go see if Christa can come watch it over lunch," Susan suggested. "Why don't you go get us some sandwiches and drinks? I'll be right back."

Art and Shannon headed for the lunchroom and picked up a selection of sandwiches and chips along with an armload of pop. They were just getting settled in the editing room when Susie returned with Christa in tow.

"I understand you're having a hard time getting the tape down to thirty minutes."

"We wanted you to see it before we try and cut it any further. I think it's as good as it gets," Art explained as he held out a chair for Christa.

"Hand me a sandwich and let's look at it."

The four of them watched in absolute silence until the end of the forty-minute tape. Shannon held her breath as the tape turned to black. She had put her heart and soul into it and she wanted it perfect.

Christa cleared her throat and turned to the three of them as they waited for her opinion. "Don't take one more minute out of the tape. It's perfect."

The three of them began to talk all at once as they explained what they had done.

"Guys, I can't understand a word you are saying. Hold on," Christa chuckled as she grinned at the three of them. They had banded together and now nothing could separate them. "You need to show it to Neely and Simone. Clean up the sound and tighten the tape up, then make a master."

"Okay Christa."

"I'll go call Neely. Shannon, you call Simone. See if they can stop by this afternoon for a preview."

"I will, what time?"

"It will have to be after four. I know Neely is in court until three or so."

"I'll let you know what Simone says."

"Guys, good job." Christa grabbed her sandwich and pop as she headed out the door. "Shannon, excellent filming."

"Thanks, Christa."

The three slapped hands as Christa headed down the hall. Now all they had to do was clean the tape up and make sure the sound was clear. They had about two more hours of work to do. Shannon took a minute and called Simone.

"Hey sweetie."

"Hi, how's the work going?"

"Good, do you think you could get away and view the tape with Neely around four?"

"Of course I can. I'll be there at four o'clock. How is the tape?"

"It's fantastic, Simone. You're going to love it. It turned out so good."

"I'm glad, honey, I can't wait to see it."

"It's going to make high school kids want to be a paramedic, I know it."

"You did a good thing, Shannon."

"We all did."

"Love you."

"I love you, and I'll see you at four."

On the dot at four, both Neely and Simone arrived at the station. Christa had invited a couple more people including Shannon's new boss, to view the tape and she had set up a viewing room. Art, Shannon, and Susan sat in the back as the tape cued up. Shannon didn't watch the video she watched Simone's face for every reaction. She laughed, she smiled, she grew serious, and at the end of the tape, she remained silent. Shannon felt tears form in her eyes as she watched Simone for any sign of her feelings.

Neely spoke up first. "That is one of the most beautiful videos I've ever watched. There isn't a student in school who won't be moved by this tape and the fact that they could choose to be a paramedic."

"I agree, the tape is first rate and very well done, excellent job by all three of you," Jim Shaw commented as he stood up to leave. "Christa, see if we can make it a special during the family hour."

"I will. Thanks, Jim."

Shannon was still watching Simone and missed the exchange until Art poked her. "Hey, your first video is going prime time."

"That's good."

"Shannon, that's not good, that's amazing."

"Art, Susan, why don't you and Neely follow me down to my office so we can check the schedule for running it." Christa all but pushed them out of the viewing room to leave Simone and Shannon alone.

Shannon got up out of her chair and approached Simone, kneeling down in front of her. Simone's face was streaked with tears. "Honey, didn't you like it?" Shannon's heart shattered as she looked at Simone, thinking she had done something horribly wrong.

Simone smiled at her girlfriend and pulled her into her lap. "You made my paramedics sound so good I didn't recognize them."

Shannon grinned at her girlfriend and hugged her. "I especially liked your comment that you don't train your medics, they train themselves, followed by your newest medic saying none of them would make it without your help."

"It's beautiful, Shannon. It does exactly what Neely and I wanted it to do. Make kids get interested in becoming a paramedic. You should be very proud."

"I am proud. I'm proud of my girlfriend who works every day to make her medics the best trained and the most sensitive people that they can be. I am proud of you, a woman who has opened her home and heart to me and my friends and never once held anything back. I'm proud to think that I will be lucky enough to have you for my lover for the rest of my life. And yes, I am proud that I was able to let everyone know what an incredibly talented girl-friend I'm going to marry."

"Yes, you are going to marry me." Simone kissed Shannon slowly, savoring the flavor of her mouth and the pleasure she got every time she kissed her. "Thank you, Shannon."

"Honey, you don't need to thank me, I enjoyed every minute of it. Now, can we get out of here?"

"I promised you dinner and a movie tonight."

"And you are going to hold my hand."

"I am, for the whole movie."

Shannon got up off of Simone's lap and helped her out of her chair. "We'd better go say goodbye to Neely and Christa."

They both walked down to Christa's office and found Art and Susan with Neely and Christa. Art and Christa were looking at the scheduled time slots in the next several weeks. Neely and Susan were talking about something in the corner of the office, oblivious of Art and Christa.

"Simone, Shannon, we're just reviewing the schedule for an open slot," Art spoke as he and Christa looked up.

Neely walked over to Simone and gave her a big hug, silencing Art's comments. "I thought the video was a labor of love, Simone," Nelly whispered as she hugged her again.

"It was, Neely." Simone glanced over to Shannon.

"Yes, and it's exactly what we need to motivate kids. I can't wait to start showing it at school. When are you going to show it to the Chief and the others?"

"If I can get a copy today, I will show them tomorrow."

"We'll send a copy with you tonight," Christa responded. "Art, can you go make a copy from the master?"

"Yes, I'll be right back." Art poked Shannon in the arm when he passed her. "We did real good."

"Do you need any of us to be there when you show it?" Susan asked as she grinned.

"I think Shannon should be there, Neely and Christa, it was your idea."

"Simone, I've got an interview tomorrow and a news special to complete in the afternoon, so I can't. Neely, what about you?"

"Depends on the time, I could clear out my morning, but my afternoon is completely full."

"Let me call the office right now." Simone stepped out in the hall and used her cell phone. She returned in moments. "How does nine in the morning work?"

"Good, I'll meet you two there."

"Susan, do you want to be there?"

"I can't, I've got to edit a show for tomorrow night and I'm backed up with a couple other projects, but thanks for asking. Shannon, call Art and I afterwards and tell us how it goes."

"I will."

Art returned in moments with a copy of the tape. "Here you go."

"Thanks, Art. Simone and I are going to get out of your hair. I'll see you two in a month if not sooner."

"Shannon," Neely called to her. "You did a terrific job."

"Thanks, Neely."

Simone and Shannon walked out grinning at each other, Simone with the tape in her hand. "You can relax now and have a vacation for a little while."

"I can."

"Come on, sweetie, I'll race you to the car."

"You're on." Shannon busted into a run and raced to the Rover, Simone in hot pursuit. They arrived at the car at the same time and burst into laughter as they both tumbled into the car.

They laughed and giggled their whole drive back to the house. The others were out for the evening on Marcus and Leo's boat, and Simone and Shannon took their time before heading out for dinner and a movie. In the theater, they settled into their chairs and when the lights dropped down low, reached for each other's hand. The movie was a dud, but more importantly, they had not let go of each other's hand for its full length. They were still in very light moods as they made the quick trip back home. The four women were still out for the night and Shannon and Simone crawled into bed, snuggling together, sharing their thoughts, and just enjoying each other. It was this night that Simone and Shannon became much more than lovers and partners, they started to become friends. Simone was the first to fall asleep and Shannon held her in her arms, just watching her sleep. She found herself overwhelmed with emotion when she thought about her future life with Simone. Every day they grew closer and more comfortable with each other.

CHAPTER 19

Shannon was even more nervous showing the video to Simone's boss and the Fire Chief than she was about showing it to Simone. It was so important that Simone's professionalism and her talent for training came through on the tape. Shannon was uncharacteristically silent as she waited in the conference room for the arrival of Simone's boss.

"Shannon, are you okay?" Simone whispered, as she sat patiently next to her.

"I'm fine."

Simone nudged her in the arm and then winked quickly at her. Simone recognized a bad case of nerves when she saw it. Shannon had no reason to be nervous. The door flew open before she could say anything more to her and Ben Strafford, her boss, and long-term friend bustled through the door.

"Simone, Chief Olsen, how're you both doing?"

"Good, Ben. How about you."

"Couldn't be better." Ben Strafford was at least six-five, with arms that looked strong enough to pick Shannon up over his head, his hair was close cropped, and slate grey. His suit was spotless, and very professional, and he carried an aura of strength around him.

"Ben, this is Shannon Dunbar. She was the film maker who made the video."

"Shannon, it's nice to meet you. Simone has filled me in on this project and the donation of your time. That's very generous of you."

"I was one of several people who worked on the video. Thank you for allowing me to spend the time with your crew. You have an amazing group of dedicated people."

"Yes we do, probably due to Simone's training and guidance."

Shannon almost smiled at the comment but contained her reaction as Simone blushed. "Why don't we start the video?"

Both men remained silent during the entire tape and Shannon grew increasingly worried that neither man liked what they saw. Simone stood up when the film ended and turned the tape off, facing both men as she finished.

"So, what do you think?"

Chief Olsen remained silent as Ben responded to Simone's question. "I think we have a recruiter tape. This is very well done, Shannon. You have illustrated the training required, and the work that the paramedics handle. But what I like most about it is that you have shown the heart and commitment good medics need to have. I would ask that we put our station house in the credits. It will help with the politics if we thank the Hawaiian Fire and Police Unions, etc. Simone, you could provide the appropriate list."

"I can do that, anything else?"

"I'd like a formal showing to all the medics, and I think we should do it with a dinner, similar to what we did for the induction ceremony."

"Where do I bill it on the budget?"

"Put it under training, we'll get more value from the good public relations this tape will provide. Simone, you mentioned that Channel Five wants to run this tape as a special?"

"Yes, I'm not sure when or how they are going to set it up, but I can find out and let you know."

"Good. Chief, what do you think?"

"I want to know when Shannon is going to do a video of the Fire Department." He grinned at her. "You can ride on a fire truck."

"Not a bad idea." Ben stood up with a smile. "Shannon, again, I want to thank you for the excellent job and I'll see you at the formal viewing. Simone, can I get a word with you before I head out?"

"Certainly." Simone followed Ben out of the conference room and down the hall to her office.

"I understand you need a week off this next month. Is everything okay?"

"Everything's fine, Ben, I just need to take a week of personal time."

"Can you get someone to cover for you?"

"Already looked into it."

"Good, how's the budget look?"

"Tight, but we'll make it, unless something unforeseen happens. Our equipment is in good shape, and we have four new medics finishing their training next month."

"What about your successor?"

"Ben, I already told you I don't want a promotion. I don't want to have to work off island, and I like what I do."

"What if I told you, you could stay here and still be in charge of all the medic programs?"

Simone was surprised at his comment. "I would be very interested."

"You'll have to attend more meetings and political dinners."

"I know." Simone grimaced at the thought.

"Think about it and we'll talk more in a month or so."

"Okay, I will."

"Simone, this video can be a real plus for us. If we can get more focus on our department, our training methods, and our skills, we may be able to leverage a larger budget next year."

"I know."

"Excellent, is there anything I need to know before I head out of here?"

"Not that I can think of."

"What about your personal life? Are you still living at the office?"

"No, as a matter of fact, I am going to be living with someone this next month. That's why I need the week off, to help her move."

"Congratulations. Now, I can tell my wife to quit bugging you."

Simone laughed as she thought of Ben's wife. She was a beautiful, vivacious, pain in the neck when it came to matchmaking, and even Simone was a target. "Tell her I'm taken."

Ben looked at Simone with a slight smile on his face. He had known Simone since she was twenty years old. He'd also known her parents and had been her mentor and guide for many years. "I'm very happy for you. Anyone we know?"

"You just met her."

"Shannon? Where is she moving from?"

"Seattle, Washington."

"I don't blame her for moving here, doesn't it always rain in Seattle? You'll have to bring her to dinner and let my wife meet her. She won't believe you otherwise."

"We'll do that."

"Well I've got to go. I have a meeting with the Police Chief in an hour."

"Thanks for making the time, Ben."

"No problem. Simone, call my wife."

"I will," Simone promised as Ben sailed out her office door. He always moved quickly when he decided it was time to move.

Simone sat quietly at her desk as she thought about everything that was happening in her life. In the last few days she had met, slept with, and committed herself to a woman she had known for less than two weeks. A woman who had produced a video that made Simone feel more loved and more respected than any other words or actions could have done. Shannon not only had captured the affection and love she had for her career and the people she trained, but had put it into a film that told everyone who watched it how proud she was of Simone and what she did. More than anything, it moved Simone's heart in a way that nothing else could have done. She smiled as she stood up and headed down the hall to find Shannon. In one month she was going to be moved and living with her for the rest of Simone's life. The rush of emotion that Simone felt was welcome, as she recognized it for what it was, love, pure and strong, and perfect.

Shannon was seated in the conference room by herself, sitting with her back to the door as she looked out of the windows into a courtyard. Shannon was so wrapped up in her worrying she didn't know Simone was in the room until she sat next to her.

"Shannon, are you okay?"

"I'm fine. What did your boss say?"

"You heard him, he loved it."

"Are you sure?"

"I'm positive. I just need to give you a list of the groups to thank on the film and it's good to go."

Shannon was slow to smile as she watched Simone. "Are you sure you like it?"

Simone recognized what Shannon was not saying as much as what she asked. She needed reassurance from Simone about their relationship. "Shannon, if I wasn't sitting in my conference room at work I would kiss you. Instead I am going to tell you that no amount of words could have told me how much you love me as strongly as the video does. You took every ounce of your love for me and wrapped it all together in that film. I know that as surely as I know that one month from now you will be living with me. A year from now, ten years, it doesn't matter, you and I will be living together for the rest of our lives."

Shannon's eyes overflowed with tears as she listened to Simone speak. "I love you."

"I know that, and you know I love you."

"Yes, I do."

"Now, get out of here, go enjoy the day."

Shannon gazed at her girlfriend and sighed before standing up. "I'll be back at five to pick you up."

"I should hope so," Simone teased, pushing her toward the door. "Go."

Shannon headed down the hall and before swinging through the front door she turned and waved her fingers at Simone who waved back at her before turning back to her office. She had a lot of work to do before she was going to be able to take the week off.

Shannon made the trip back home without incident, her thoughts on moving and what she needed to take care of. She was going to start her list as soon as she got back to Simone's house. She parked Simone's Rover and entered the quiet house, heading straight for the bedroom and her pack.

"Shannon, how did the video screening go?" Janice asked as she poured a glass of ice water in the kitchen.

"Good, very good. They didn't ask for any changes."

"That's great." Janice grinned at her friend, but couldn't help but notice Shannon's subdued mood. "What's up, honey?"

"Nothing, I am just preoccupied with all the details of moving."

"Shannon, this is Janice you're talking to."

Shannon turned to her friend and then spoke. "I'm just scared. What if I get everything moved and Simone changes her mind?"

Janice snorted in disbelief. "You've got to be kidding. I've never seen two people so much in love. She won't do that, but what about you?"

"I love her so much it makes me ache. I can't imagine my life without her."

"Than quit worrying and take a break. You haven't had any vacation to speak of, and everything has been pretty hectic. Why don't you take a day or two off and just enjoy yourself?"

"But…"

"But nothing, two days of vacation aren't going to kill you." Janice shoved her down the hall. "Go put your bathing suit on and join us on the beach."

"Maybe I will."

"Shannon…"

"Okay, I'll be right out," Shannon chuckled. Maybe it was just what she needed.

CHAPTER 20

"Simone, I don't need a brand new one," Shannon explained as they wondered through the Range Rover car lot. It was the Saturday before Shannon's first day of work and they were looking for the appropriate car. Shannon's Miata had sold almost immediately and she was now in need of a new car. Shannon and Simone had taken care of almost everything in the week that Simone spent with her in Seattle, packing her stuff, putting her condominium on the market, and selling her car. In the week after Simone left, Shannon had supervised the movers as they packed her things and spent several evenings saying goodbye to friends and colleagues. She had flown back to Hawaii and Simone late Friday for the final time.

"Why buy someone else's problems?" Simone asked as she continued to look at the shiny, new, smaller version of her Range Rover.

"Simone, this is an expensive car."

"Yes and a good one. It should last many years and be very safe for my girl-friend while she drives around the island chasing stories."

"I doubt if I'm going to be chasing stories."

"Of course you will. Why do you think you now have a cell phone, a beeper, and a computer hanging off your hip?"

Shannon had been equally surprised at everything that awaited her at the house when she had settled in. The station was expecting her to be connected at all times and left a huge amount of equipment at her house. Her badge was prepared with her picture; she had a portable computer at her disposal, a state of the art cell phone that did many other things besides act as a telephone, and her very own camera and bag. She appreciated that they wanted her to get familiar with it since she was to start work Monday morning. She had the choice of using her own car or a company van as she went from story to story. Shannon would much prefer her own wheels, hence the need to pick one out.

Shannon didn't respond to Simone with anything but a grin and a hug but Simone knew how she felt. Shannon was bubbling over with emotions. She had burst into tears the minute she had seen Simone at the airport, and she was still having difficulty controlling her emotions. Simone felt the same way as she grabbed Shannon, holding on tightly, while she felt the rush of emotion move swiftly through her body. Even though they had talked several times a day during that last week, they had missed each other terribly. They couldn't go very long without touching each other. They were really living together and it was so incredibly overwhelming.

"Shannon, this is the perfect car for you. Plenty of room and storage for your camera and everything, it has four wheel drive, so you can go anywhere. And it's small enough to get reasonable gas mileage."

"It's expensive."

"It comes in your favorite color," Simone pointed out, a grin on her face as she saw Shannon look longingly at the steel blue car. "Why don't you test drive it?"

"I don't know."

"Come on, what will it hurt?"

Shannon and Simone finished their dinner on the patio and washed the dishes together standing hip to hip, frequently turning to kiss each other.

"I still can't believe we bought a new car today."

"In both our names," Simone reminded her.

"I know, it's so cool." Shannon's eyes filled with tears as she looked at her lover of less than two months. Simone had also put Shannon's name on the house as joint owner and Shannon had cried for twenty minutes before Simone could settle her down, even making the bed together made Shannon teary.

"Shannon, we love each other, and we have the rest of our lives together."

"I know." Shannon turned and wrapped her arms around Simone's waist. "It's so overwhelming how much I love you."

"It's the same for me." Simone promised with a kiss.

"I have an idea."

"Let's hear it."

"How about some late night swimming tonight, I think a little lovemaking in the ocean is in order," Shannon flirted with Simone, her lips sliding along her neck.

"I think we can do that," Simone sighed as she reacted to Shannon's actions and her words.

"Simone, do you think you can wear your uniform down to the beach? You know what seeing you in uniform does to me."

Simone couldn't help but laugh as she picked Shannon up and kissed her deeply. She would never tire of loving Shannon, and she certainly enjoyed her sense of humor. "I can do that."

CHAPTER 21

A Year Later

"Simone, boy is it good to see you." Mel and Janice hugged her as they came off the plane. "Where's Shannon?"

"She's on a story. She'll meet us at home as soon as she can finish up." Simone hugged them both back.

"You look fantastic. I can't believe it's been a year since we were last here."

"Thanks. You both look terrific, and I know Shannon was disappointed she couldn't pick you up."

"How is she?"

"Wonderful. She's doing incredibly well at her job, which puts her in constant demand for her camera work. She's had three pieces nominated for awards, and she spends her free time helping Neely in what ever cause she needs help with," Simone shared with a grin, as she led the two women out to her car.

"And the commitment ceremony, is everything ready?"

"Yes, thanks to a lot of help from Neely's family. It's a traditional Hawaiian wedding ceremony on the beach, so we left everything in Christa and Neely's hands."

"We can't wait. Are Olivia and Hanna here?"

"Yes, they are out with a real estate friend of mine looking at property. They will meet us back at the house."

"Congratulations on your promotion, Captain."

Simone looked down at her badge and grinned. "Thanks, I keep forgetting about that."

"You deserved it."

"So how's the fire business?"

"Busy, but we still love it."

"No chance of moving over here?"

"No, but keep asking." Janice hugged Simone again. "We're so glad to be here."

"We're glad to have you here. Shannon and I want all of our family with us."

"We wouldn't miss it."

The three of them visited like old friends as they made the trip from the airport to the house. They piled out of the car and Simone led them into the familiar house. "You both know where your bedroom is, so I will leave you to unpack while I change out of my uniform. We're meeting Christa, Neely, Marcus, and Leo for dinner."

"Simone, Janice and I are very excited for you and Shannon."

Simone stared at Mel and Janice for a moment, her eyes filling up with tears before responding. "Not as excited as Shannon and I are. We're so glad you can share it with us."

Simone turned and walked down the hall to the bedroom while Mel and Janice unpacked. "She looks great, doesn't she?"

"Yes, and did you see her eyes when she spoke of Shannon. They are something, aren't they?"

"Yes, they are. Now, hurry and unpack, I want to go down to the beach."

That's exactly where Hanna and Olivia found them as they sat on towels and visited while they all waited for Shannon to get home. "We'd better go and get cleaned up before dinner. If Shannon doesn't get here soon, she'll miss it."

"Did you see her studio yet?"

"No, we thought we'd wait until she could show it to us."

"It's impressive. She does a lot of her editing at home because she has the right equipment."

"How is she, Hanna?"

"I'll let you decide, but she is pretty close to someone who thinks she won a thirty million dollar lotto."

"That good?"

"Yes, she's delirious and so is Simone."

"Good, I'm glad." The four friends trooped up the path and to their respective rooms to get cleaned up. Simone was in her office where they passed by her. She was on the telephone and waved at them as she continued to speak.

The five women were seated out on the patio visiting when Shannon shot out the patio door with a big smile on her face. "Mel, Janice, give me a hug. I have missed you guys." Shannon's eyes grew wet with unshed tears as she hugged first Janice and then Mel. "I'm so glad you came."

"We wouldn't have missed your wedding for anything."

Shannon was swamped with emotion as she went to Simone and bent to kiss her hello. Simone hugged her tightly knowing how close to crying Shannon was. Shannon sat down next to her at the table.

"So guys, are you ready to go have dinner with a crowd?"

"We are, what time do we need to head out? Janice and I would like to see your studio."

"We don't need to leave for another hour, so you have time," Simone responded, her voice full of affection. "Shannon, go show them your studio."

"Okay, and then I have to get cleaned up I'm pretty filthy from running around today." Shannon stood up and bent to kiss Simone again. Simone and Shannon held hands for a moment, their eyes locked on each other before Shannon turned to Mel and Janice. "Come on guys, and see what my girlfriend made for me."

The three headed across the patio chattering like magpies as Simone watched them with a smile on her face. "She needed to see Mel and Janice. She misses you all so much."

"She does, but she's so happy with her life."

"So am I."

"Jeez, Shannon, this is incredible, how big is that monitor?"

"Twenty-one inches, and it's perfect. Simone and I worked for several months to get it set up correctly. It's as good as anything you'll find at work."

"Are all those videos yours?" Janice pointed to a shelf with row after row of labeled tapes stacked next to each other.

"Yes, I keep a copy of everything I've shot in case I need any of the original footage."

"Does Simone have to come drag you out to see you?" Mel teased her with a hug.

"I work a lot, but so does Simone." Shannon grinned. "Since Simone's promotion she works a lot more than before. We both work odd hours but we can't complain. We make sure we spend as much time as possible together."

"Simone said you won three awards for your camera work." Mel was very proud of her friend.

"Not yet. I have three clips that have been nominated, but I won't know until after the first of the year."

"So things are going well?" Janice watched Shannon carefully.

"Things are perfect. I have to pinch myself just to make sure everything is real. Simone and I are so happy." Shannon began to cry. "I'm so glad you could make it."

Janice and Mel hugged Shannon tightly as she cried on their shoulders. It was several long moments before Shannon was able to stop crying. "So tell us what can we do to help?"

"Nothing, everything is done. Neely's family has done most of the work. We're going to have the ceremony here on the beach on a week from today and following the ceremony, we are going to have a big luau. You guys get to spend a week just hanging around."

"Are you sure you want all of us in your home? We certainly can get a hotel." Mel didn't want to intrude.

"We want you here."

"Are you going on a honeymoon?" Janice grinned at her.

"No, we're going to spend a couple of nights on Lanai, but we both decided to hang around until we can get a couple of weeks off. Then we are going to a stay on a couple of the other islands. Neither one of us could get too much time off right now. But we wanted to have the ceremony as close to the year anniversary of our meeting."

"We're very happy for both of you."

"Life couldn't be better. I honestly thank God every day for all that I have in my life."

"We like your studio, Shannon. Maybe you could give us a tour of your station while we're here?" Janice was very curious about the television station.

"Of course, I'd love too. We'd better get going for now. I need to go change my clothes and clean up."

The three headed back out to the patio and while the rest of them remained outside visiting, Shannon went in and washed up and changed into a sundress for dinner. She joined them about twenty minutes later, just in time for all of them to pile into Simone's larger Rover after all of the women took a moment to exclaim over Shannon's year old smaller one.

The dinner was loud and full of affectionate conversation as they all caught up with each other. It was a very fun evening and none of them left to go home before midnight. It was after one before Shannon and Simone had any time alone as they prepared for bed.

"Shannon, are you okay, sweetie?" Simone had noticed that Shannon had been a little subdued at dinner.

Shannon was seated on the bed unbraiding her hair. "I'm fine, honey. I am just a little overwhelmed with everything that's going on." She smiled up at Simone as Simone stood next to her.

"One more week until we are married." Simone bent to Shannon and kissed her slowly.

Shannon dropped her brush and pulled Simone on top of her on to the bed. "I can't wait. I want to be married to you," Shannon whispered against Simone's mouth before capturing her in a kiss that made Simone's head spin.

Shannon and Simone's love life had only improved over time, as they had gotten to know each other, and their love and trust had deepened. Shannon's kisses were no longer soft or gentle as hunger for Simone clawed to be let loose. She was always astounded at how quickly she and Simone combusted with lust for each other.

"I want you naked." Simone demanded as she struggled with Shannon's night shirt, all but tearing it off of her body so that she could put her lips on her breasts. Shannon gasped as Simone's mouth found her nipple and arched against her hot mouth. Simone's tongue teased, as did her fingertips, while Shannon welcomed the heat and the pleasure that speared through her body. Simone made quick work of stripping Shannon, and her mouth and hands were everywhere as she drove Shannon crazy with a touch of her tongue, the feather like feel of her fingertips, and her moist lips, branding Shannon where ever she kissed.

Within minutes, Shannon's body was burning with a craving that only Simone could relieve. Simone leaned up and kneeled between Shannon's thighs as she looked down at Shannon's body open to her view and her pleasure. She smiled as she ran her fingers over Shannon's breasts, fascinated by how they reacted to her touch. Bending over she ran her tongue down the center of Shannon's stomach as her hands covered her breasts, loving the weight of them in her hands. Shannon's hips pushed against Simone's thighs as she communicated to her lover what she wanted. Her body was wet and throbbing in anticipation of Simone's lovemaking.

"Simone, please." She pleaded as Simone gripped her hips tightly in her hands.

Simone was still in her pajama top and underwear and she moved away from Shannon and stripped her clothes off before returned to kneel between Shannon's thighs. "Shannon, come here."

Simone wrapped her arms around Shannon and pulled her up until she was tight against Simone's body, her legs surrounding Simone's hips. Shannon locked her arms around Simone's neck as her mouth covered Simone's. Simone entered her so quickly that Shannon groaned against her mouth as her hips began to pound against Simone's. Simone could feel Shannon's body welcome her with a ripple of her body and a flood of moisture. Simone moaned herself as Shannon's body pulled on her fingers while she stayed deeply inside her, letting Shannon's hips pump against her hand. Faster and harder Shannon worked her hips until she exploded with a scream muffled against Simone's neck and a slumping of her body. Simone turned to meet Shannon's seeking mouth as they kissed slowly, Simone still deeply held inside of Shannon. Her thumb began to rub Shannon's clitoris, teasing the already sensitive tissue until Shannon was once again engulfed in an orgasm that made her shiver against Simone's body.

"Oh, God, honey, you're going to kill me," Shannon gasped, trying to catch her breath.

Simone just smiled as she pulled Shannon up to her knees in front of her. Shannon knew what her girlfriend needed and she reached down and ran her fingers through the blond curls that covered her wet, trembling center. Simone spread her legs to accommodate Shannon's hand as she reached down and grasped Shannon's hips. Shannon moved a thigh between Simone's legs and pushed it against her probing fingers and Simone's body. Simone gripped Shannon's hips and ground her body hard against Shannon's hand and her thigh. Shannon flipped Simone on to her back and with her fingers embedded in Simone, she ran her tongue hard against her, savoring the flavor that she loved almost as much as the woman it belonged to. Simone's body shook in response as Shannon ran the tip of her tongue against the hardened tissue until she felt Simone's body ripple around her fingers. Shannon's hot mouth and tongue drove Simone quickly into a series of orgasms that made her tremble from head to toe.

"Shannon..." Simone's voice broke as she pulled on Shannon's shoulders until she could bury her face in Shannon's neck. Simone held on tightly as her body was buffeted with another wave of pleasure moving through her body.

They lay wrapped together in the center of the bed for a long time before Simone turned to Shannon and spoke. "Do you think they heard us?"

Shannon's eyes twinkled at her girlfriend as she responded. "Yea, I think they heard us."

Simone blushed with embarrassment. She and Shannon had gotten used to being by themselves in the house and normally it didn't matter how loud they were. But with both bedrooms full of company, they would have to tone down their lovemaking.

"I love you."

"I love you. Are you going to be off island tomorrow?"

"No, I'm in the office most of the day. What about you?"

"I'm probably going to catch up on some editing with Art and Susan in the morning, depending upon our assignments. It's been pretty quiet for the last couple of weeks."

"Did Mel and Janice like your studio?"

"Yes very much, and they would like a tour of the television station. I talked to Christa tonight and she suggested they come in on Tuesday when she is doing her weekly island special."

"Good, they'll enjoy that." Simone yawned as she lay tucked against Shannon.

"Honey, you're exhausted, let's go to sleep."

"I am tired." Simone pulled the covers over the two of them and turned to kiss Shannon goodnight. Shannon rolled on to her side while Simone tucked up behind her, her arm slung over Shannon's hip. Within minutes they were both asleep, comfortable with their familiarity and their love.

CHAPTER 22

The weekend came and went quickly and by Monday morning Shannon and Simone were back at work while the four visiting women when out on the boat with Marcus and Leo for a day of snorkeling. The day was a beautiful clear eighty degrees by mid-morning and the six on the boat were having fun getting in and out of the water, laughing much of the time.

Shannon's day had started out fairly quiet with one call for her to go to a flower show to film some of the world's most beautiful orchids. It took her most of the morning to get to the hotel and to take some good footage. It was close to lunch when she burst through the door of the station intent on getting her film to Susan for editing.

"Shannon, dump your film and grab some fresh video tapes. I need you to go with me to the beach to film a rescue," Christa called to her. "Meet me at the front door in five minutes.

"Will do." Shannon raced down the hall and quickly unloaded her bag, handing the tapes to Susan with a brief explanation, before stuffing her bag full of new blank tapes.

She met Christa at the door and they went through it together. "We need to take the van because we might go with a live feed on this one," Christa explained as she tossed the keys to Shannon. Christa and Shannon had gone on many news stories together and had a system worked out together.

"What happened?"

"Two teenage boys are trapped in lava tubes on the Makole'a Black Sand Beach. The tide is coming in and they can't swim out. If the tide comes in completely they might drown. The search and rescue team is already on its way."

Shannon's head jerked when she heard the statement. Simone was on the search and rescue team because of her diving skills and her medical training. She didn't say a word but Christa knew what she was feeling, and placed her hand on Shannon's arm. "Simone is well trained, honey."

"I know." Shannon's heart shuddered as she envisioned what Simone might be preparing to do.

It took a long thirty-five minutes to get to the beach and while Christa went to find out what was going on, Shannon unloaded the van and began to set up. Once she had everything organized and ready to go, she swung her camera on to her shoulder and went to find Christa. She wasn't surprised to see three fire trucks, two medic units, and Simone's Rover parked next to three police cars. There was a crowd of fire and police officers talking to each other on the cliffs above the beach, while Simone and another young man were pulling on their diving equipment. One of the fire units was also unloading water bikes into the water.

Christa was busily talking to a policeman off to the side as several firemen unloaded coils of rope from their truck. She waved Shannon over to her, as Shannon scanned the area with her camera to start preparing the background.

Shannon hustled over to Christa who quickly checked her notes and motioned Shannon to start the tape.

"Good afternoon, this is Christa Neiland with Hawaiian network KQRT, reporting live on the shore of Makole'a Black Sand Beach in Kona, where drama is unfolding. Two young teenage boys have become trapped by the incoming tide in the old lava tubes formed by the Hu'ehu'e lava flow in eighteen hundred and one. The Hawaiian search and rescue team is preparing to send in their best divers to see if they can locate and remove the two young men before the tide comes in any further. We have not been able to find out the names of these two boys but will continue to monitor this rescue as it unfolds."

Christa signaled for Shannon to end filming and then checked her notes one more time before grabbing her cell phone and dialing the network news editor. Shannon knew her job and she popped the tape out and entered the van where she prepared to submit the tape via a satellite connection back to the station where it would be played on the network news. She also began to make preparations for a direct link via her camera. She was expecting the news editor to request a live feed.

"Shannon, they want you to send the tape ASAP."

"Done, Christa."

Christa grinned at Shannon before responding. "I'm not surprised. I suppose you're already set up to go live."

"Yep." Shannon grinned back at Christa before turning to watch for Simone.

"Shannon, do you want me to have another cameraman meet us here?" Christa touched Shannon's arm as she spoke, concern laced her voice.

"No, I'll do my job. Do you know what's going on?"

"Not yet, but let's go see if we can find out."

Shannon shouldered her camera and followed the rapidly moving Christa as she zeroed in on the Fire Chief as a target for her interview. "Chief Olsen, can you tell me what your rescue team is going to do?"

"Right now we are preparing to put two search divers into the water. They will head into the cave and try and locate the boys. From there, depending upon where they are, and how much time we have, we will extricate the two boys."

"Do you have any idea where they are?"

"We know what cave they entered but the problem is there are several branches that they could have followed. The caves go back several thousand feet, some of them currently flooded. There are so many lava tubes they could have followed it's hard to predict where they ended up."

"Do you have the names of the two boys?"

"Yes, but we're notifying their parents right now. We're going to keep their names out of the media until we have talked to the parents."

"What about your rescue divers, can you tell me who they are?"

"We are sending in our senior divers, Simone Moreau and David Cleary, both who have more than twenty years of experience as search and rescue divers and paramedics."

"Can you tell me what the procedure is for their search?"

"They'll be tethered to a rope as they swim into the cave and conduct their search. Once they locate the boys and assess if they have any injuries they will bring them out. It is extremely difficult to bring them out against the incoming tide, especially with two boys that have never scuba dived before. It is very dangerous and serious work, but they are well trained. Now, that's all I can share with you, I need to get back to the control center."

"Thanks Chief."

Christa turned to Shannon to see her still filming the Chief as he walked to the crowd of police and firemen where Simone stood in her wet suit along with another man in diving gear. They were talking earnestly to a man who had spread a map on to the trunk of a police car. Shannon's face was white with fear and anxiety but she didn't stop filming until Christa touched her on the back. "I think we have enough for right now, Shannon. Do you want to go send it to the station?"

"Sure Christa." Shannon turned and swiftly walked back to the van, but Christa had seen the sheen of tears in her eyes. Christa could only imagine how terrified Shannon was.

Christa headed for the nearest fireman and spoke quickly to him. With a nod of his head he walked up to Simone and got her attention. Simone turned and saw Christa standing thirty yards away from her. Simone turned to her partner, speaking quickly, and then walked over to Christa.

"Where is she?"

"In the van."

"Thanks Christa."

"No problem, just be careful."

"I will."

Simone walked over to the van, opened the slider, and entered. She shut it behind her. "Shannon."

"Simone, what are you doing here?"

"I came to get a hug."

Shannon tried to control her emotions but she couldn't prevent her tears as she threw her arms around Simone. "I'm so scared."

"Everything will be okay, I promise. I am very well trained and so is David. We have practiced this many times. Besides, we're getting married on Saturday."

Shannon struggled to keep from begging her not to go. "Yes, we are. Go save those two young boys."

"I will, and you'll be waiting for me because I want a night alone with you."

"I'll be waiting." Shannon kissed Simone slowly. "I love you."

"I love you." Simone exited the van and returned to the waiting team.

Shannon settled her emotions and finished transferring the video and loaded up her camera again. She returned to where Christa stood. "Any word from the network?"

"Not yet."

They both stood silently watching, Shannon with her camera rolling as the team went over the map and their plan. Fifteen minutes later the water bikes were started up and Simone and David climbed on the back behind two other members of the team. A helicopter circled overhead as they headed out into the ocean's heavy surf.

The water bikes stopped about two hundred yards out in front of the cave and Simone and her partner got into the water, a rope tied around the waist of both of them. As they swam to the cave mouth one of the men on the water bike held the ropes steady. A rescue boat joined them as they fed the rope out to the two divers. The rope was transferred to one of the two men on the boat and they continued to slowly play it out as Simone and her partner drew nearer to the cave opening that was currently almost totally under water. As they neared the cave, Simone raised her arm signaling to the boat and her team that they were going in. Shannon's heart pounded loudly in her chest as she filmed the two divers while they disappeared from view. She began to breathe deeply and bit her lip to keep from crying as she continued to film the men in the boat who had the only connection to her lover.

"Shannon, are you okay?" Christa placed an arm around her waist.

"I'm fine." Shannon turned to face Christa as she turned the camera off. She was unaware of the fact that tears ran down her face.

"Oh Shannon." Christa's heart wrenched at the sight of Shannon's silent agony. "Simone knows what she's doing."

"I know." Shannon looked at Christa, her heart filled with fear. "I just can't lose her. I just can't."

Christa threw her arms around Shannon and hugged her tightly, rocking from side to side. There were no words she could offer to Shannon that would console her at that moment. Christa knew how she felt because as she had watched Simone disappear her heart had also reacted. She loved Simone and was equally as terrified.

"Let's get this tape to the network. I think they are going to want to go live when they bring the boys out." Shannon would be an eternal optimist. She couldn't think of any other outcome.

Christa remained silent as she watched Shannon head back to the van. She dialed her cell phone quickly to the news editor. "This is Christa. They have sent two divers in the caves to look for the boys. I'm going to try and get more information but Shannon is sending the tape as we speak."

"Christa, as soon as you can get one of the big wigs on a live feed. Tell Shannon we go live in two minutes."

"Will do." Christa entered the van. "Shannon, we're live in two minutes. I need to go grab the Chief for an interview."

"I'll be right out. I've got everything up and running." Shannon was nothing but a professional as she exited the van, swinging her now live camera on to her shoulder, and followed Christa.

"Chief, I would like to get a live interview with you about the rescue. Can you give me a couple of minutes?"

"I've got work to do," he snarled at her, but Christa knew him well.

"Oh come on Chief Olsen, just a couple of minutes. Your team is good. They can do without you for a little bit."

"Okay, but just a couple of minutes." He straightened his uniform as Christa stepped up next to him, a microphone in her hand.

"Okay Christa, in ten seconds, counting now, ten, nine…" Shannon pointed to Christa when she was live and Christa began to speak.

"Good afternoon, this is Christa Neiland speaking live to you on the cliffs above Makole'a Black Sand Beach. With me is Chief Olsen, who is leading the search for two young boys who are currently trapped in the lava tubes below. Chief, could you explain the rescue efforts?"

"We have two divers currently entering the caves to locate the two boys. Once they are located, the divers will assess the situation, and commence with the rescue."

"Chief, with the mouth of the caves under water, how do the divers get the two boys out?"

"Each diver has an extra tank on their back and they will bring each boy out with them. The divers are tethered to a rope so we know how far in they are, and the rope will also help lead them out. There are many places inside the cave that do not get filled up with the tide and we believe the two boys have taken refuge in the cave in an air pocket high above the water line." What the Chief didn't say was that the pocket was probably rapidly filling up with water.

"How long do you believe the rescue will take?"

"Each diver has enough oxygen for an hour and a half. This means that they have forty-five minutes to find the two boys and forty-five minutes to get out safely. They have their orders. When their watches show they have searched for forty-five minutes they return."

"Thank you, Chief Olsen." Christa turned to the camera. "As you can see there are quite a few emergency personnel here as they orchestrate this rescue. I was informed earlier by one of the police officers that these particular set of caves are actually lava tubes that go back several thousand feet, with many branches and turns. It is difficult to navigate without the incoming waves, but even more treacherous when filling up with water. I will try and get more information to you as this rescue continues."

Shannon counted Christa down and turned off the camera. "Good job."

"Thanks, what's the network saying?"

Shannon tuned into her headset that was connected to the news editor. "He says we will go again in fifteen minutes, and great job."

Christa began to respond but she was distracted by a cry of pain from a woman, who collapsed as she was helped out of a car. Three women and two men were quickly ushered over to the control center but not before Shannon filmed the absolute anguish on their faces. Christa and Shannon could hear the woman sobbing as one of the men tried to console her, his face drained of all color and complete terror on his features.

Shannon turned the camera off and faced Christa. "The parents, I sincerely hope that they will see their boys again."

"So do I." Christa turned to Shannon. "I need to go try and interview them and I hate this part of my job."

"But you will do it with gentleness, not all news people would treat them with the dignity they deserve. You will."

"Thanks, Shannon. I needed that." Christa smiled and picked up her mike. "Come on, we have work to do."

The next two minutes on air included a tearful plea for prayers from both parents of the two young boys, one of them Steve Mazito was a fourteen-year-old and Mike Foreman, a fifteen-year-old boy. Christa was able to get each set of parents to describe their sons, while showing how much they loved them. It was a good interview, and a compassionate one. As they were shutting things down for another fifteen minutes, there was a shout from the boat, and a scurry of activity at the control center. Shannon and Christa watched as the medics, police, and firemen held a conference at the control center.

"I am going to find out what happened." Christa headed for the crowd with Shannon trailing behind her.

"Officer, can you tell me what is going on?"

"The rescue rope was severed and the divers are completely on their own. They need to turn around and head out in the next ten minutes or they will be in trouble."

Shannon continued to film the interview but her hearing had shut down. She felt panic invade her body at the thought of Simone lost in the dark cave with no way to get out. She couldn't keep her heart from jumping in her chest, let alone her hands from shaking. It was all she could do to keep filming while Christa completed the interview.

CHAPTER 23

Simone and David were not having good luck in locating the boys. They were down to five minutes before they were scheduled to turn around and head out of the cave, a difficult job, especially since the rope that had been tied to the two of them had been caught on the cave wall and cut. Simone stopped and motioned David to come closer to her in the submerged cave. She pulled out a board to write on and scrawled quickly. Tank and a question mark. David motioned that he was showing sixty minutes of air left. Simone checked hers and it had close to the same amount. She wrote quickly again. Ten minutes and we head back. David shook his head yes and they continued their search of the cave. They had found six pockets of air as they had traveled, none of which showed signs of either boy. They were running out of time for the boys and themselves. Simone checked her watch ten minutes later and was going to signal David to return, when a movement in front of her caught her eye. It was two legs moving in the water. Poking David, she swam quickly to the spot and was happy to find the two boys clinging to the cave, their heads barely above the rapidly filling air pocket. Both David and Simone flipped their masks and regulators off.

"Hello, I am Simone, and this is David. We're going to get you out of the cave."

The two boys were exhausted and scared to death as they flung themselves in Simone's direction.

"Whoa, slow down, are you okay? Is either one of you hurt?"

"No, we're cold and hungry, but we're okay."

"Now, you need to listen to me carefully. The tide is coming in very fast and will fill this cave up completely in no time. We have brought tanks and regulators with us for both of you. You're going to have to swim out of the cave with David and I, and it isn't going to be easy. We're going to have to swim against the tide and it will take awhile. But we are going to get you out. Do you understand?"

"I've never skin dived before." One of the boys spoke softly, his fear evident on his stark white face.

"Then you're in luck, I'm an instructor," Simone smiled at the scared young boy. "You stick with me, and David will help your buddy here. What's your name?"

"Steve, and that's Mike."

"Okay Steve, David is going to take good care of Mike, and I need you to pay attention to me. This is the regulator and it goes into your mouth. You breathe regularly from it. We have a mask for each of you, and a pair of flippers to strap on."

While David and Simone prepared the two boys, the water rose to just under their chins. Simone figured they only had ten minutes at best before the cave filled up.

"David, are you and Mike ready?"

"Yes, Simone."

"Okay Steve, are you ready?"

"I guess so."

"All right, let's tie these light sticks on so we can easily spot each other in the water. David, you and Mike need to tie off, and then Steve and I will bring up the back."

"Now remember guys, just breath normally through your mouth and the regulator will do all the work."

It took Steve three attempts before he could submerge and stay with his head underwater. Claustrophobia was very common with most people and in order to skin dive they had to overcome the natural instinct to panic. Simone knew he was going to panic when they first headed back down the cave, and she didn't blame him. She was close to panic herself at the thought of swimming in the dark water, being pushed back by the incoming tide. Thoughts of Shannon waiting impatiently for her return made it a little less frightening as she consoled the terrified young boy. David looked at Simone and she stared back at him. They both knew there was a chance they would all drown. They faced that possibility every time they went on a rescue. He tapped on his watch and signaled to her. David and Mark started without incident back down the cave.

"Okay, Steve, we need to go, buddy."

The frightened young boy started to cry as he stared at Simone. "I'm scared."

"You know what Steve, so am I. But if I wasn't, I wouldn't be a good rescue diver. It makes me be very careful. Now, why don't you give me a hug and let's get out of here."

Steve hugged her tightly and Simone felt her own tears as she hugged him in return before pulling her mask in place. Steve mimicked her movements as she put her regulator in her mouth and began to breathe. Giving a thumbs up to Steve, she turned with him and dove under the water pulling him along. He began to struggle as they started down the cave, completely surrounded by water and darkness. Simone faced him so he could see her calm eyes and stroked his back until he gradually began to swim with her. The tide pushed on them as they swam, making it slow going as they moved to what Simone thought was the path home, after checking her compass.

CHAPTER 24

Shannon gravely checked her watch as she prepared for Christa's next live update. Simone and David had been gone for over an hour, and the whole site was becoming very concerned, especially with the rope severed. The rope still trailed into the cave, but was no longer attached to Simone and David. They had to rely on their compasses and their wits.

"Shannon, how are you doing, honey?" Mel, Janice, Hanna, and Olivia piled out of Neely's car.

"What are you doing here?" Shannon hugged them all tightly.

"Christa called Neely and told her to bring us here."

Shannon looked at Christa who was standing next to Neely watching them. Shannon smiled in thanks to her. She began to answer the four women's questions as Christa and Neely conversed.

"They have been in the cave for over an hour and they only have air for one and a half hours total," Christa explained to Neely.

"Does anyone know if they found the boys?"

"No, there is no way to communicate with the divers while they are inside the cave. Simone is in charge of the rescue inside the cave."

"Is it totally under water?"

"Completely, and with the tide coming in it's very hard for them to get out, especially with two very young boys."

"How is Shannon doing?"

"She's broken hearted and scared to death for Simone."

"How are you?"

"Equally as scared, Neely, they have been in there so long, and they're just about out of air. They have to swim against the incoming tide the whole way."

Neely hugged her girlfriend tightly before responding, "Honey, Simone is one of the best trained divers in all of the islands. If anyone can save those two boys it's her."

"Christa, we're live in five minutes," Shannon called to her as she hefted her camera on to her shoulder.

"I'm ready," Christa smiled at Neely. "I'll be right back."

"I'll be here." Neely watched as Shannon and Christa made their way over to where the control center was located. The parents of both boys sat in their car waiting as did the ambulance, paramedics, and all the other emergency personnel. There was very little talking as the time slid by under the watchful eye of everyone. Christa approached the silent crowd while Shannon turned the camera on.

"Chief Olsen, could you give us an update on the rescue."

Chief Olsen sighed before he began to speak. The strain and worry for his two divers was evident on his face. "We're expecting our divers to be surfacing in about fifteen minutes."

"Does anyone know whether they found the boys?"

"We won't know until they surface, but we're assuming it's taking them so long because they did find them."

Christa hesitated before asking her next question, but she knew her job required it. "If the divers don't come out in fifteen minutes, what is the next plan?"

The Chief didn't want to state what he had to say, but he couldn't dodge the question. "We'll assess the situation, but our original plan was if the divers didn't make it out during the allotted time we would wait until the tide goes out and resume our search. The divers know that if they were close to running out of air they would take refuge in an air pocket if they can't get out of the caves."

"Thanks, Chief Olsen. Well, as you have heard, we are waiting for the divers to surface. They currently have less than fifteen minutes worth of air. We will continue our live coverage of this rescue after a five minute break."

Christa turned away from Chief Olsen and walked closer to Shannon. "Do you think we can get a good shot of the cave opening from over there on the cliff?"

"I think so."

Christa and Shannon headed to the cliff down from the actual cave and Shannon zoomed on the breaking waves above the cave opening. The two water bikes were back in the water and were patiently waiting along side the rescue boat. Christa turned to Shannon and grabbed her waist hugging her quickly.

"I know she's okay, Shannon."

"She's going to have the boys with her." Shannon tried to reassure herself and Christa.

"Yes, she will. We'd better start up."

Shannon turned the camera on as Christa raised her microphone. "This is Christa Neily, and we're watching the rescue attempt of two young boys by Kona's talented rescue divers. They're carrying an hour and a half of air with each diver and their time is about up, as we watch for their safe return."

A yell from the beach interrupted Christa's dialogue, and Shannon focused the camera on the rescue boat and the two water bikes, as there appeared to be some activity. She saw a diver's head in the water, a hand raised above the surf. One of the water bikes moved in and threw a rope in the same direction and within moments the diver and one of the boys was pulled out of the rough surf and into the rescue boat. A cheer went up from the emergency personnel as the radio crackled with the information that the young boy named Mike was fine. They would be bringing him to shore shortly. There was a short pause as the crowd watched the water above the cave for Simone and the second boy to appear. The time grew long as they all waited.

"It's been over ten minutes." Shannon whispered to Christa. "Won't Simone run out of air?"

Christa didn't know what to say as she clutched Shannon's hand in silence while they watched. Ten minutes stretched to fifteen and fifteen grew to twenty as everyone watched in complete disbelief and silence.

"Chief, I want to go back in," David's voice crackled over the radio.

"David, you know what your orders are. No one goes back in."

"But she is probably slowed down by the boy. He was petrified of diving." The panic in David's voice was loud and clear.

"David, you have your orders." Chief Olsen's voice was stern, even though he wanted to say yes. Simone was a dear friend of his and a very brave paramedic. If the Chief could have gone himself, he would.

CHAPTER 25

Simone checked her regulator and felt the panic as she realized that she and Steve were almost out of air. She had no idea if they were anywhere close to the cave entrance. She prepared herself. Steve would instinctively struggle when his air stopped flowing. She prayed and fought against the current, dragging Steve behind her. All she wanted to do was get out of the cave and see Shannon once more. She couldn't die now, not after finding the love of her life. Please God, let me see Shannon again. She made up her mind she would continue to swim as long as her body could. She would not give up. Nothing would make her give up. She would die trying. The blackness was so frightening and her light only pierced a little ways in front of her. She fought against the strong current, her body tiring as she forced herself to keep moving.

The rope tied around her waist jerked and Simone turned around to find Steve struggling to breathe. His air had given out and he was suffocating. Simone grabbed him to her and held on as he fought hard to get a breath. His movements became sluggish and he slowly slumped inert in Simone's arms. She felt pain deep in her heart as he drifted unconscious in the tide.

It was now up to Simone to get him out of the cave and as rapidly as possible. She only had a little time before she too would run out of air. It was even harder for Simone to swim through the current with Steve's unconscious body pulling on her.

"I need to see you, Shannon, please God, just one more time," Simone whispered over and over in her head and she forced herself to continue moving. Fear made her think about letting go and giving up, but she couldn't. She continued to move one foot at a time, her arms growing heavy with each stroke.

She'd only gone another fifty feet when her air stopped abruptly and she was totally without air. She felt the pain in her lungs as she continued to swim burning up her energy. Just when she thought her chest would burst, her light caught the drifting rope as it fluttered in the water. Even if she couldn't get them out of the cave, she could tie the rope to them. They could recover the bodies. Wrapping the rope around her waist, she tied it tightly as she fought the urge to gasp in water and end her trip. Her chest burned, her arms and legs heavy.

"Shannon, I love you." With very little strength left, Simone pulled the two of them along the rope, knowing it would take them out of the cave. She lost all coherent thought as she focused on placing one hand in front of the other, pulling on the rope with whatever strength she had left.

She felt herself losing consciousness and started to cry as thoughts of missing Shannon became too much. She had to make it. "Please God, let me make it. Help me, please."

CHAPTER 26

Five more minutes slipped by as the waiting crowd watched the water, prayers being said out loud and in private. Shannon's chest felt heavy, and her body ached while she tried to stem off the rising panic she felt. She couldn't lose Simone, not now. "Please God, help Simone."

"There she is!" A yell went up in the crowd as Simone's familiar wet suit appeared in the waves in front of the cave, the young boy being dragged behind her.

The rescue worker on the water bike threw a rope to her, and she grabbed hold and tied it around her body. Protecting the young boy's body with her own, she was pulled closer to the waiting rescue boat. As soon as she was close enough, she yelled to the waiting medics.

"He's not breathing!"

The medics dragged the boy into the boat and began working on him immediately as one of the other members of the rescue team pulled an exhausted Simone from the water. She slumped on to the floor of the boat, gasping for air. David kneeled down in front of her.

"Simone, are you okay?"

"I'll be fine in a minute. We ran out of air the last two hundred yards or so. I'm afraid he took a lot of water in his lungs. He panicked when he lost his air and pulled the regulator out of his mouth. David, I watched him drown."

David's eyes filled up with tears as he looked at Simone's distraught face. He had enormous respect for her as a diver and a person and he knew there was no one who could have done what she did. He reached out and touched her cheek gently in support. Steve began choking and spitting up salt water and they both turned to watch. The two medics working on Steve grinned, and a sigh of relief went through both of them. "He's fine, Simone, he's going to be just fine."

The radio crackled to life as one of the medics spoke over it to the control center and the waiting crowd. "The young boy and our rescue diver are both just fine." The man's voice broke with emotion as he completed his statement.

A cheer echoed across the cliffs and moved across the water to the boat as they made their way to the beach. Simone stayed seated on the deck, too tired to do anything but grin at the group.

Shannon heard the words on the radio as she was filming Simone and the paramedics working on the boy on the boat, as they all waited for news. Her heart flipped in her chest and as the cheer went up from those waiting she started to cry. Christa was in tears herself as she picked up the microphone to speak.

"As you have just witnessed, the young boy and his rescuer are being taken care of on the rescue boat, and both are okay. We'll bring you more of this successful rescue as soon as we can. This is Christa Neilson with the Kona news network, bringing to you the happy news about the daring rescue of two young boys from a water filled caves off Makole'a Black Sand Beach. We will now go back to our regularly scheduled news cast."

Christa dropped the microphone on to the ground and turned to Shannon, who lifted the camera off of her shoulder and placed it at her feet. They looked at each other with grins, and then grabbed each other in bear hugs, as they both began to cry. Neely and the rest of the women joined the two of them, as they took turns hugging and kissing each other. There was no shortage of tears as they let loose with their emotions and their fears.

"God Shannon, I was so scared," Janice admitted as she wept.

"So was I."

Neely hugged Christa tightly. "That was too close."

"Yes, it was." Christa hugged her girlfriend as tears ran down her face. "Yes, it was."

It was several minutes before any of them could do anything other than hug and grin at each other. Shannon watched as the boat pulled up on to the beach and both young boys were handed off to the waiting paramedics who would check them both out. David and Simone were also helped out of the boat by other members of the rescue unit. Shannon's eyes didn't leave Simone's figure as she responded to questions from the rescue group, but her eyes ran over the waiting crowd until they found Shannon's, and they locked on her. It was a long gaze, as people around them grew silent, showing them the respect due two people who loved each other. And anyone who looked at them knew they loved each other deeply.

Simone began to walk toward Shannon, her strides long and rapid. Shannon dropped her camera and started walking toward her. Within two steps, she was running, closing the gap as they met in a hug as Shannon threw herself at Simone and was caught in Simone's arms.

"I love you, I'm so glad you are okay. I thought I was going to lose you," Shannon babbled as she clung to Simone.

"I love you, Shannon. Shush I'm okay, and everything is fine." Simone couldn't let go of Shannon and she couldn't stop shaking. She'd come so close to never seeing Shannon again. "I need to go and finish reporting to the team."

"Go, honey." Shannon hugged her tightly once more. "I'll wait for you. Simone, I'm so proud of you."

Simone's eyes filled with tears as she stared down at Shannon. "I love you."

"You go give your report." Shannon pushed her gently in the direction of the control center where the two boys were being hugged and kissed by their parents.

Shannon watched her lover walk back to the rest of her crew and a feeling of love, pride, and awe filled her from head to toe. Simone would always amaze her with her commitment, her pure and honest nature that was driven to help others, and her love for Shannon.

Christa and Neely approached Shannon along with the rest of her friends. "She's amazing isn't she?"

"Just as amazing as her partner, who stood and watched as her girlfriend's life was in unbelievable danger while she saved two other lives. You still did your job, an incredible one I might add, while your lover was in danger. I'd say that makes you two perfect for each other." Christa grinned. "And we need to finish up here so we can get the last tape into the network, and call it a wrap. Are you up to a few interviews with the boys and their families, and the rescue unit?"

"I can do that." Shannon reached down and picked up her camera. "But when we finish up, I'm taking my girlfriend home and putting her to bed, with me in it."

The laughter that followed Shannon and Christa as they headed toward the family made them both grin. It was happy, stress releasing laughter, and it made them feel good just to hear it. It warmed Shannon's already full heart.

The interviews with the families went quickly as both boys wanted to thank Simone and David for being alive. The parents were too busy holding their children to say much more than thanks and God bless. But Steve wasn't shy in telling his story, and it caused Shannon to freeze with cold stark fear while he spoke.

"It was so dark you couldn't even see the walls of the cave. We were hanging on to the wall and the water was up to our chins when we saw Simone and David. We thought we were going to die." Steve's mother cried on her husband's shoulder as she listened to her son speak, shocked and awed by what her son was saying. "Simone explained to us that we were going to swim back through the cave, and she taught me out to use the scuba gear. David and Mike went first because I was scared, and didn't want to go. But Simone promised me we would be okay, and she was right. I had a hard time swimming because the current was so strong, but Simone would stop and hug me, and write little notes on her underwater tablet. She told me she had to hurry up, because she had a date."

The smile on Steve's face was one of a young boy with a huge crush and a little awe. Shannon smiled as she filmed another one who had fallen under Simone's spell.

"She kept telling me I was doing good, but I know I wasn't going fast enough. She told me we would run out of air, and she needed me to trust her when we did. She said she would get me out and she did. When we ran out of air, I got really scared. But she held me tightly until I wasn't scared and then she kept swimming. I don't remember much after that accept waking up on the boat."

"Thanks, Steve. I am very glad you're okay."

"I am, too."

Christa turned to the Fire Chief who looked a little less stressed than he had appeared earlier. "Chief Olsen, your rescue team was very successful today. Can you explain a little of what your two divers did?"

"We will have a complete report by mid-day tomorrow but currently we believe the two boys were fairly deep into the cave, and found a cavern where a pocket of air was available, when the tide came in cutting off their escape route. Our divers were just about to return and go back out, when they found the two boys clinging to the walls of the cave, up to their chins in water. Our rescuers estimated the cavern would have filled with water within ten to twenty minutes of their arrival. Both boys were prepared for extraction from the cave by our rescue divers, and they started the swim back out of the cave. David left first approximately ten minutes before Simone. It took David an hour to make the trip out of the cave. Simone's trip took a little over an hour and twenty minutes to make the trip. Simone and David had approximately forty-five minutes of air remaining in their tanks. The boys had the same amount of air. Both divers made it out successfully, bringing the young boys with them."

"Thank you, Chief Olsen. You must feel very proud of your team."

"That I am."

Shannon turned the camera off at Christa's signal and lowered it before speaking. "Chief Olsen how did Simone and the young boy make it out when they ran out of air before exiting the cave?"

The Chief looked at Shannon and his face betrayed his exhaustion and his respect for the people he commanded. "Shannon, Simone and David know how to slow down their breathing and make their air last longer than what the regulator reads."

"Thirty minutes worth?"

"Shannon, this is one of those times when I don't have a scientific answer for you. Let's just say Simone had a reason for getting the young boy and herself safely out of that cave. She swam the last two hundred yards with little if any air. That takes a tremendous amount of courage, strength, and will power."

"Thanks Chief."

"Thank me next Saturday night, when I give you the gift my wife picked out for you and Simone. I think its butt ugly." He grinned at Shannon and squeezed her arm.

"I owe you a drink."

"I'll take you up on that when I can enjoy it. Right now I need to go thank my team for a job well done, and send them home."

Christa and Shannon smiled as they watched the obviously relieved and very well respected Fire Chief speak to his team, before sending them on their way. The team went about the job of picking up and stowing their equipment, before dispersing back to the station. Simone and David removed their wet suits and loaded up their equipment, after rinsing everything off. Shannon piled everything in the van to return to the station with Christa after hugging her friends and Neely goodbye. Simone came over to the van with David just as Christa and Shannon were preparing to leave.

Christa hugged Simone while Shannon hugged David. "You both were amazing, David. We're so glad you're okay and that you found those two boys."

"So am I, Shannon." David wasn't his usually talkative self. He looked exhausted physically and emotionally.

"You need to go home to your girlfriend and crawl in bed."

"That's exactly what I'm planning on doing." David and his girlfriend had spent many a night over at Simone and Shannon's for dinner.

"Shannon, I'll meet you at home as soon as I can get this stuff back to the station."

"Okay honey." Shannon smiled up at her girlfriend. "And then I want you all to myself."

"Sounds perfect." Simone looked as exhausted as David but she had a huge grin on her face.

Shannon and Christa pulled out of the park and started the drive back to the station. Neither one spoke for the longest time as they made the over forty minute trip. They were within ten minutes of the station before Christa spoke softly to Shannon. "It's times like this when I realize just how wonderful my life is. We could have lost four people today, but instead two lost boys were found by two very brave people, one of which is my very best friend. This is the type of story that makes all the other stuff just fade away."

"Christa, what you do every day makes a difference in people's lives. They turn on the television to watch you because they know that they'll get an honest, thorough story every time."

Christa was surprised and embarrassed by Shannon's comment. She didn't know quite how to respond. "Thanks, Shannon that means an awful lot to me that you think that."

Shannon was surprised at Christa's insecurity. "That's why I agreed to be your cameraman. I know you aren't going to take any shortcuts, you always do your homework, and provide an accurate well-rounded viewpoint."

Christa was bright red from embarrassment. "Thank you, I thought you might dislike my requesting you as my cameraman because of my history with Simone."

Shannon laughed and flipped a smirk at Christa before responding. "I might have felt that way a year ago but now I don't. I really like you and Neely together and I love how Simone and I are with each other. I have no need to worry about anyone else when it comes to Simone, and she has no reason to worry about anyone else with me. And I like you, Christa. I know the side of you that very few people get to see, you are a marshmallow."

Christa snorted with laughter. "I have to tell you I had some reservations when I first met you and Simone told me she was going to marry you after one week. But she reminded me that Neely and I moved in together after a week. I also saw how you treated Simone, and I no longer worried. I can't wait to see you and Simone get married. I like you too. You're a good woman."

"Thank you. I'm going to count my blessings for a very long time and I can't wait for Saturday."

"Amen to that."

Shannon pulled the van into the station parking lot and parked it in the lot. "Christa, I'll unload the video tapes and camera and lock up. You go on in."

"Thanks Shannon, I need to polish up my notes before heading home."

Shannon knew that Christa worked long into the night on stories to get them right. "Don't work too late, Neely is waiting at home, and I'm sure she knows how lucky you both are."

Christa flashed her trademark smile at Shannon as she walked quickly to the door. "I'm not spending a moment longer than I have too."

Shannon finished unloading the van and locking up when Art joined her as she swung the camera and bag over her shoulders. "Hey Art."

"Hey Shannon. Here let me help." Art grabbed the camera bag and walked with her back into the building. "Exciting day."

"Very."

"Your video was excellent."

"Thanks Art."

"Was it as nerve wracking as it looked?"

"It was worse," Shannon admitted as they headed down to the editing room to drop the videotapes off.

"I'm glad everything worked out."

"So am I. Tomorrow I need to go over the video with you and see if we can make a better story. I'm sure Christa is going to want to run a follow up to the rescue."

"Sounds good. Shannon, I'm very glad Simone was okay."

"So am I, Art. So am I. I didn't realize until today how brave and unbelievably talented she is. It's humbling to see people put their lives on the line to save two young boys. It makes what I do pale in comparison."

"I don't know about that. It would be hard for people to understand how incredible the rescue was without talented people like you filming it."

"Thanks Art."

"You're welcome, you do excellent work."

"I appreciate that, I have good teachers." Shannon grinned at him. "I'm going to lock this camera up and head home."

"You do that."

Shannon was on her way home within ten minutes, impatient to get there before Simone. She was going to make sure Simone crawled in bed and got a good night's rest, right next to her very relieved girlfriend.

Simone was having similar feelings as she headed out of her office toward the front door of the station.

"Simone, can I have a quick minute of your time?"

"Sure Chief."

"I just wanted to say how proud I was of your work today. That was a very difficult and grueling rescue. Not everyone could have done what you did."

"We're all very well trained, and any one of us would do the same thing."

"Captain, you are, and will always be one of the most talented paramedics we'll ever have. I consider it an honor and a privilege to work with you. Now, I have one request of you, and I told David the same thing. I do not want to see either of you in this building before ten o'clock. Is that clear?"

Simone grinned at the Chief as she responded, "Yes sir."

"Goodnight."

"Goodnight." Simone's feet dragged as she walked to the car, she was exhausted and stiffening up. She knew she would be very sore in the morning. All she wanted to do was to go home and crawl in bed.

"Hi guys."

"Shannon, you look beat."

"I am a little tired. I hope you guys don't mind, but I'm going to take a shower."

"Honey, we don't mind at all. I fixed you and Simone some cold chicken and a salad for dinner. You can eat it in bed."

"Thanks Olivia. Simone is going to be exhausted when she gets here. I'm going to convince her to crawl in bed as soon as possible."

"I think that's a good idea. We're going to go down on the beach and leave the two of you alone for awhile."

"You guys don't have to leave."

"We aren't leaving. Shannon, we're so glad Simone is okay, and that she was able to find both boys. She's amazing."

Shannon couldn't keep the tears from filling her eyes or the ones that tracked down her cheeks. "Yes, she is."

"Go honey, and take a shower." Janice and Mel hugged her, then Olivia and Hanna. They watched in silence as Shannon slowly made her way down the hall and closed the bedroom door behind her. They knew she was struggling to contain her emotions. Olivia prepared two plates for dinner and then the four headed out the back door. Simone and Shannon needed an evening alone after the day they had experienced.

Shannon stood in the shower long after the water turned lukewarm. She needed to wash away the emotions that churned inside her body. She was still reeling inside over watching her lover almost die while saving a young boy's life. And she knew Simone wouldn't hesitate to do it all over again. It was as much a part of her as her very generous heart, and it was one of the many things that Shannon loved about her beautiful girlfriend.

Simone entered the quiet house and looked around for their houseguests. They were nowhere to be seen, so she headed down the hall to her bedroom. Shannon was still in the bathroom, spreading lotion on her legs and arms. She didn't hear Simone enter the bedroom or the bathroom until she saw Simone's wan face in the bathroom mirror. Without a word, Shannon and Simone reached for each other, their lips devouring each other. Shannon murmured as Simone's hands raced over her body, producing flashes of heat, as her touch ignited all of Shannon's senses, while they rolled against the door and then fell into the bedroom. Shannon's hands struggled to remove Simone's uniform and finally gave up trying to unbutton her blouse. She tore it open as Simone moaned and Shannon stripped it off her body, her lips sliding over the swell of breasts above her bra. Simone's lips covered Shannon's face, neck, and shoulders, her hands stroking Shannon's hips. Shannon removed Simone's bra and kissed her breasts and nipples as she unzipped Simone's shorts, dropping them to the floor. Simone had kicked her shoes off and Shannon ran her hands under her panties sliding them quickly down her legs. She kissed Simone passionately, their tongues sliding against each other's as the need just grew larger. Simone's hands were everywhere and before Shannon could suggest they find the bed, Simone's hand cupped her between her legs, her fingers sliding into the welcoming wetness as she licked and tasted Shannon's nipples. The orgasm that ripped through Shannon's body took her breath away as she slumped against Simone.

"Shannon, I love you. I love touching you and making love with you. You were all I thought about as I swam through the cave. I had to make it I knew you were waiting for me." Simone's words and her lovemaking tumbled Shannon into another orgasm that rolled through her body. She wrapped her arms around Simone as her body slumped against her.

Shannon reached down and ran her hands over Simone's muscular backend before lifting her right leg up and holding it against her hip. Her left hand slid down Simone's stomach and through the blond, moist curls, before shoving her fingers deeply inside Simone's waiting body. Simone's hips slammed against Shannon's as Shannon plunged deeper and faster into Simone. Simone's hips pounded against Shannon's, as she cried out in pleasure, her arms tightening around Shannon's shoulders. Her mouth covered Shannon's in a renewal of life, of love, total commitment.

"I thought I was going to lose you today." Shannon's eyes glistened with tears as she touched Simone's face.

"Never, you'll never lose me."

"I can't. You are my heart, my soul."

"And your mine, I love you Shannon." Simone and Shannon stood in each other's arms for a long time, not willing to relinquish one moment away from each other.

They moved slowly while they put on robes, and took advantage of Olivia's prepared dinner and they spent forty minutes in the kitchen eating it. Simone was hardly aware of eating, exhaustion and emotions overwhelmed her, as she fought to stay awake.

"Simone, I'm going to put you in bed, honey."

Simone didn't argue as Shannon took her by the hand and led the way to their bedroom. Shannon removed Simone's robe and pulled the covers back on the bed. Simone sat down and looked up at Shannon with such love that Shannon started to cry as she leaned over and hugged Simone.

"I love you so much."

"Could you hold me for a while?" Simone's voice was barely a whisper but Shannon heard the need in Simone's voice and her heart ached.

"Of course, you lie down." Simone crawled under the covers and rolled over to face Shannon as she removed her robe and slid into bed beside Simone. Shannon reached for her and gathered Simone in her arms. Simone wrapped her body around Shannon, laying her head on Shannon's shoulder. "Go to sleep, sweetie, you're safe."

Simone never responded as she quickly fell sound asleep, her body limp with exhaustion. Shannon lay awake for a long time reliving the last five hours before she slid into restless sleep, images of Simone swimming in the pitch black cave, struggling to get the young boy out.

"How are they?" Janice asked as she and Hanna sat in the living room, quietly reading.

"Both of them are dead to the world," Mel responded as she sat down next to Janice.

"Good, they need their sleep after today. Boy, it sure seems like every time we come to Hawaii someone almost drowns."

"Just bad luck."

"I hope so. So what do we need to do tomorrow?"

"Neely will be here at nine in the morning, and we're going to follow her over to her mother's home. We're going to string flower leis and make the decorations for the tables. We'll set up the tables Friday and decorate them on Saturday morning. I think we're going to help them cook on Wednesday and Thursday. We need to clean the house on Friday and we're taking Simone and Shannon out for dinner on Friday night."

"Are we giving them their gift on Friday night?"

"I though we would."

"So do you think I could talk you into going to bed with me?"

"I think so." Mel grinned at Janice.

"Goodnight." Hanna wanted to finish her book before she turned in and joined her sleeping girlfriend.

Shannon slept soundly with Simone curled around her body, her mind and body at rest, but Simone wasn't so lucky. She began to cry out in her sleep and turned from Shannon as she thrashed back and forth. It was a cry so full of anguish it jerked Shannon awake as she sat up and turned to Simone. Simone's face was awash with tears her eyes clenched shut, her skin clammy to Shannon's touch.

"Simone honey, wake up. You're having a bad dream." Shannon stroked her face to try and wake her.

Simone didn't wake up quickly she struggled in Shannon's arms before she slowly began to respond to Shannon's whispered pleas. She fought hard, gasping for air as her eyes fluttered open.

"Honey its Shannon. You're okay, sweetie. Everything's okay."

Simone sat up and looked at her girlfriend, before bursting into tears. Shannon wrapped her arms tightly around Simone and rocked her as she cried her heart out. Her weeping was full of pain and fear. It was a long time before Simone settled down enough to where Shannon could understand what she was trying to say.

"I keep dreaming I'm trying to swim out of the cave and I get to the opening and there is a locked gate that I can't get through. I keep trying to open it and I can get through to you." Simone began to sob again.

Shannon started crying as she listened to Simone, the panic in her voice and her frightened face made her ache for her lover. "It's all over you're safe here with me."

Simone buried her face against Shannon's shoulder and hung on to Shannon as if her life depended upon it. Shannon stroked her back, soothing her with her touch as well as her words.

"Why don't you lie down and I will hold you tightly so you know you are okay?"

"Shannon, I'm sorry."

"You have nothing to be sorry about." Shannon bent and kissed Simone softly. "I love you."

Simone settled down next to Shannon, her eyes barely open as she struggled with exhaustion and fear. Shannon held Simone against her body, speaking softly, as her eyes drifted shut, and her breathing deepened. Shannon willed herself to stay awake in case Simone had another nightmare. She couldn't keep the tears from sliding down her cheeks as she realized just how terrified Simone had been in the cave. It was sheer will power and the need to save the two young boys, that made her do her job. And that made her efforts just that much more amazing. Shannon watched Simone sleep for several hours. As she became agitated Shannon would speak softly to her, while holding her tightly to sooth her. Simone didn't slip into quiet sleep until about four in the morning and even then Shannon lay next to her, unable to drop off into complete sleep. She slept restlessly with Simone draped around her body, Shannon's arms holding her tightly.

"Shannon," Simone's voice was raspy due to exhaustion, her eyes red rimmed and swollen. "Did you get any sleep?"

"I got plenty, honey. How are you doing?"

"I'm fine. I'm sorry I kept you awake last night." Simone leaned over Shannon, smiling down at her.

"Sweetie, I just glad you are here to keep me awake." Shannon reached up and slid her arms around Simone's neck, pulling her close. "I love you. Could I get a good morning kiss?"

Simone and Shannon kissed slowly, their lips soft and tender, drawing the kiss out. It went a long way to soothing the ache in Shannon's heart. Simone and Shannon continued to kiss, less in passion than in love and promise.

"Five more days."

"Isn't that amazing?"

"I love you," Simone pledged as she hugged Shannon tightly. The alarm went off next to Shannon before she could do anything more than groan.

"I can't wait until Friday." Simone sat up and prepared to get out of bed. Shannon quickly stood on her feet. She had an hour to shower, dress, and be at work. "Simone, you don't have to be at work for several more hours, why don't you stay in bed?"

"I'm fine I would like to get my report written before this morning's meeting. Besides, I need to make sure I have the schedules completed for next week. Today should be pretty quiet, so I can get a lot of work done."

Shannon just listened quietly to Simone. She didn't say a word but Simone could read the expression on her face. "I promise I will come home a little early." Shannon just raised her eyebrows in response. "I'll be home by three."

Shannon smiled before she entered the bathroom to take her shower. She had made her point to Simone, and Simone would keep her promise. Shannon was going to try to get home early herself.

Simone's day was uneventful, if three network interviews, and hundreds of telephone calls, on top of her usual full day was normal. And that was by lunchtime.

"Simone, have you finished the schedule for next week?"

"I did, Randy. It's being printed as we speak. You should have a copy within the hour." Randy Cartwright was going to be handling things while Simone was out of the office. He was a talented medic and shift manager that Simone was grooming to take her position when or if she was promoted or moved. "You and I need to set some time aside tomorrow to go over any last minute issues that might come up, especially with all of this media attention."

"I'll set up a meeting in the afternoon for an hour or so. Is there anything you want me to look into today?"

"Can you check with David and see that we have re-outfitted the diving team equipment?"

"Sure will."

"Thanks." Simone turned back to the pile of paperwork on her desk and was just settling down when her cell phone rang on her hip. She grinned when she saw the caller id.

"Hi sweetie."

"Hello, how is your day going?"

"Good, I am just going to finish a little bit more paperwork and I have one more meeting before heading out the door. I promised my girlfriend I'd go home early."

Shannon chuckled as she responded. "Are you tired?"

"I am. And I'm sure you are, since I kept you awake for most of the night."

"I think I'm running on adrenaline, but I'm on my way home and I am planning on sneaking a nap on the beach. How does that sound to you?"

"Perfect, but don't we have something to do tonight?"

"No, everything is being handled by Neely and her work crew. Christa warned me to stay out of her way."

"I love you, Shannon."

"I love you, and I will see you soon. Meet me on the beach."

"I'll do that." Simone was grinning when she hung up the telephone. It continually surprised her how well she and Shannon got along especially when she stopped to consider that they had met, fallen in love, and moved in together in less than a month. One year later, they were even more in love and their respect for each other had only grown. They were best friends and soul mates, soon to be married in the eyes of their friends and each other.

"I thought you told me you were leaving early?" Chief Olsen bellowed from the doorway. Simone had just returned from her last meeting.

"I am."

"Then get out of here. There is nothing on that desk that requires immediate attention."

Simone grinned at him as she stood up, grabbing her briefcase. "I'm going right now."

He walked with Simone to the door of the station house. "Simone, we need to begin re-training for more rescue divers on our team when you get back from vacation. You need to share your knowledge and what you've learned with a broader audience."

"I agree. I'll start looking at some tentative dates this week."

"Simone, I said after you get back."

"Okay, I'll wait."

"Simone, I want to tell you again, that you are one of the most talented and dedicated paramedics we've ever had. I'm continually amazed at your capabilities as a rescuer and a manager."

"Thanks Chief." Simone colored with embarrassment.

"You're welcome. Now go and get some much needed rest."

Simone walked swiftly to her car the idea of spending an afternoon snoozing on the beach with Shannon was extremely appealing. Shannon was already putting her plan into action. She entered the empty house and quickly changed into her bathing suit. Her next stop was to grab a blanket, a couple of pillows, and several bottles of cold water. Ten minutes later she had everything ready, including a small bag of snacks to munch on. She sat silently enjoying the beach as she began to unwind after a fairly busy morning. She could feel the tension leave her body.

"Hey you." Simone flopped on to the blanket next to her, gathering her in her arms as she hugged her tightly. "I missed you today."

"I missed you too. You look exhausted." Shannon ran her fingers over Simone's face.

"I am tired. How about you lie down with me and we both try to take a nap. I left a note on the refrigerator for the girls to come wake us when they got home."

"I like that idea."

Shannon and Simone snuggled up to each other on the blanket and within minutes they were both sound asleep. They were still deeply asleep when Hanna went to check on them an hour later.

"They're both still sleeping soundly," Hanna commented to her friends as they all congregated in the kitchen.

"We should probably let them sleep for another hour or so. I don't think either one got too much sleep last night."

"Are they going to get sunburned?"

"No, they're in the shade. So what's planned for dinner and whose turn is it to cook?"

"We're barbequing hamburgers and there's fresh potato salad in the refrigerator. Mel's doing the cooking."

"Great, so what do you say to a little snorkeling before dinner?"

"I like that idea, Mel and Janice and going to go for a walk and stay around the house."

"I bet I beat you into my bathing suit!" Olivia boasted as she took off down the hall with Hanna rapidly following her.

CHAPTER 27

The rest of the week, in comparison to the beginning, was uneventful, as Friday afternoon arrived, signaling the start of the weekend festivities. The evening was an elegant dinner hosted by Neely and Christa in celebration of Simone and Shannon's impending ceremony. Held at a restaurant in a private dinner room, there was a lot of toasting, some gift giving, and some emotional moments, as friends of both Simone and Shannon shared memories and good wishes for the two of them.

Shannon spent most of the evening moving between laughter and tears as she listened to the stories from Simone's long time friends. Mel and Janice got into the act by sharing some revealing, and very humorous stories of Shannon, along with some very touching moments. Simone and Shannon held hands tightly throughout the evening, overwhelmed by the generosity and love they received from everyone. The night ended fairly early, since many of the party goers were scheduled to set up for the following day's luau. Shannon and Simone were being sent off to a spa for a massage and lunch to get them out of the way for the decorating and early preparations. Since people were going to start arriving later in the afternoon, they were scheduled to return by three in order to get dressed for the occasion. Neely, her family, and her work crew had thought of everything.

"Shannon, I can't find our rings?" Simone voice was raised in panic as she rummaged around in their dresser.

"Honey, Neely and Mel have them stashed away for safekeeping."

Simone turned and looked at Shannon, who was seated on the bed calmly brushing her hair. "Aren't you nervous?"

"Not yet, but by tomorrow afternoon I am going to be a basket case."

Simone flopped down on the bed next to her. "I'm so nervous I feel sick to my stomach."

Shannon looked at her girlfriend in surprise. "Are you nervous about the commitment?"

"No, I'm scared you are going to change your mind." Simone wasn't teasing her eyes were large and locked onto to Shannon's face.

Shannon's heart melted as she gathered Simone's hand in her own. "I'm not ever going to change my mind. I love you more today than last month and it just gets better and better every day."

Simone's smile was slow but Shannon could see the relief roll away. "I don't know why I'm so nervous."

"You can go into an underwater cave in the dark and save two boys without an ounce of fear, and getting married to me makes you nervous?" Shannon teased as she rolled over to lie next to Simone.

Simone turned so they were facing each other before she responded. "The first one I am trained to do. Marrying you is so much more important to me."

"So your not going to chicken out on me, are you?"

"Me chicken out, not on your life." Simone hugged Shannon. "You're stuck with me, baby."

"You bet your life I am," Shannon vowed, kissing Simone gently.

They were content to just lie quietly on the bed holding hands, their faces tucked against each other's as they slowly drifted off to sleep, love and commitment already a large part of their life together, just waiting to be stated in front of family and friends.

CHAPTER 28

"Can we come out now?" Shannon called from the bedroom door as she and Simone waited impatiently in their room. It was after four and they could hear people arriving, but had been locked in their room waiting to be told they could join the growing crowd.

"Just a little bit longer," Hanna called back as she and Christa finished some last minute preparations in the kitchen. Everything had gone amazingly well due to Neely's expert planning, and the many volunteers who helped.

Simone sat on the bed fidgeting while Shannon meandered around the bedroom, both of them nervous and excited. Simone's eyes roamed over Shannon and she couldn't prevent the heat from rushing through her body at the thought that Shannon was marrying her today. She was such a good person, full of love and laughter, and she was so beautiful. Shannon was wearing a bright blue and green lava lava, her shoulders bare and the slit showing a well tanned thigh. Simone's lava lava was a mix of yellows and white swirling together in a tropical pattern found in wild orchids. Neely's family had supplied the beautiful traditional garments for them. They were both barefoot with no jewelry on. Simone's blond hair was full of loose curls that swirled around her beautiful face. Shannon's long hair was tied back in a French braid that trailed down to the middle of her back, with a green and blue matching cord strung through it. Simone had never seen her dressed more beautifully than today and she continued to gaze at her as Shannon moved restlessly around the room. Shannon turned and caught the look on Simone's face and she reacted to the love and attraction she saw. Her body heated up as she realized how much Simone wanted and needed her.

"I love you Simone." She walked over to stand in front of her.

"I love you. You're so sexy in this dress."

"I like the way you look." Shannon pulled Simone to her feet. "Do you think we have time?"

"For what?" Simone looked closely at Shannon and then began to chuckle as she realized what Shannon was intimating. "I don't think anyone would appreciate our arriving to the party late because we had better things to do in our bedroom."

Shannon just grinned and hugged her girlfriend tightly. "You know what my first choice would be."

Simone knew, and it was also hers. It pleased her immensely that they felt the same way about each other. They were still standing in each other's arms when there was a knock on the door.

"Come in."

Christa and Mel stood in the doorway smiling. Each had white flower lei in their hands. "There is one for each of you and one for your ankles."

Simone and Shannon helped each other with the ankle leis and then first Christa and then Mel placed them around their necks. "Are you two ready?"

Simone and Shannon grinned at one another and clasped hands. "Yes."

"Okay, follow us."

Simone and Shannon followed the two women through the house and out the back door on to the patio. There was a line of people standing on either side of the path and they clapped at the sight of Simone and Shannon. Flower petals littered the path down to the beach as they joined Christa and Mel and the waiting Hawaiian minister, while their friends called out greetings. The crowd followed the two women down to the beach and surrounded them as they stood holding hands in front of the minister.

"Good afternoon to everyone. Simone and Shannon, we're all here to witness your vows of commitment to one another in front of God and your family and friends. When two people choose to spend their life together in love, it is a special day to mark. Here on the beach, where God's beauty surrounds us, Shannon and Simone will make a promise to one another. Before we begin, I would like to encourage all of you who are standing with your loved one to renew your love along with these two women. The Hawaiian culture has always recognized that love and commitment is most important when it is made in the presence of God's beauty. There is nothing more beautiful or more eternal than standing here with the waves crashing on the beach. Shannon and Simone, would you turn and face each other to say your vows, Simone you can go first."

Simone's hands shook as she faced Shannon and prepared to speak. "I didn't realize how much I was missing in my life until you entered it. I grew up watching my parents love and respect each other for over thirty years and I always hoped I would find the same. You came to Hawaii and literally overnight changed my life. You filled my heart completely and I fell in love with you. You are my partner in every sense of the word. I will spend my life loving you and being loved by you. And I will thank God every day for the blessings in my life."

Shannon took a deep breath and began to speak. "I knew when I looked into your eyes the first day I met you that you were special. You place the welfare of others above your own, in your work, and your home. The day we met, I fell in love with you. You are my family and my partner. I will love you forever and longer, and I thank God every day for putting you in my life. You are brave, and beautiful, and perfect."

"Simone will you repeat after me, I promise to love and respect you for the rest of my life, forsaking all others, and being a partner in all things with you until death due us part."

Simone smiled at Shannon as she repeated the words, clasping Shannon's hands tightly in her own.

"Shannon will you repeat after me, I promise to love and respect you for the rest of my life, forsaking all others, and being a partner in all things with you until death due us part."

Shannon began to cry as she repeated her vows, her eyes full of love and emotion as she looked up at Simone.

"Simone and Shannon, will you each exchange rings and then turn to face me."

"In so much as the rings represent the commitment of love that is eternal, the two of you are exchanging rings to remind yourself every day that each decision, every choice you make, is made with two people in mind." Shannon and Simone slipped wide gold bands on each other's ring finger and turned to face the minister.

"And now comes my favorite part of the ceremony. In front of God and the people that are special to you both, I join you in mutual love and commitment until death do you part. I call on the Gods of fire, water, air, and earth to bless this union of hearts and minds. Would you like to kiss each other in celebration?"

Simone and Shannon didn't have to be asked twice as they kissed slowly, savoring the emotion that swirled around both of them. Shannon's face was streaked with tears as was Simone's.

"And now another Hawaiian tradition is for the two of you to take your leis off and tie them together, placing them in the ocean to represent your union."

Shannon and Simone removed their leis and twisted them together, knotting them before walking into the surf and placing them in the water where they were pulled out into the ocean. They walked back to the minister.

"Now, everyone please join me as we clap in celebration of their commitment and life together." The crowd whooped and hollered as Shannon and Simone hugged tightly. "That concludes the ceremony. Everyone is encouraged to stay and celebrate with Shannon and Simone in a tradition luau."

Shannon and Simone kissed again and then turned to hug their waiting friends. Neely approached them with two more colored leis to replace the ones they had released in the ocean, before kissing them both. "Come on and sit down, the party is just starting."

Neely couldn't have been more truthful. Her family knew how to stage a luau and the food never seemed to run out. The music and dancing went on for several hours before culminating in Neely and her grandmother doing the traditional hula to the Hawaiian Wedding song. It brought tears to Simone and Shannon's eyes as they watched, clutching each other's hand. It was beautiful and special. Many other people were equally as moved as they watched the old Hawaiian tradition.

The party wound down around midnight and as rapidly as the party had been set up, it was cleaned up, and everything was cleared away. Simone and Shannon walked up the path with Neely and Christa, Hanna and Olivia, and Mel and Janice, having hugged everyone else goodbye.

"We can't thank you enough for today," Simone spoke to the group as she and Shannon entered their home.

"It was our pleasure. Neely and I are going home. Thanks for all the help, ladies. We did good." Christa ushered Neely out the front door after hugging everyone.

Mel, Janice, Hanna, and Olivia hugged Shannon and Simone and sent them off to their bedroom.

Simone and Shannon had no more entered the room when they realized that the room was full of candles. There was a cold bottle of champagne sitting in an ice bucket next to the bed, and flower petals were strewn all over the room and the turned down bed.

"Simone, look at what they did." Shannon's eyes glowed as she looked at their surprise. They were not officially on their honeymoon until the following week when they headed to the island of Lanai for a couple of nights. But their friends had wanted their night to be special.

Simone shut the bedroom door and turned to Shannon. She didn't care what was in the room she was only interested in Shannon. "Shannon, I love you."

Shannon came up to her and slid her arms around her neck before she responded. "I should hope so, you just married me."

Simone grinned at her. "Would you like a glass of champagne?"

"Sure."

Simone poured them both a glass and she handed one to Shannon before picking hers up. "A toast, to us and our life together."

"Together forever." They both took a sip and placed their glasses on the dresser.

"I want to see you out of this dress," Shannon requested, running her hands up Simone's arms.

"I can do that, if you will join me." Simone placed a kiss on Shannon's shoulder.

Slowly Shannon untied the lava lava to reveal her almost naked body. The only thing she was wearing was a pair of thong underwear. Simone reached up and untied her lava lava to reveal her near naked body. "God, you are so beautiful."

"Shannon, I can't tell you how much today meant to me." Simone's soft blue eyes glittered with tears as she and Shannon slid into each other's arms.

"I think I know. It meant a whole lot to me."

"Will you make a video from the film today?" Shannon had reluctantly turned the video taping over to a cameraman from the station.

"I will, with your help."

"Do you mind staying home until Monday?"

"Not at all, this is where we started." Shannon began to kiss Simone's cheek, her lips slowly covering her face with sexy little kisses.

Simone clasped Shannon's left hand and lifted it to her lips where she kissed her ring. "I pledged my love to you when you looked at me and told me my name fit me because it was beautiful."

"I pledged my love to you when you took my hand at the hospital and held it for the very first time."

Shannon and Simone slowly stretched out on the bed, their eyes locked, and their hands clasped as they shared a kiss, full of love and promise, that had begun over one year earlier, and would last a lifetime.

The End

0-595-32046-5

Printed in the United States
27347LVS00001B/94-108